"It isn't just—" James blew out a breath. "I'm angry, yes. And confused. And...this changes everything."

"That's what I'm trying to tell you. Zeke doesn't have to change anything for you. You can still run for sheriff. I think you'd make a great one. You don't have to worry about supporting us, not on a county sheriff's salary, because I have a great job with good benefits—"

James shut off the engine and got out of the Jeep, slamming the door shut behind him. Mara took a few steps back.

He advanced on her, pointing his finger at her chest.

"I'm not going to walk away and pretend I don't know I have a kid in this world."

Dear Reader,

Welcome back to Slippery Rock! Although *Rebel in a Small Town* has both secret-baby and reunion-romance hooks, at its core the book is about accepting who we are, flaws and all. Mara and James both have preconceived notions about the other, and neither has been 100 percent honest. For baby Zeke, they'll have to be honest, about what they want and about who they are.

Mara and James (and baby Zeke) stole my heart from the moment they appeared on my computer screen...and I hope they steal your heart, too.

I love hearing from readers. You can catch up with me through my website and newsletter at www.kristinaknightauthor.com or on Facebook, www.Facebook.com/kristinaknightromanceauthor, and if you're a visual reader like me, follow my books on my Pinterest boards—you'll get some behind-the-scenes information and lots of yummy pictures.

Happy reading!

Kristina

KRISTINA KNIGHT

Rebel in a Small Town

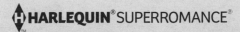

Recycling programs
for this product may
not exist in your area.

ISBN-13: 978-0-373-64035-5

Rebel in a Small Town

Printed in U.S.A.

Kristina Knight decided she wanted to be a writer, like her favorite soap-opera heroine, Felicia Gallant, one cold day when she was home sick from school. She took a detour into radio and television journalism but never forgot her first love of romance novels, or her favorite character from her favorite soap. In 2012 she got The Call from an editor who wanted to buy her book. Kristina lives in Ohio with her handsome husband, incredibly cute daughter and two dogs.

Books by Kristina Knight

HARLEQUIN SUPERROMANCE

The Daughter He Wanted
First Love Again
Protecting the Quarterback

A Slippery Rock Novel

Famous in a Small Town
Rebel in a Small Town

For Shelby, Ace, Tyler, Josh and Kayla, you are my favorite little people in the whole world, and for Megan and Mandi, who were the first little people to steal my heart. Zeke is a little bit of all of you.

PROLOGUE

Two years ago

"TONIGHT WE ARE going to take this slow?"

Mara Tyler couldn't find the words to answer, so she only smiled, letting her hands trail over the broad shoulders of James Calhoun—the very last man she should be having a clandestine affair with.

The very last man for whom she should be having feelings of anything but the physical variety. Yet here they were, in Nashville. It had been nearly a week since she logged her last speaking engagement at the securities conference. James was supposed to have returned to their hometown of Slippery Rock, Missouri, three days earlier. He kept making excuses for why he was staying, but to be honest, Mara didn't care.

They stood at the window overlooking downtown Nashville. Neon signs twinkled in the darkness, and masses of people wandered from bar to bar and lounge to lounge.

They'd been down there with the crowd until a half hour before, just like any other couple.

They weren't any other couple, though. He had been voted most likely to succeed in their high school class, was now a sheriff's deputy and was next in line to become the sheriff. She had been voted most likely to blow something up, and although she'd changed, no one in their hometown would believe the girl who had broken several laws as a teen was now a respected securities consultant. Or that one of her partners in crime had been the sheriff's son.

None of that mattered. They were in Nashville, not Slippery Rock, and none of this was real. It was just for fun.

James cocked an eyebrow, the back of his hand teasing the side of her breast.

God, this was so much fun.

"No answer?" he asked. "Then we'll see how long you can take slow."

He lifted her in his arms and laid her gently on the bed. Slowly he unzipped one knee-high boot, letting it clatter to the floor, and then the next.

Her hands found his shoulders, urging him up, but James seemed perfectly content between her legs.

With one hand he pulled the zipper of

her skirt down, down, and with the other he teased the bit of exposed flesh between her skirt and blouse. Mara's muscles clenched and she fisted her hands against the soft, hotel room duvet. James pulled the skirt from her hips, tossing it over his shoulder. Her silk cami followed, and she was nearly naked before him. Only the green lace boy-briefs and matching bra covering her.

Mara was torn. She wanted the lace gone, too, but she liked that dangerous look in his gaze. The look that said this was going to last a long time.

She wouldn't mind if it lasted forever. She could stay in this hotel room or even a desert island forever, just as long as James Calhoun was right there with her.

That thought was nearly as dangerous as the look in James's eyes, though, because this thing between them wasn't real. It wasn't forever. This was a fling. It was hard to remember that when his heat was burning her to the ground.

Time to get this *thing* between them back on solid, nonthreatening ground.

"When you said *slow*, I didn't think you meant glacial," she said and used his tie to urge him up. James planted a hand on either side of her, grinning.

"You say glacial, I say leisurely," he said. Then he covered her mouth with his, and his legs tangled with hers.

Mara wrapped her arms around his neck, wanting to hold him here, right here, for as long as she could.

They had done this a hundred times, and still she wasn't tired of it. Of him. Still, she wanted more of him. Wanted to feel the hardness of his chest against her, wanted the heat from his skin to warm her, wanted to lose herself in him until she forgot that no matter what happened in a hotel room in another city, it didn't mean anything could ever happen between them in real life.

She didn't want to go down that road quite yet, though, so she loosened his tie, pulling it from his neck, and then unbuttoned his shirt, letting her hands meander over the wide expanse of his chest for a few moments.

"I can go glacial, too," she said, before pushing the shirt from his shoulders.

James reached for the buckle of his belt, but Mara put her hand over his and stopped him.

"Slow, remember?"

He lifted one eyebrow. "You were just complaining about the glacial pace."

True, but now that she thought about it, glacial could be fun. As long as he was on the receiving end, just for a little while. She found the tie on the bed and held it up.

"Maybe you've convinced me that glacial has its interesting points."

Mara pushed against his shoulders until James was flat on his back, and she dangled the tie from her fingertips.

"Hands up, Officer."

James grinned, but he raised his hands above his head, grasping the spindles of the headboard in his hands.

"That's 'deputy,' ma'am, not 'officer.'"

"Deputy Calhoun, do you know why you're being confined?" she asked mildly as she tied the tie loosely around his wrists.

"Speeding?"

Mara chuckled. "The speed limit in this room is 'leisurely.'"

"And I was going glacially?"

"Something like that." With his arms secured, Mara reached for the buckle of his belt. She slid the leather from the clasp, and then unsnapped his pants. She kissed his sternum, and couldn't resist licking her way down his washboard abs.

"You going to—" he was grinning at her "—fine me, Deputy?"

Mara glanced up. His hands were clenched and his eyes were closed.

"Is this your way of asking for a ticket? You don't want to plead your case?" Mara pushed his pants over his hips, and James kicked them to the floor. He wasn't wearing boxers, and for a moment, Mara wasn't sure what to do. She'd been expecting one more slow removal of clothing, and instead she saw him, thick and hard.

"I think I'll just take the fine."

Mara swallowed. The fine. The fine. She had no idea what to say next, how to keep this role-playing thing going when all she could think about was taking him in her hands. In her mouth.

Snap out of it, Mar, this is just fun and games.

She unsnapped the clasp of her bra, letting the lace fall to the floor, and then stepped out of her panties. Mara kneeled on the bed, putting her hands on either side of his head and straddling his hips before she took his mouth with hers. Screw the game, she only wanted James.

He pulled her body against his, the hairs on his chest tickling her breasts.

"Hey, I tied you up," she said between kisses.

"You'd never survive in the wilderness with those knot tying skills. I'll teach you a simple tie. For next time," he said, pushing her to her back.

"Next time," she said, and the words sounded dreamy to her ears.

Every time she met up with James, she told herself it would be the last time, but it never was. He was like that last bit of birthday cake—impossible to resist.

His mouth found her breast and Mara arched her back, wanting more.

"James," she said, pressing her hips against him, urging him to hurry.

James reached into the drawer of the bedside table and pulled out a foil packet. He tore it open with his mouth, and rolled the thin covering over his length.

And then he was inside her. Mara wrapped her legs around his waist, loving the feel of his body against hers, inside hers. This was all she needed.

James Calhoun was everything she wanted, even if she could never be the woman that he needed.

MARA WATCHED JAMES sleeping soundly on the hotel room bed. The lights were off, but the glow of the neon on the street below was enough to illuminate the room dimly. His mouth was open slightly, his left hand over his heart and his legs tangled in the sheets. The tie draped over the pillow. A lock of hair fell over his eyes. She pushed it back.

This wasn't just fun.

She swallowed. She wanted to slide under his arm and rest her head over his heart. Wanted to lie there for hours, listening to his heart beating.

God, what had she done?

They'd been meeting like this, in hotel rooms around the country every few months, for nearly three years. Every time it had just been about the sex. Good sex. Excellent sex.

Why did she have to go and let her heart ruin it? This was a great arrangement. He liked his small-town life, and she liked her on-the-road life. They met up for sex, they each went back to their lives, and no one expected anything more.

She took a deep breath. She shouldn't want more, so why did she? It wasn't fair. She should have been able to love him and leave him, the way she had every other time they'd met.

Mara pressed a quick kiss to his cheek. James rocked his head slowly to the side, but he didn't wake.

"I don't want to mess this up," she whispered to the man on the bed. The man who had been her best friend for most of her life. The man she should never have fallen in love with. "This will lead to broken hearts and anger, so I'm ending it now without the anger and without breaking anything. It's better this way."

She slid off the bed, picked up her satchel and laptop, and quietly left the hotel room. She would arrange for the hotel to pack her things and ship them to her office in Tulsa, because if she waited for him to wake, she wouldn't be able to leave. She would tell him how she felt about him.

He might tell her he felt the same, but it wouldn't matter. She didn't want his kind of life any more than he wanted hers.

More than that, he deserved better.

He deserved someone who wasn't broken.

CHAPTER ONE

Present day

MARA PULLED INTO the parking lot of Mallard's Grocery in Slippery Rock, Missouri. The lot with its cracked pavement sat at the corner of Main Street and Mariner, a few blocks north of Slippery Rock Lake. The grocery store still had the image of a duck on its sign, the paint dividing the parking spaces was still off-center from the cement blocks at the head of each space, and the same cracked glass was in the revolving door.

Despite the light breeze along the shore, it was oppressively hot in the town center. She had forgotten exactly how muggy and uncomfortable a southern Missouri summer could be. Since slipping out of town the night after her high school graduation, Mara had allowed herself only a handful of visits, all around the holidays, when the weather was significantly cooler.

She turned off the ignition and tossed her

keys into the large tote she carried for work. Although the store stood several blocks from the waterfront, where a horrible tornado had leveled several buildings a few weeks before, she could hear the hammering and sawing going on in the downtown area.

This section of town had experienced a few uprooted trees, but most of the damage had been to roofs and windows. The grocery store still had one big plate-glass window boarded over, and one of the cart corrals looked as if a tree had landed on it. Maybe one had.

She hadn't expected to feel sympathy for the town when she decided to come back, but sympathy was the only explanation she had for the tightening in her chest. Closing her eyes, she took a few deep, centering breaths. The tornado was an act of God. It wasn't her fault. Not like so many other happenings that had befallen this town because of her. Now she was in a position to help this place that had saved her as a child.

And ideally, while she was helping the town at large, she could fix a couple of personal messes, too.

Mara activated the locks on the SUV as she exited. A few cars and trucks sat in the lot, and she decided to begin her security sweep here rather than checking in with the office first. She didn't need a store manager distracting her from her job with talk of how little crime they'd experienced. If the stores she visited weren't in need of a security upgrade, she would not have been dispatched to their area.

On a small notepad, she jotted the locations of several security cameras situated to capture the inbound and outbound foot traffic to the store, but as she crossed to the rear, near the row of Dumpsters and a big cardboard baler, she noted only one camera. It appeared to be slightly askew, and she wondered if it worked at all. Not a great setup despite the low crime rate in Slippery Rock. She made a notation in the notebook.

Air-conditioning blasted her as she pushed through the two-sided revolving door into the store, a nice relief from the heat of the blacktop parking lot. The clerk, a middle-aged woman with salt-and-pepper hair, ignored her as Mara passed through the automatic doors. The woman's hair might have changed color since Mara left Slippery Rock ten years before, but that frown on her face was as familiar as the bored tap-tap-tapping of her fingernails against the counter. A teen with red-and-blue-striped hair—the high school colors—sat on the end of the check stand, chewing gum while he waited for a customer to come through the line. A few glass-domed cameras looked down over the front of the store, but again, in the back there was little security. She scribbled more notes. To test the system, she put a box of cookies in her bag along with a small carton of milk.

She waved to the clerk as she left the store. The clerk ignored her. No sirens sounded, and the teenage bagger remained at his perch at the end of the check stand.

Not good. No wonder the grocery store wanted an upgrade. They were probably losing a small fortune in junk food to kids who either didn't have the money to buy it or simply didn't want to pay. The fact that the beer aisle was one over from the cookies probably pushed their loss ceiling even higher. A man with only a couple of dollars in his bank account and a tremendous thirst for a Budweiser wouldn't think twice about risking a run through the less-than-secure store.

Mara turned around and headed back inside, and as she stepped into the revolving door, buzzers began beeping, and the mechanical door stopped moving altogether, trapping her in between a wall of glass and the inner door. Mara tried to stop, but her shoe slipped against the floor, and she lost her balance. Her shoulder slammed into the glass, making her wince in pain. Mara regained her footing only to find she was trapped inside the door. She had never encountered a system that trapped only people who returned to a store with stolen merchandise. For that matter, she didn't think such a system existed. Probably some kind of kink in the software.

The gum-smacking teen pointed a broom handle at her as if she were under fire, and the bored clerk talked animatedly into the phone, waving her hands as she said something Mara couldn't make out from her side of the thick-paned door.

She motioned to her bag and tried to shout above the racket of the beepers. "I'm with Cannon Security," she said, but the teenager kept wielding the broom handle at her like it was a machete. "I'm on a security check," she said, trying again, but neither of the employees seemed able to hear her. Maybe the two of them didn't want to hear her.

Damn it. She checked her watch. She needed to be at the bed-and-breakfast in twenty minutes, and she didn't see that happening. Crap, crap, crap. She never missed Zeke's postnap snack. Never.

A crowd gathered behind the check stand, mostly middle-aged women wearing jeans and T-shirts and probably boots, just like their husbands would. A few had small children with them and pushed the kids behind their carts as if Mara might be dangerous. "Turn off the buzzers," she yelled, putting her hands over her ears.

The checker hung up the phone and came over to the glass. She said something that sounded peculiarly like "Criminals deserve discomfort" before backing away to the safety of her check stand. As if Mara was about to draw a gun or something.

"Now I know what the goldfish at the office feels like," she muttered, still holding her hands over her ears. She pushed one foot against the inner and outer doors, but neither budged.

Finally the beepers stopped and everything quieted. Mara took her hands from her ears and tried the doors again. They didn't budge. She repeated her call through the thick glass.

"I'm here on a security check. I need to speak with Michael Mallard." The clerk shot a glance behind her toward an area marked Employees Only. No one appeared. The crowd began to disperse, lessening the goldfish effect.

She tugged at her earlobe when a low siren began to wail. Was this some kind of second-tier warning system? The clerk crossed her arms over her chest as if in triumph. The wailing became louder, and it wasn't coming from inside the store. Mara pressed her face against the outer door, looking left and then right.

"No, no, no. Please, no."

The siren grew louder, and a few cars passing on the street pulled to the side.

"Let it be a fire. Let it be a fire."

But it wasn't a red fire truck that entered the parking lot. It was a big black SUV with Wall County Sheriff plastered along its side. She was definitely not making it to the B and B for snack time.

As the SUV came to a stop, she could make out the driver, a large man with brown hair and big aviator sunglasses over his eyes— eyes she knew would be the color of molten chocolate. This man had been interrupting her dreams since she'd hit puberty and began to figure out why male and female body parts were made so deliciously dissimilar.

"Crap, crappity crap."

JAMES PULLED INTO the parking lot of Mallard's Grocery and sighed. He could see a tall, thin woman caught between the double doors, and she looked annoyed. Her long hair was pulled through the back of her Kansas City Royals baseball cap, which obscured her face. Probably another customer who'd reentered the store after making a purchase. He'd been called out here at least a dozen times since Christmas, when the store's security system started going wonky. Not once in all the calls he'd answered had anyone actually been stealing from the store. Of course, that didn't stop CarlaAnn from acting like she'd been deputized every time. And, crap, was the bag boy wielding a broom at the woman?

That alarm system was a menace. Mike should invest in better locks and leave it at that. There was no need for expensive—and defective—security systems in Slippery Rock.

He got out of the SUV, blistering afternoon sunshine reflecting off the pavement. Since the tornado, the summer temperatures had been relatively mild, but according to the local weatherman, this heat wave would continue for at least a week.

James knocked on the glass of the entrance, his attention focused on the woman still caught between the doors. She turned and faced the store, her shoulders and spine seeming rigid beneath the vibrant blue of the tank top she wore. Cropped jeans hugged the curves of her lower half, making his mouth go a little dry.

CarlaAnn, the clerk at the checkout, pressed the button that disabled the alarm, allowing the doors to whoosh open, but the woman caught inside didn't budge until the door pushed her gently forward. She stepped from the doorway, holding on to her oversize shoulder bag with both hands, gaze focused intently on the empty aisle leading to the butcher counter. Maybe she wasn't a typical customer. James put his hand on his holster just in case as he motioned for her to follow him to the check stand.

"We'll get this straightened out in a moment," he said.

"I wasn't stealing anything. I had a reason for being in this store," she said, and her husky voice sent a shiver down James's spine. He knew that voice. Even after two years, he knew it.

"Mara?" He turned his shocked gaze to her. She'd let her hair grow, and she wasn't the stick-thin girl he remembered either from high school or the day she'd walked out on him two years ago.

"I swear," she said, reaching into the bag and pulling out a box of cookies and a small carton of milk, "I have a really good explanation for this."

Well, that much, at least, was familiar. Mara Tyler always had a good explanation, both before she acted and after the fact. While in high school, the six of them—he and Mara, her brother Collin, Levi Walters and the twins, Aiden and Adam Buchanan— had pulled a number of pranks on the town. They'd painted Simone Grainger's phone number on the water tower after she dumped Aiden before the last basketball game of their senior year. They'd all brought dogs to school on the same day, and had switched the cables from the principal's computer to the secretary's. They repainted the downtown parking spaces and put up Tractors Only parking signs. There were countless other pranks, but each one had been orchestrated by Mara, and every single one of them he'd gone along with because he would rather have been with her than without her.

Whenever Mara came around, his law-abiding side warred with his reckless side, and usually the reckless side won, leaving his law-abiding self to clean up the mess.

Like the mess the two of them made graduation night.

Correction: the mess he'd made all by himself when he took one of her pranks to a whole other level.

No one except him and Mara knew exactly what happened that night, and he planned to keep it that way.

"Yeah, it just figures Mara Tyler would set off the store alarm." CarlaAnn had joined them. "I thought I recognized her when she walked in, but I wasn't sure until the alarms went off." She shook her head, her shoulder-length, salt-and-pepper hair shaking from side to side. "This alarm system isn't good for much, but it finally caught *her* in the act." She stabbed a finger toward Mara's chest. James stepped between them.

CarlaAnn was Simone's mother, and she'd always blamed their group for the water tower incident—with just cause. A few weeks after that incident, Simone ran off with the biker she'd dumped Aiden for, and she had never returned to Slippery Rock. CarlaAnn blamed only Mara for that offense, and her blame had turned into a raging hatred before the six of them graduated.

"I have a perfectly good explanation for

being here, and for setting off the alarms. I tried to tell you that through the glass," Mara said, stepping around James's arm. "I need to speak with Mike." She glanced at her watch, and she tapped the toe of her shoe against the tile.

CarlaAnn crossed her arms over her chest. "Mike is on vacation. You'll have to deal with me."

Mara kept her gaze trained on the other woman for a long moment. CarlaAnn was the first to look away. "Then I need a phone number or email address where he can be reached."

CarlaAnn pressed her lips together and scowled. "I don't have either of those," she finally said.

James noticed the crowd of shoppers gradually inching closer to Mara and CarlaAnn, probably expecting some kind of girl fight now that Mara had been identified. Small towns meant there was always a helping hand around, but they also meant long memories. Everyone remembered the water tower prank, among others. The love-hate relationship between Mara and the town had turned to flat-out hate after the fiasco of graduation night, though.

Since then, James had done his best to prove he was a man worthy of being the next sheriff. Mara setting off alarm bells at the grocery store would only reinforce their belief that she was a felony charge away from jail time.

He knew she wasn't a felon, and their pranks had been generated out of boredom rather than malice, but that wouldn't matter. Nor would the fact that James graduated at the top of his class in both college and the police academy. His anonymous restitution to the school would be irrelevant. None of those things would matter to the townspeople, just as those things didn't truly assuage his conscience. He could only hope that someday the man he'd become would matter more than the boy he'd been. Maybe that was how Mara felt, too.

"We'll take care of this, everyone." He motioned to the crowd to continue shopping, then turned to Mara. "Why don't you and I go into the office area and talk this through?"

Mara checked her watch again. "Can we make it quick? I, um, have an important, uh, conference call in fifteen minutes."

"Don't you need my statement, too, Deputy Calhoun? Or is this a purely cursory investigation?"

James thought he heard a silent *too* on the end of CarlaAnn's last question, as well, and remembered his mother confronting his father after CarlaAnn accused him of conducting a "cursory investigation" into Simone's disappearance with the biker. James took Mara's arm and pushed past CarlaAnn.

"Hey," Mara said in protest, but he ignored her until the door to the back office closed behind them. "I'm not a criminal. And I have another appointment."

"No, you're a mischief maker. And important conference call or not, I'm going to investigate why you're setting off alarm bells at my grocery store."

"I thought it still belonged to the Mallard family, or have the Calhouns gone into groceries as well as law enforcement?"

"You know what I meant. This is my town, and the people here are my friends, my family. The businesses they run, I protect."

"They were mine once, too."

"Until the day you ran out on everything."

Mara jerked her arm from his grasp. "You, of all people, know why I left."

James clenched his jaw. Yeah, he knew. Only it hadn't been her leaving ten years ago that he'd been talking about. She didn't need to know that, though. He opened the door to the room that held the security equipment and motioned her inside. "Want to show me your reasonable explanation for stealing five dollars in snacks when I know for a fact that you don't eat generic cookies and are lactose intolerant?"

"I can't." Mara looked uncomfortable. "But if you would let me get to my—"

"You'd better, or CarlaAnn out there is going to do her damnedest to make sure this misdemeanor offense not only lands on the crime blotter of the *Slippery Rock Gazette* but also sounds like a felony." God, but she was cute when she was upset. Her face took on a pretty pink hue, and she wrung her hands together nervously. Mara was almost never nervous, so seeing her this out of balance was nice. Especially since she was so good at putting *him* off balance.

Mara motioned to the equipment on the counter. "The system doesn't catch where I was in the store, and it misses a lot of the parking lot." She pulled an ID badge from her bag, the move pulling her top taut over her breasts. James's mouth went dry. Stupid reaction. He'd been hung up on Mara Tyler for most of his life, but he was not going to let himself get hung up on her again. He was a responsible adult with a responsible job, and she'd walked out on him two years ago without so much as a goodbye. He was over her.

"I work for Cannon Security." She named a firm he had heard about during his training in Jefferson City a few years before. "Mike hired us to do a security overhaul, and I was here to conduct a cursory check before telling him what needed to be done. No one told me he was on vacation. I have emails on my computer at the B and B."

"You work for a security company?" That was new. He had always figured Mara had gone into hacking or some other not-quite-legal profession. Although they'd had an on-again, off-again relationship, they never talked about anything important. She'd seen his badge, and knew he had always wanted to become the sheriff, but they had never talked about her plans. Or dreams. Hell, he couldn't really call what they'd had a relationship. It was more like a five-year series of booty calls when she was near Slippery Rock or when he went to law-enforcement conferences in the cities where she worked. "I didn't realize you were one of the good guys now."

"Well, I don't wear a cape, but I do have a lot of really cool techy toys that come in handy from time to time."

Great, now he was picturing her in tights and a cape, and in his imagination her body looked so much better than any of the good guys from the comic books. Not that she was one of the good guys. Er, girls. Women. Whatever. He refocused as she continued talking.

"I do camera and detector installs, but I also write specific programs for some of our clients." She sat at the counter and ran through the tapes from the ancient camera system.

The images were grainy and fuzzy, but he could tell they focused on the check stand and the front of the store. He moved closer, putting his hand over hers. Warmth from the touch spread up his arm, but Mara didn't seem to notice. He shook himself. He was not going down this road, not again. Mara only ever saw him as a friend or a booty call, and even if that changed, his job didn't. Her reputation wouldn't. Getting tangled up with her again would be…irresponsible. James hadn't been irresponsible, at least not inside the Slippery Rock city limits, since graduation night.

"This was to be a custom job because Mallard's is the only store on this particular block. He has specific needs."

So did James, not that his needs had anything to do with the images on the screens before them. Those needs had everything to do with the heat that seemed to seep into his skin from hers. He stepped back. "Like more cameras and a new door."

"Yes, as well as computerized entry codes and new systems for opening and closing the registers. The store has lost a lot of revenue from shoplifters, but Mike also mentioned something about registers not adding up. It's a big job."

"And they picked you to run it." He was impressed. Mara Tyler was not only a good guy but also a good-at-her-job good guy.

"Actually, I volunteered." She stood. "I needed to make sure my family was okay after the tornado, and…" She paused. "It seemed like a good time to come home for more than a day at a time." She twisted her mouth to the side as if she might say more.

James waited a long moment, but she didn't continue. "I thought you hated Slippery Rock."

"Sometimes the things you hate the most as a kid are the things you miss the most as an adult." There was something in her voice that made him look at her more closely. This wasn't personal—that couldn't be it. But there was something different about Mara. Something had changed over the past two years, and that change was interesting.

Not that he would act on *interesting*. Still, it might be nice to have her around for a while, if for no other reason than to give uptight old CarlaAnn a hard time.

"Are you ready to face the music with CarlaAnn?" He checked his watch. "By my count, you have ten more minutes before the big conference call."

Mara shrugged. "I kind of figured her antipathy toward me would have lessened."

"You've forgotten how small towns work, haven't you?"

Together they returned to the check stand, where CarlaAnn was scanning a woman's groceries while the teenager bagged them. Once the woman had paid, James motioned CarlaAnn to the side.

"Meet the new security consultant for Mallard's Grocery."

"Well, doesn't that just figure?" CarlaAnn said, annoyance in her voice. "Mike didn't say anything about security changes."

"I'm sure he'll tell you all about it when he gets back."

Mara moved to the check stand and took the cookies and milk from her bag. "To show there are no hard feelings, I'll pay for these. It really was part of the initial security check."

Reluctantly CarlaAnn scanned the items and slid them onto the conveyor belt. The teen put them in a small plastic bag.

"I'll see you Monday morning," Mara said, "and I'll have my boss call your boss, just to let him know we've gotten acquainted."

CarlaAnn harrumphed. James walked out of the store with Mara.

"It's Tuesday," he said. "Why wait until Monday?"

"Just an assumption that I won't be able to get much done until Mike returns. And another assumption that he'll come back to work on a Monday. My boss at Cannon will have contact information for him. If he isn't back Monday, I'll wait a little longer. I can do a lot of the programming from my computer at the B and B."

"You aren't staying at the orchard?" Usually only tourists stayed at the motel or B and Bs in town. He'd been so focused on his reaction to her, he'd ignored those other references to staying in town rather than at her family's farm.

That uncomfortable look flitted over her face again. "I, ah, thought it might be simpler to be closer to Mallard's." She reached into her bag and pulled out a set of keys, which she began fiddling with. "You know, glitches and things."

They arrived at her car, and James wasn't sure what to say. He wanted to ask how she'd gotten involved in the security industry. Wanted to ask why she hadn't come back to town before now. Wanted to know what she'd been doing for the past two years.

He didn't believe for a second that *glitches and things* were the real reason she was staying at the Slippery Rock Bed-and-Breakfast in town rather than in the ample space of the farmhouse at the orchard.

If she were a friend, he would push the issue. But she wasn't a friend. Friends didn't cut friends out of their lives the way she'd cut him out. James decided to let it drop. Mara might make his blood run hotter than Bud's Fourth of July chili from Guy's Market, but James was through allowing her to make him do irresponsible things, like trying to push his way into her life.

"I guess I'll see you around, then. Try not to set off any more alarms, okay?"

She grinned, but that uneasy look remained in her clear blue eyes. James fought the urge to try to make that look leave her face. "I'll do my best," she said and slid behind the wheel of a navy SUV with darkly tinted rear windows. She gave him a finger wave as she pulled out of the parking lot.

Asking any of those questions would imply he was interested, and he wasn't. Was not interested in Mara Tyler. At least, he shouldn't be.

CHAPTER TWO

MARA HAD RENTED a suite at the Slippery Rock B and B. Well, *suite* was a bit of an exaggeration, but there were two rooms with an adjoining door. It was the best option she had. The only other hotel in town looked like it had been through a war, and she didn't think it was entirely due to the tornado. This B and B was one of the few buildings on the west side of the downtown area that hadn't been hit hard by the tornado. Joann, the new owner who had moved to town a couple years before, told her they lost the roof and a little bit of siding, but that was the extent of the damage. She didn't question Mara about why she was staying at the B and B instead of the orchard—the question Mara knew James had been dying to ask at Mallard's.

Mara opened the door to her suite with her happy mommy smile plastered to her face, ten minutes after Zeke's usual wake-up. When Mara started to say something, Cheryl Johnson, Zeke's nanny, shook her head.

"Still sleeping," she whispered. "I think the drive tuckered him out."

Mara crossed the room to the small Pack 'n Play she traveled with, wishing for the thousandth time that Zeke had a proper crib. Cribs didn't transport well, not even in an SUV. Since her work required regular travel, this was the best solution. She ran her fingers lightly over the little boy's brown hair. It was soft and silky and baby-fine, unlike the thick mass of hair his father had.

She blew out a breath. The office of Mallard's Grocery hadn't been the right place to tell James about Zeke. She knew that. So why did she feel so guilty about her silence? She'd come here to tell him about his son, to introduce them, and she would do it. But not when she was on the verge of being arrested for stealing a carton of milk and a box of generic cookies.

Mara took the items from her bag, put the milk in the small fridge inside the oversize bureau and tossed the cookies on top.

"Thanks for sticking around until I got back. You didn't have to do that."

"Are you kidding me? If today and tomorrow are the last days I have with Zeke, I'm going to pack as much of his sweet baby face as I can into them. Are you *sure* you don't need me to stay? My contract with the school district in Tulsa doesn't start for another two months—"

Mara held up her hand. "And you're going to spend two of those weeks helping your sister plan her wedding, and after the wedding, you're taking your father on that trip to Ireland he's always wanted. Zeke and I will be fine." She couldn't ignore the little spike of fear that hit her belly, though.

She'd hired Cheryl to be Zeke's nanny when he was three weeks old. Cheryl had traveled with them all over the United States, but earlier this year her father had been diagnosed with Parkinson's. Cheryl wanted to be closer to her family, and Mara couldn't blame her, especially with a wedding coming up and a parent whose health was in decline. She might not have the close familial ties her nanny had, but Mara could empathize.

Part of her hope for this trip was that she would be able to repair those ties with her own family. That, and tell James he had a son. She also planned to tell him she could raise Zeke on her own so he could continue with his postcard-perfect, fairy-tale life as the heir apparent to the Slippery Rock Sheriff's Department and forget he'd ever been so reckless as to have an affair with her.

"But you'll send me pictures, right?" Cheryl's hazel eyes clouded with tears, and her voice cracked. Mara wrapped her arms around the woman who was her only friend.

"Are you kidding? Who else is going to understand just how cute the little monster is when he's destroying his dinner like Godzilla destroyed Tokyo?"

"Okay. Okay then." Cheryl pulled back, grabbed a tissue from the box on the bureau and dabbed at her eyes. "I swore I wasn't going to get choked up. This isn't forever. The contract is only for a year, and then, who knows? Dad will be settled by then. He might not need as much attention."

"Sure," Mara said, pushing more confidence into her voice than she felt. She had no doubt that she and Cheryl would stay in touch, but she was very doubtful this sabbatical would last only for the length of the school year. Cheryl's father wouldn't get better, and her sister would begin having children. Unlike Mara, normal people weren't made to live out of suitcases in a series of boring hotel rooms. "Until you come back, I'll text and email more pictures than you ever wanted to see. You'll have to block my numbers to stop the flow of toddler silliness."

Cheryl dabbed at her eyes again, but she

seemed to have regained her equilibrium. "I'm going to collect those takeout menus the manager promised when we checked in." She closed the door, and Mara was alone with her son.

She sat on the edge of the bed and sighed. She could do this. She'd taken all the parenting courses, enrolled herself in therapy to deal finally with the baggage from her childhood. She was now in the same town with her baby's father, and she was ready to tell him that he could have a place in his child's life or not. Either way, she and Zeke would be just fine. Simple enough conversation.

Zeke made a small noise, and his little fingers began their usual scrape-scrape-scrape down the mesh sides of the playpen. His favorite stuffed toy, an ugly black-and-brown lemur, was wedged under his hip, but he wrestled it free and began talking in mumbles to it.

She was stronger now than she had ever been. She could do this.

"BUT WHY ISN'T she staying at the orchard?" James called himself ten kinds of fool for asking Collin the question, but he couldn't resist.

He'd stopped by his house to change out of his uniform, but somehow the old jeans and gray T-shirt weren't any more comfortable than the layers of stiff, starched cotton, body armor and gun belt he wore to work every day. The fact that Collin, Mara's brother and one of his best friends, looked incredibly relaxed in a pair of cargo shorts and a similar T-shirt only made him more uncomfortable. He, Collin and Levi were sitting at their usual Wednesday night booth in The Slippery Slope, the waterfront bar. It still felt odd not to see Adam across the booth, but he was in the hospital recovering from the injuries he sustained in the tornado. The doctors weren't certain he would walk again.

"She says it'll make things easier with the odd hours she's keeping working on the security system at Mallard's," Collin said. "And to be honest, I don't need the distraction of my sister underfoot. I've got enough to do with the new plantings."

Tyler Orchard had been hit hard by the tornado. Collin had lost about half of their apple trees and several peach and pear trees, too. Still, when family members visited Slippery Rock, they didn't stay at a B and B.

"The orchard is all of a ten-minute drive to town," James said. "Don't you think that's odd?"

James hadn't seen Mara since Tuesday

morning—apparently she'd had no more run-ins with the wonky security doors at the grocery store—but he couldn't get her out of his head. He'd worked with one of the construction crews this afternoon, putting up the new roof of the farmers' market just down the street, and he could have sworn he saw her standing on the corner. Of course, when he took a closer look, he'd seen Mrs. Bailey, the Methodist minister's wife. Mrs. Bailey was short, had iron-gray hair and carried a pocketbook from 1959. No sane man would mix her up with the tall, thin Mara Tyler carrying a canvas tote bag.

"What's with the third degree over where Mara chooses to stay while she's on a business trip?" Levi asked, coming to the table with a tray of beers and a bucket of peanuts.

James sat back as if he hadn't just been interrogating one of his best friends about said best friend's sister, while the best friend was unaware that James had been having an affair with that same sister. "No third degree, just curiosity," he said, hoping neither Levi nor Collin would push the issue.

"Look, you have the black-and-white sitcom version of the perfect family. Having family stay with you is normal. The Tylers have never been anyone's version of normal,"

Collin said, but his words didn't hold their usual rancor. Since he'd fallen for Levi's sister, Savannah, Collin's anger at his parents seemed to have dissipated. "If Mara says it's easier to stay in town, I'm fine with that. If she decides to come to the orchard, we have plenty of room."

"She hasn't even been to the orchard yet?" Not going to see her family was weirder than weird. Who came home for work and didn't immediately check in with the family? Sure, she'd been only a sporadic visitor, but he knew Mara loved her grandmother and her siblings. None of this made sense.

Collin, who emanated that happy-in-love countenance usually seen only on the guy characters in chick flicks, shrugged. "She called to let us know she was in town. She'll probably be out this weekend." He popped a peanut into his mouth and chewed.

"And you don't find that just a little bit strange?"

"Not really. You know Mara. She does things at her own pace."

"Usually that pace rivals the Indy 500 drivers," James said, sipping his beer. It was one thing for Mara to check into the Slippery Rock B and B, but not even to go to the orchard to see her family? That was unlike the woman he'd known.

Of course, he'd never envisioned that woman walking out on him, changing her phone number or ignoring his emails, and she had done all of those things. Maybe he didn't know Mara Tyler at all. James opened his mouth to say something, anything to get Collin to tell him what was going on, but Levi spoke.

"If we aren't going to play, I'm going to head back. Pulling double duty with the cleanup crews and at the ranch is killing me. I had no idea twenty-eight could feel so old." Levi wove a single dart through his fingers.

"We'll play," Collin said, and James nodded.

All three of them—hell, most of the people in town—were working around the clock to get the town back in shape. A few weeks before, Savannah and some friends from Nashville had hosted a benefit concert to help with renovations. Now the town was pulling together to complete the projects in the hope that the Bass Nationals would hold a major tournament at Slippery Rock Lake this fall. As part of the benefit, they'd held a smaller fishing event, but having their lake on national television would do a lot to promote tourism and show the world that Slippery Rock remained a good vacation destination.

The three of them played a couple of rounds of darts, but without Adam, their usual round-robin style of play wasn't as fun, and Levi bowed out and left after the third game. Collin and James nursed their beers across the table from one another.

"Jenny called this afternoon. The doctors say he'll need surgery eventually, but that Adam is going to walk again," Collin said after a long moment.

That was the best news James had heard in a while.

"Any word on when they'll release him?"

Collin shook his head. "Jenny said they needed more testing, and the doctors are still tweaking the treatment of the seizures. I thought I might drive up to Springfield to see him, but Jenny says he doesn't want visitors still."

"That's not like Adam."

"How would you feel about gawkers if a tornado left you partially buried under the rubble of a church? And if the head injury left you with seizures?"

James didn't have to think about the answer. "Pissy."

"So, we leave him be. We can bug the beje-sus out of him when he's home."

Collin finished his beer, and James watched the clock tick off a couple of min-utes. No songs played over the jukebox, and Juanita, the waitress, was snacking on the cherries and oranges Merle kept on the bar to garnish the fancy drinks. He wanted to ask about Mara again, but couldn't think of a way to do it without sounding like a con-cerned boyfriend.

"You want to tell me why you're so all-fired interested about where my sister stays this visit?" Collin finally asked.

"Curiosity. You know it killed the cat. Ap-parently it's trying to kill a deputy sheriff now, too."

"Acting sheriff, soon to be elected sher-iff," Collin added. "Unless you've changed your mind?"

James shook his head. His father, the cur-rent sheriff, was off work on disability and couldn't come back to the department. He'd gotten caught in the tornado and broken a hip; Jonathan Calhoun wasn't ready to step down from his position, but he had to. "You know my dad's legacy speech." James deepened his voice to imitate his father. "Three genera-tions of Calhouns have protected this town from predators." James finished his beer. "If I don't become that fourth generation, I think he might disown me."

"If you didn't want to be sheriff, you wouldn't care about being disowned."

There was truth to that. He'd wanted to be sheriff for as long as he could remember, long before graduation night, and not just because it was his father's dream. James finished his beer. "Sorry about the third degree."

Collin shrugged. "Enquiring minds," he said, a teasing note in his voice.

"Yeah, well. I have an early shift tomorrow, and you've probably got trees to plant or something."

"I'll be at the farmers' market in the afternoon, finishing up the roof."

"See you there."

Collin left while James went to the bar to pay the bill. The four of them—three of them, he corrected himself—took turns paying rather than making Juanita print separate checks every Wednesday. Merle made change from the old-fashioned register. Then James walked onto the familiar street.

He could smell the lake and the pine trees surrounding it. He even thought he might smell the cattle from Walters Ranch, where Levi and his family lived, and the fruit from

Tyler Orchard. He knew that was fanciful thinking, and he wasn't a fanciful guy. He was straightforward. Conscientious. Responsible.

He'd spent nearly all his life trying to live up to the legacy his father established; the one time he'd stepped outside the boundaries, he'd nearly ruined his entire life. Put the local school in financial jeopardy. Stepping outside the bounds wasn't worth it. He should have remembered that before he'd started meeting Mara on the sly years ago.

Maybe, with Mara back in town, he would finally learn that lesson.

CHAPTER THREE

"AND THAT—" MARA pointed to the tilted neon sign that read The Slippery Slope "—is the town bar where everyone goes on Friday nights. Of course, it's only Thursday so no big crowds tonight." One of the green *P*s was burned out, along with the word *The* on the sign, just as it had been when Mara was a teen. Some things never changed. The thought was comforting, especially considering the amount of change she was bringing to Slippery Rock.

"There's a church on either side of it and one across the street, too." Cheryl laughed. "God, small towns are great."

"If the beer doesn't save you, the brimstone sermons might," Mara agreed. It was Cheryl's last night in Slippery Rock, and Mara had convinced her to come out and really see the town. She used an online service to find a local babysitter for Zeke, a teenage girl who didn't seem to associate the

Mara Tyler she was working for with Tyler Orchard outside town.

Mara and Cheryl had dinner at the Rock Café overlooking Slippery Rock Marina, and had been walking around for the past few minutes while Mara pointed out the local landmarks. They weren't due back at the B and B for another hour.

"If you want to see real small town, you have to go inside the Slope. Mahogany everything, a jukebox from the 1970s that still has mostly old stuff on it and enough neon to light up downtown."

Cheryl grinned. "I'll buy the first round, and if I go for a second, remind me I'm driving to Tulsa at the crack of dawn tomorrow morning."

"I make no promises," Mara said, holding up her hand.

The bar was mostly empty when they walked in. A few old-timers sat at the tables scattered around the dance floor. No one noticed Mara and Cheryl as they entered. Mara went straight to the bar.

"Do you still have the best apple shandy in southern Missouri?" she asked the older man behind the bar.

Merle flipped the dishrag he always carried over his shoulder as a grin split his face. "Did you get kicked out the one time you tried to con some salesman passing through to buy for you? Never tried that one again, did ya?"

"I'm a fast learner, and now that I'm legal, I'll have the shandy." Merle came around the bar quickly and wrapped his arms around Mara's waist, squeezing her tight. He'd been one of her grandfather's best friends, and although he readily allowed her and the guys in back in the old days, he'd never served them. Not even the shandy, which was more apple juice or cider than beer.

"Me, too," Cheryl added, hopping onto a stool at the bar.

"I'll make it two," he said. "I hadn't heard you were back in town."

That was surprising. Mara had figured CarlaAnn and her gossiping cronies would have spread the news of Mara's near arrest all over town by now.

"I'm here for work," Mara said.

"Come to think of it, some civic-minded soul might have mentioned you and a package of stolen cookies?" Merle winked at her as he slid the drinks across the bar. Mara shook her head. She would bet money CarlaAnn or another of her ilk were spreading the news.

"It was a misunderstanding. I'm actually working on Mallard's security system."

Merle shrugged and went back to work. Mara took a good look around. A few of the neon signs had changed, but the juke was the same, and the polished dance floor still gleamed in the dim light. Juanita roamed among the tables, waiting on her customers.

"This place is exactly what I thought it would be," Cheryl said as she turned in her seat. She sipped from the frosty glass. "And the drink is better."

"He won't tell anyone his secret, and I've never had a better one. Not in any of the über-hip clubs, not in the dive joints and not in any of those bottled options you find at grocery stores."

The jukebox turned on and a wailing, twangy tune warbled through the bar's speakers.

"You're not really leaving at the crack of dawn, are you?" Mara asked.

"By ten, that way I'm home by early afternoon. No rush-hour traffic." Cheryl didn't like driving in heavy traffic. She'd gotten around as Zeke's nanny because Mara usually chose to stay in downtown areas where everything was in walking distance.

"You'll call when you get in?" Mara asked.

Cheryl nodded. "And you'll call when…

well, when the little man does anything of consequence? Or not of consequence?"

"Yes." Mara would not get maudlin. Cheryl leaving was a good thing. She would love her job with the school district, the wedding planning and the trip with her father. Mara was a grown woman with a good job who could easily hire another nanny for her child if she needed to. Hiring someone as good as Cheryl, that was the problem. Of course, there was the other option. The staying-in-Slippery-Rock option.

She wanted… God, it didn't matter what she wanted. It mattered that Zeke was well cared for, and she was equipped to do that caring, even after her job took her to another strange hotel in a distant town. A town that didn't have a decent apple shandy, or a bar that might have been caught in a time warp.

She slid a few bills across the bar but didn't finish her drink.

Staying in Slippery Rock wasn't really an option, it was a pipe dream. A second thought, and this wasn't the time for second thoughts. She'd given in to enough of them over the past two years. She'd nearly called James a dozen times early in her pregnancy, and again after Zeke was born. But telling the man he was a father over the phone seemed wrong, and she had known she wasn't strong enough to do it in person. Even after her therapist assured her she should face this last demon, she'd told herself that she was too busy, that Zeke was too little, that "later" would have to do.

Cheryl's voice cut through her thoughts. "You're going to be okay, you know. You and Zeke, you and your family."

"I know."

"Don't run, not now."

Cheryl knew almost everything about Mara's past. She knew about the pranks and graduation night; she knew about the neglect that marked Mara's first few years of life. She knew everything except who the father of Mara's baby was, but she had probably guessed it was someone from Slippery Rock.

Mara took a deep breath. "I'm not going to run. I ran from here once before, but I'm not going to run this time." Mara took one more sip of her drink. "I just want to." Because not telling James would be so much simpler than telling him.

James with the perfect family history, the perfect job and the ability almost always to do the right thing might never understand why she'd walked away from him. Why she had needed finally to confront those first few years of her life, and why she needed to do that without him in her life.

"Are you ready to leave?" she asked Cheryl. "We haven't been to the marina yet, but you'll see most of it from the street."

Cheryl nodded, and as they started for the door, she left Mara with her thoughts, seeming to understand that she needed to think.

Samson and Maddie Tyler were horrible parents. They had been too wrapped up in one another to give any attention to their children. She could remember many times in whatever cramped apartment Samson was renting when she and Collin had stayed alone while their parents went out. When Amanda, their younger sister, was born, Samson and Maddie were gone even more often. Mara never doubted that her parents loved one another, but the lack of love they had for their children had scarred her. Even after the three of them came to live at the orchard with their grandparents, Mara would worry when Gran would go to the grocery store or when Granddad was late coming in for supper.

As a teen, she covered that worry with a carefree attitude, and in all of her personal relationships, she did a good job of keeping people at a distance. All except one: James Calhoun. She'd never told him the worst of

what had happened before she and Collin and
Amanda came to Slippery Rock, but she had
told him other things.

It was a chance meeting during her first
year in grad school and his year at the police academy when things between them
went further than friendship. When she'd
started thinking of James not just as one of
her brother's cute friends but as a man who
made her stomach do funny little flips, and
whose touch made her skin burn. After that
first weekend, it had been hard to separate
herself from him, hard to keep things light
and easy between them.

How many times had she heard Maddie
on the phone with one girlfriend or another,
talking about how crazy she was for her husband, how he made her stomach clench and
how his touch burned? Those were the same
feelings she had for James, and the knowledge made her nervous.

James was part of the reason she chose the
job with Cannon. He made her want things
that she knew she couldn't have, and if she
lived on the road while he was tied to Slippery Rock, it was simpler to keep things easy
between them. To convince herself that her
feelings for him were the result of really good

sex or the fact that seeing him only sporadically kept things fresh.

Mara didn't want her entire life to be wrapped up in one person. She wanted a career, financial security and to know she could take care of herself. When she found out she was pregnant, she went from scared to terrified in a heartbeat.

"Which way?" Cheryl asked, pulling Mara out of her thoughts as they exited the bar.

"Right," she said, and they started toward the marina. Mara pointed out the pontoon boats and speedboats in the marina and the ample dock space available. Obviously some of the tourists were still staying away after the tornado.

"The air is so clean here," Cheryl said, breathing deep. "I'm going to soak in as much of it as I can before I head to Tulsa."

"I've always thought they should bottle it. Pine and lake and, I know it's only my imagination, but I swear there is a hint of fruit under it all."

"I'm just glad there is no undertone of manure. Didn't you say there is a big dairy farm here?"

"Other side of town, and out in the country so—" Mara walked into a solid wall of muscle as she spoke. A hint of sandalwood joined those other scents, sending her senses into overdrive. She knew that scent, knew the feel of the muscles under her hands. She tilted her head up and saw those same chocolate-brown eyes that had glared at her less than twenty-four hours ago. "Hi, James," she said, stepping carefully away from him and his muscles.

"Mara."

"Are you on patrol?"

"Do you need to be arrested?" His voice held a teasing note, but then his gaze caught on something—or someone—to her right and narrowed. "Hello," he said, using the voice she associated with his professional side. Kind, courteous. The way he'd spoken to CarlaAnn at the grocery store, not the way he spoke to friends.

"I'm Cheryl—"

"This is Cheryl," Mara said at the same time Cheryl stuck out her hand. "Cheryl is my n—" She hadn't told James about his baby on the phone or in the middle of him almost arresting her, and she definitely couldn't tell him about the child on the sidewalk after visiting a bar. "My friend," she said, insisting to the quiet voice inside that it wasn't a lie. Cheryl *was* her friend, in addition to being her nanny.

"I'm just in town for the night," Cheryl

added helpfully, "and Mara was showing me around a bit."

Tension crackled between Mara and James. Even in the darkening evening, she could see his eyebrows draw together and his lips form that thin line they'd had at the grocery store the day before. Which was silly. It wasn't as if Mara was not allowed to have a friend, or she and her friend had been doing anything illegal. Even if they had been, James wasn't in uniform, which probably meant he was off duty.

"Another security expert for the grocery store?" he asked.

"No, I'm a na—"

"Cheryl works for a school in Tulsa," Mara said. "She decided to hook up with me before she gets roped into her sister's wedding plans."

Cheryl raised an eyebrow at Mara's explanation. Then understanding dawned in her expression. She turned her attention to the man before them, probably comparing his features to the baby waiting at the B and B. After a moment she nodded like she understood everything.

"I'm going to finish my walk while you two—" she pointed her finger between them "—get reacquainted."

Mara wanted to call her back, but that was silly. She could exchange a few pleasantries with James in the twilight, with the last rays of sunlight shooting golden flecks into his brown hair. She swallowed.

"So, I guess CarlaAnn is outing me as a kleptomaniac around town," she began, keeping her voice light.

James watched Cheryl walking down the street for a moment, and the interest in his gaze hit Mara hard in the belly. He couldn't be interested in *Cheryl*. That would just be too… What did Mara care who he was interested in? She'd spent the past two years getting over James Calhoun. She didn't want to get under him again.

"I guess going back into the store to reassure her Mike did hire you, or at least your company, and that you weren't an actual shoplifter didn't do the trick."

"Did you really think the truth would stop CarlaAnn's rumor mill? But, thanks. You didn't have to do that." His gaze remained trained on Cheryl. Annoyed, Mara snapped her fingers. "Hello, I'm over here."

"What?" He turned to Mara as if realizing she was still standing before him. Just the confidence booster her vanity needed. "Sorry, I just… Is she…" He pointed to Cheryl, who was halfway down the block already. "Are you and she…"

"Friends? Yes, I believe I introduced her as my friend."

"So that's it." The words sounded almost excited, and Mara couldn't figure out why.

"That's what?"

"You're friends. That's it." James shook his head. "This is weird. Should I apologize?"

The conversation seemed to be going around in a circle that Mara couldn't see.

"Aplogize for what?"

"You're *friends*. And I kept coming around—"

"Yes, we're friends. I don't know what is *it* about that fact. And why should my having a friend mean you shouldn't have come around?" This circle talk was making her dizzy. Maybe she hadn't been ready for Merle's apple shandy.

"Not that you have a friend. That you have a *friend*," he said, emphasizing the word. "I always wondered what made you walk away like that. Now I know. It wasn't me."

Mara's eyes widened and her mouth dropped open. Not a friend. A *friend*. James thought she was, what, bisexual, and that made her walking out on him okay? "I don't know what you think you understand, but you are completely and totally off base—"

"It's okay to be a lesbian—"

"I'm not a lesbian."

"Okay, a bisexual—"

"If that look means you think you might be joining in a little three-way action now that I'm back in town, think again, Deputy Doofus. I'm not bisexual and I'm not a lesbian. I am a straight, CIS-gendered female who likes men."

James blinked. "But she's... And you're... You said she was here to hook up with you."

"I didn't mean *hook up* hook up. God, why do men assume women can be friends with one another only if they're also hooking up?"

"It was a natural assumption from the way you introduced her."

"Are you sure you passed that police academy test? Your deductive reasoning could use a little work."

"Yes, I'm sure I passed it, and my deductive reasoning isn't flawed. You insinuated—"

"—that she was my friend. She's also my employee, and no, that doesn't mean I pay her for sex." Mara intentionally lowered her voice even though there were no other people on the sidewalk. "There is no sex between Cheryl and me. I thought you'd already gotten the memo that my preferences lean toward men."

"I didn't know friends randomly meet up

with other friends in strange towns where one or the other of them is working."

"Then you obviously don't have very good friends." Mara crossed her arms over her chest. "Or you live in a town with a single stoplight, and so do all your friends."

"Touché." James put his hands in his pockets. "You look good."

"So now that I'm not an attached lesbian-slash-bisexual, you're going straight into hook-up mode?"

James grinned. "It was a statement of fact," he said, "not an invitation for either of us to go jumping into whatever lake we were swimming in up until two years ago."

Two years ago. Zeke. Fatherhood. Arguing with James about her sexuality was another no-no in the parenthood talk they needed to have. "Yeah, well, that was a pretty deep lake."

"I was thinking it was kind of shallow," he said, reaching to curl a lock of her hair around his finger. "We kept things light and simple, and you walked away."

She could feel his heat even across the distance between them. Wanted to feel the soft pads of his fingers against the skin of her cheek. Wanted to drink in that sandalwood smell that was James Calhoun. "I...thought you wanted simple."

"What the hell did I know about what I wanted? Other than more time with you," he said, and his brown eyes seemed to darken. Mara closed her eyes. She could lean forward just a little bit, could stand on tiptoe and her lips would meet his. She would have him, one more time, in her orbit. God, she wanted that.

She snapped her eyes open. That was not how this was going to happen. She was not hooking up with James one night only to tell him he was a father the next. She couldn't do that, not to him. Not to Zeke. She was better than this, stronger than the kind of person who let herself get wound up in a man and forgot about all the responsibilities in her life.

Like the baby in her room at the B and B.

"Cheryl is my nanny," she said, blurting the words out as she took a deliberate step away from James. His eyes widened and she immediately wished the words back.

"You have a nanny?" He cocked his head to the side, confusion evident from the slight drop in his jaw.

"Technically, my son has a nanny. I employ a child care provider who also happens to be a friend."

"You have a son?" James pulled away from

her, both physically and emotionally. She watched it happen in a smooth motion that started when his hand dropped from her hair and ended when his eyebrows beetled in that cold cop expression she'd seen the day before. The same cop expression his father used in any number of school assemblies and during "conversations" with her outside the principal's office in high school. James was just as good at that condescending look as his father, but coming from Jonathan Calhoun, the look had never hurt like this. Like a bomb had exploded in her belly.

"He's fourteen months old," she said, forcing her voice to remain crisp and clear. She could pretend to be just as calculated and cold as he; she would not break in front of him. Mara closely watched his expression as he counted back. Fourteen months, plus nine for the pregnancy, would land him at the conference he'd attended in July in Nashville. She'd been writing a new security protocol for a musical publishing company in Nashville. That was the last time they'd seen one another until this week. Realization hardened his gaze into an impenetrable brick. "Yes," she said, "I got pregnant in Nashville."

James took another step back, putting more breathing room between them. "We used protection," he said, his voice wooden. "Every time."

"Condoms break. The pill isn't one hundred percent effective. Even used together, things can happen." Mara started to reach for him but quickly drew her hand back. He wouldn't welcome her touch, not now. Maybe not ever again, and she was going to have to deal with that. She hadn't wanted to tell him in the middle of the street, but she'd felt cornered. She'd used their son to put a wall between them, and she hated herself for that.

Her hands itched to touch him, to comfort him. She crossed her arms over her chest, and tried to put all the remorse she felt into her voice. "I didn't realize I was pregnant until I was almost five months along."

"And, what, between that five-month mark and now you couldn't pick up a phone?"

His expression closed. No anger, no annoyance. Not even panic at finding out he was a father. There was nothing, and the nothing made Mara's chest ache.

"I couldn't tell you on the phone," she began.

James snorted derisively. "No, you didn't *want* to tell me on the phone," he said and spun on his heel.

"James, wait," she called after him, but he

kept walking. She couldn't move. At the corner, he turned. When he was gone from her sight, it was as if an engine turned on inside, making her legs move to follow. She hurried after him, but he had disappeared by the time Mara reached the corner. "Damn it," she whispered, and smacked her hand against the brick of the building. She winced and shook her hand. "Damn it."

JAMES PACED THE living room of the small house he'd bought overlooking the lake. It sat on the far western edge of Water Street, and the view of the calm lake never failed to center him. To remind him of the things he wanted. A good career. A family. Making his parents proud. Being a good friend.

Tonight the calmness of the water mocked him. He had a son. A son he had never met because, when Mara walked away, he let her.

There were things he could have done to find her, but instead of going after her, instead of forcing her to talk to him, he'd let her walk away.

And tonight he'd walked away from her because he didn't know what to do with any of this. Her coming back to town. How she made him feel, even after two years. The child he didn't know.

Dear God, he had a son, and he didn't even know what the child looked like. He didn't have Mara's phone number to call her to apologize.

To ask her if he could meet the kid. Did he want to meet him?

James didn't have to think, he already knew the answer to the question. He wanted to meet his child.

The sky had turned a brilliant orange, the last rays of sunlight glinting off the surface of the lake like a million tiny diamonds. Like the diamond he'd bought two years ago. The one currently hidden in the oak credenza that had belonged to his great-grandfather when he was sheriff of Wall County.

James had fooled himself, thinking that the on-again, off-again relationship with Mara went off simply because of the distance. That weekend in Nashville, when they had wandered Music Row for hours, when their bodies had come together like puzzle pieces, had been different from their other encounters. Mara was softer that trip. She'd talked a little more about missing her family. He made the mistake of believing her homesickness was about him as well as her grandmother and siblings. A sunset not unlike this one had made him think of the family he wanted, and for the first time he added a face to the shadowy figure of the woman he'd always envisioned by his side.

It was always Mara.

And then she was gone, and a hotel bellhop arrived to pack her things. James had searched the airport and train station, but hadn't found her. He'd called at least a hundred times before getting that first 'this number is no longer in service' message. That was when he tried email. Over and over and over until he realized she wasn't going to answer.

James pulled open the small desk drawer next to the envelope slot. The little black jeweler's box had dust on it, but he didn't bother to wipe it off. Instead, he shut the drawer a little too hard, and a small corner of wood popped off the drawer face. He picked up the shard and tossed it into the trash can.

This was not what he wanted, not what he needed. Not now. Two years ago…he had been crazy in love enough to try to make it work, at least. But now there was too much at stake. James grabbed a beer from the fridge, then crossed to the back porch to drink and watch the sun go down. The beer was icy, the last rays of sun hot, yet they didn't soothe him. He was still twisted up over Mara's revelation.

He might still be attracted to Mara, but he'd gotten over loving her long ago. He was now the acting sheriff, and she'd nearly been arrested yesterday. It wouldn't matter that she'd done nothing wrong. Perception was what mattered, and thanks to CarlaAnn the perception was that Mara Tyler was caught shoplifting her first day back in town.

Then, there was the complication from their graduation night escapade.

Over all of that was the baby. He wasn't in love with Mara, and he wasn't foolish enough to think only people in love could raise a child together, but did he even register in her thought process over the past year? He had gone along with Mara's insistence of keeping things light and friendly. He hadn't chased after her when she walked away. There was no way he could walk away from a child, though, and there was no way he could trust that Mara wouldn't disappear on him again.

Everything about seeing her, about this situation was a mess.

The fact that Mara hid the baby from him for more than a year, and the fact that their years-long series of booty calls led to a baby? Those things would lead to gossip, and gossip about the present would quickly reignite gossip about the past, which could lead to his part in the school bus prank.

Thousands of dollars in damage had been inflicted on the bus fleet because, instead of just leaving the lights on as Mara had planned, James took it upon himself to deflate the front tires on several of the buses. The weight of the vehicles on the wheel wells had warped them beyond repair. The cost of the repairs pushed what would have been an annoyance for the school district into the realm of felony. James had anonymously paid restitution for the bus damage, and the statute of limitations was long past, so he couldn't actually be charged with the felony. Still, who would vote for a sheriff who'd committed a felony—even an uncharged felony?

Who would want even a deputy with that kind of history, and without a job, what kind of father could he be?

He finished the beer and let the bottle hang from his fingertips while the porch swing gently swayed in the evening air.

There was the possibility the baby might

not be his. James didn't like to think of Mara with other men, but the fact was, the two of them hadn't been in an exclusive relationship. They hadn't been in a relationship at all. They'd hooked up throughout the Midwest whenever they were in the same areas. But then he returned to Slippery Rock and she went on with her hotel-hopping life. She could have had a man in every town.

James rolled his eyes. Now he was acting like some cheated-on wife in a bad movie. Mara was a lot of things, but she wasn't the type to have a man in every city in the Midwest. If Mara said the baby was his, then it was, and he would have to deal with that. Would have to deal with the schmucks her parents had been and the damage they'd done to her. Would have to deal with her envy of his traditional childhood. Would have to deal with his parents, who had very specific ideas about what the life of James Calhoun should look like. He doubted those ideas included a woman like Mara.

The sun sank past the pine and spruce and oak trees lining the lakeshore, throwing the water into darkness.

What either of his parents thought about him having a child with Mara Tyler, though, didn't matter. What mattered was that he had the child. Mara was the mother. James was the father. It might not be the family he'd envisioned when he bought this house, but it was the family he had.

He would figure out a way to make this work.

CHAPTER FOUR

MARA STOOD LOOKING around her suite at the B and B on Friday morning, trying to find anything that could delay her trip to the orchard. There was nothing. The beds were made, the breakfast dishes on the tray in the hallway. Zeke was clean and dry and happy. Cheryl had left a half hour before. There was nothing more Mara could do on the Mallard's account until Mike returned from vacation on Monday. She straightened the shampoo and body wash containers on the small vanity.

She had been in town for only a few days but had yet to make the trip to the orchard. Had spoken to Gran and Collin briefly on the phone once, but hadn't told them about Zeke. Hadn't told them about James.

All that would change in less than twenty minutes. She could only hope they wouldn't walk away from her as James had done last night.

There was a big chance they would, and

that would be on her. Because she hadn't told them how very much she had missed them over the past year and a half. She had just cut them out. She'd invented reasons to cancel trips to the orchard, skipping phone calls and video chats. She had avoided them just as she had avoided James.

Damn it, if she could do the past two years over, she would have done them differently. Scratch that—not just the past two. The past ten, because from the moment she left Slippery Rock for college, she had been avoiding any kind of emotional entanglement, especially those that might mean pain. She kept their interaction superficial on those quick holiday visits. If her time with them wasn't light and fun, her family would realize just how much she wanted to be part of their unit, and that would make it harder to stay away. Back then, she couldn't be part of them, though, not without putting James's future at risk because of that stupid prank. With her out of town, the investigation into what had happened that night had gone cold. But the town had their assumptions and even those quick trips home at first had started the talk up again. Then, once she was pregnant, she couldn't because that would entail revealing the baby's father. Telling them about James would put her—and him—right in the middle of town gossip. Could land one or the other of them in jail, and what good would that do? Was there a statute of limitations on vandalism?

Mara crossed the room to fluff the pillows on the bed and watched Zeke for a moment. He was sitting up, banging his baby fists against the tiny piano keys on his favorite mirrored activity set. His hair was the same color as James's, but his eyes were more hazel. He was a good boy, a smart boy, and he deserved a father who would love him.

James was meant to be a lawman, destined to be sheriff. At some point he would find a pretty woman who would make the perfect sheriff's wife, who would work with local charities alongside the ministers' wives. He deserved that kind of life and, while she might crave the June Cleaver fantasy of life, Mara knew fairy tales rarely came true for people like her. If James couldn't love Zeke, then she would love Zeke enough for both of them. But James had to be the one to walk away, and not just because he'd been caught off guard by the news. She would have to talk to him again, and soon. Right now, though, she needed to talk to her family.

She would have to face not only her lies of

omission to James but also her family's judgment. And she could only hope the gossip about graduation night would stay buried. If it didn't, it wouldn't matter that she was now a security expert or that James was a fine sheriff's deputy. The only thing that would matter to Slippery Rock was that they had put the school in jeopardy.

Once she repaired her relationship with her family, she would fix this thing with James. Would make him understand that she'd needed to get herself into an emotionally healthy place before she could face him. God, that sounded like a lame, made-up excuse. She really hadn't thought this whole thing through. There were thousands of times she could have told James he was a father. Phone call, text message, Skype, social media. She had all his contact information.

And if those weren't immature solutions to an all-too-adult problem, Mara wasn't sure what was. Her therapist would have a field day with her trying to tell James he was a father by cell phone, social media or Skype. She might as well fully revert to her teenage self and break up with a guy by text message.

She considered contacting him to set up one of their clandestine meetings, and then telling him once she had him alone. That had seemed just as awful as telling him over the phone. So she didn't call at all. The longer she'd put off contacting him, the harder that call became until she'd convinced herself she would simply go home to break the news. There had been plenty of reasons not to come to Slippery Rock—her work, her therapy, Zeke cutting teeth, having a bad cold. Damn it, it was Cheryl quitting that had finally started Mara seriously considering coming back. Not because she needed babysitters, but because of Cheryl's commitment to her family. Mara wanted that connection, that commitment for herself. Then the tornado hit, and she'd known she couldn't keep making excuses. She had to tell James. Had to face her family. She couldn't continue to be the kind of runaway her own parents were.

James had already walked away, and, God, why suddenly did James not wanting to be part of Zeke's life hurt so bad? Until she'd seen him do it last night, the possibility of him stepping out of Zeke's life had seemed so much simpler than sharing parenting duties.

There was every chance her family would walk away, too.

"Okay, Mara, you have the plan. Now get out of this B and B and set things in motion," she said, standing. She turned off Zeke's activity stand, and he shook his fists at her in annoyance. "We have an appointment," she said, and he grinned as if he knew what that meant. Probably it was just gas. He still smiled when he had gas.

Mara blew out a breath, picked up Zeke and slung the colorful tote she used as a diaper bag over her shoulder. She could keep looking for a reason to stay holed up in the B and B or she could be a grown-up and face the music with her family.

She was saving the rest of her conversation with James for another time, though. After last night, she was unprepared to tell him he had no responsibilities where Zeke was concerned. Where she was concerned. She gently tweaked Zeke's nose.

"Okay, little guy, here we go. Don't worry. They're going to love you," she said, hating the slight emphasis on that last word. Gran hadn't turned her, Collin and Amanda away when they were little, but Mara was an adult now. An adult who shouldn't have kept this part of her life secret for so long.

Zeke put his pudgy hands on her cheeks and mumbled something that sounded peculiarly like, "Don't worry, mama." It was impossible. Zeke had two words in his vocabulary at this point, and neither was *don't*, *worry* or *ma*. He said *dog* periodically and had said *ball* a handful of times.

Still, his mumbling steadied her, and she rested her forehead on his for a moment, breathing in the scent of powder and lotion and little boy. After a moment, her stomach muscles relaxed, and breathing no longer felt as if she were dragging air through passages lined with sharpened sticks.

Downstairs, she locked Zeke into his car seat, then buckled herself into the driver's seat. He waved his hands as he watched the world go by out the rear window. The narrow streets of downtown Slippery Rock rolled by, opening up to the wider state highway that led to the orchard. Despite being a weekday, there wasn't much traffic on the road. She passed a couple of farm trucks and a few minivans, but the cattle and alpacas—she would have to ask Collin when alpacas had come to Slippery Rock—outnumbered the humans she passed. Everyone lifted their fingers in the familiar steering wheel wave she remembered from her teenage years.

No one staffed the small roadside stand her grandfather built the year Collin turned twelve and she turned eleven, and she pulled into the drive leading to the orchard.

A few stumps were still visible in the apple

orchard, but saplings outnumbered the stumps. She spotted the red roof of the big barn in the distance, and as her SUV cleared the drive, the old house came into view. Red-roofed like the barn, the two-story farmhouse hadn't changed. A porch swing rocked in the light breeze. The steps leading up to the door were lined with Gran's snapdragons. The tall oak still stood in the middle of the drive with a rope swing hanging from a branch.

She'd learned to swing on the old tractor seat. Had pushed Amanda when she was little. Had hidden in the branches with Collin when their parents had shown up unexpectedly one spring. She and Collin had been petrified their parents would make them go to whatever cramped and dirty apartment they lived in, but a few hours later their parents drove away. Granddad came to sit in the swing, pretending to talk to himself as he reassured the two of them that they didn't have to go anywhere.

She wanted to go inside. Wanted to push open the door and announce herself like she belonged there. Well, Gran had always said this was her home.

Mara gathered Zeke and the baby bag and walked up the steps and into the house. The same hardwood floors greeted her, the same overstuffed furniture. The TV was still in the corner near the fireplace, the sofa under the big picture window. To her left, the dining room led to the kitchen and the family room.

"Anybody home?" she called out, because usually there was some kind of noise inside the house, but today there was nothing.

"Back here, sweetheart." She heard her grandmother's voice from the kitchen and started in that direction. "Just putting a pie for the weekend farmers' market in the oven. They're finishing up the new roof this afternoon and—" Gran stopped talking when Mara crossed the threshold. "You have a baby."

Gran's blue eyes, so similar to Mara's own, widened. Zeke waved his fist in the air, then buried his face in Mara's shoulder. He was a happy, well-adjusted baby, but new people always made him a bit shy.

"I do." Mara was unsure what to say, how to read the shock on Gran's face. Good shock? She seemed a little pale, and the knuckles had turned white from their tight grip on the countertop. Gran broke her hip earlier this year, and Collin had been very worried. Mara didn't want Gran to collapse. Maybe she should have waited until Collin was at the house before walking in. "Gran, why don't you sit down?" Mara took her grandmother's arm, leading her to the Formica-topped table while balancing Zeke on her hip.

Gran brushed Mara's hands away. "You have a baby." She squeezed Mara's hand. "He has your grandfather's chin." Then she smacked her hand against Mara's shoulder. She winced, more from surprise than pain. "Why didn't you tell us, Butter Bean?" Her eyes narrowed and she glared at Mara for a moment, but behind the glare was something that looked a lot like love. Support.

This, this almost immediate acceptance was beyond any of Mara's expectations. She closed her eyes for a moment. It was going to be okay. It would take time, especially with James, but things would work out. She could do this. She would do this.

"Mara?" Gran's voice brought her back to the cozy kitchen, and she sat in the chair across from her grandmother.

All the reasons she'd kept Zeke from her family tumbled through her mind. She wanted to get herself together. She hadn't told James. But all of those reasons skirted around the truth she'd been afraid to admit even to herself. And in this kitchen, the one where she'd eaten butter beans and declared they were the only bean she would ever like, where she'd cried when the school put her in the advanced program, where she'd run after every minor and major scrape in her life, she couldn't tell a half-truth.

"I was afraid," she said. She hadn't even told the therapist about her fear. That Gran would think badly of her, that this would be the thing that caused her family finally to turn away from her. She knew it was silly. Babies brought families together, at least in books and on television. In her specific case, though, babies made adults do crazy, irresponsible, unforgivable things.

Gran's soft hand cupped her cheek, and her expression softened. "Butter Bean, what did you have to be afraid of?"

So many things. That she would ruin her life or James's. That Gran wouldn't understand.

"That I couldn't do it. That I wasn't made to be a mother. That you'd be disappointed." She paused, ran her hand over Zeke's baby-fine hair and said, "That I'd leave all the child-rearing in your more-than-capable hands."

Gran clucked at that. "When have you ever left anything you really wanted for someone else to handle?"

"I'm so like them, like Samson and Maddie, though. I like traveling, I like living out of my suitcase, I like not being tied down—"

"I could never be disappointed in you. Worried for you, yes. Disappointed? Not in a million years." Gran seemed to consider her next words carefully. "I love my son, but I stopped…trying to understand Samson a long time ago. And you are like him, but in all the good ways. You inherited his excitement for the unknown, his natural curiosity. He could never seem to find a balance, but you? Sweetheart, you travel for work, but you've worked for the same company since college. You might not live here or visit often enough for my liking, but you call every week. You remember birthdays and anniversaries. You are a responsible, kindhearted woman, and I'm proud that I had a hand in raising you."

Mara smiled and leaned into Gran's gentle touch. She closed her eyes and sighed. "I'm here now. Zeke and I are going to stop being afraid of things. We're going to face everything head-on."

Gran put her hand over her heart and her eyes glistened. "Zeke?" The word was a whisper in the quiet room.

Mara nodded. "I named him for Granddad. Ezekiel Tyler—"

The back door opened before she could

say his last name, which was probably just as well. Until she got things hammered out between her and James, it was best to keep that to herself. She turned and saw her brother, looking tanned and relaxed, in the doorway.

Collin looked from Gran to Mara and the baby. He blinked and shook his head as if he couldn't believe what he was seeing, and then stood a bit straighter. Collin tilted his head to the side as if considering all the options for a baby being in their kitchen.

"I guess you weren't kidding when you said you had something to tell us," he said. Collin put the ball cap he wore in the orchard on a peg in the mudroom, then continued into the kitchen. He grabbed a bottle of water from the refrigerator and took a long drink.

"Collin," Gran began, but Mara stopped her.

"It's okay. Yeah, pretty big news. Something I thought needed to be shared in person," Mara said. Her voice shook only a little, and for that she was thankful. Gran was the first hurdle in her family; Collin would be the second and probably the biggest. She and he had been close until she became pregnant. "I have a son."

"He doesn't look like a newborn."

Mara swallowed. "I know. I had some

things… I needed to figure out a few things. Before I told you and Gran and Amanda."

"And the *things* are figured out now?"

Mara opened her mouth to say yes, but she didn't want to lie. "Mostly."

"You're okay?"

She nodded. "Good job, good health benefits." Mara wasn't sure what more she could tell either Gran or Collin without first talking to James. "And now I'm home."

Collin put the water bottle down and crossed the room. He put his index finger under Zeke's chin, and the little boy grinned at him. "He looks like Amanda did when she was a baby."

"He has your grandfather's chin," Gran added. "And his name."

Collin's eyes widened, and Mara nodded. "I call him Zckc."

"Hello, Zeke," Collin said after a long moment. "I'm your uncle, Collin."

CHAPTER FIVE

JAMES SAT IN his Jeep outside the Slippery Rock B and B—hands at ten and two despite the SUV's parked position—with the air-conditioning blasting. Her SUV wasn't in the lot, and he wasn't above tracking her down in town, but he'd rather have this conversation in private. If he hadn't stormed off last night, they could have talked then, but he'd been too floored by her revelation.

He rubbed his hand over his neck.

Angry, a little.

Scared, maybe. About the baby, about what the baby meant for his future in the Slippery Rock Sheriff's Department. About what the baby meant for his future with Mara. Or what his future might look like without her. There had to be some dark reason she'd kept the baby from him for two years.

For the life of him, he couldn't figure out what the reason was. He had a good job, came from a good family, had the same core group of friends he'd had since high school. For Pete's sake, he was still a member of the Slippery Rock Methodist Church along with his parents and grandparents. He didn't attend regularly, but he donated at all the usual holidays. He wasn't a mean-spirited drunk, and he wasn't a crazy, let's-jump-off-a-cliff drunk, either. He actually wasn't a drunk at all, despite the weekly dart games at the Slope. One or two beers was his limit, and not only because he was a cop. Because he didn't like the feeling that came with having a few too many beers or shots.

For her to have kept knowledge of the baby from him for all this time didn't make sense. It didn't fit into his plans on how he'd start a family, for sure. More than that, her secrecy didn't fit into the Mara he knew. No, their relationship hadn't been serious, but she'd never lied to him before. Not intentionally and not by omission. The Mara he'd known for most of his life was fearless. She did what she wanted, when she wanted and to hell with the consequences. In that respect, keeping their son from him made sense, but under that brave, rebel exterior, Mara had a kind and soft heart. She couldn't bear to watch

Dumbo because the circus kept the elephant calf from Mrs. Jumbo.

James clenched his jaw. None of this made sense.

A dark SUV turned the corner and pulled into the B and B's lot. James exited his Jeep and strode across the pavement, waves of heat rising up and making him sweat.

"We need to talk," he said without preamble as Mara got out of the driver's seat. The woman from last night wasn't there, and the baby seat in the back seat was empty. A quick stab of disappointment hit his belly.

Mara didn't blink. "Why don't you come inside?" she said as if she were inviting him into her home instead of a rented suite.

He followed her up the walk, reaching around her to open the door.

"Thank you," she said, her voice starchy.

"You're welcome," he returned, his voice just as firm as hers.

Mara unlocked the door to room seven. It was empty. No baby. No nanny. Just a green square playpen thing with mesh sides and dinosaurs on the fabric. A light blanket lay on the bottom, more dinosaurs on it, and a stuffed T-Rex sat in one corner.

Well, at least he knew the baby thing was

for real now. Not that he'd doubted it. Mara wasn't one to make up stories.

She folded her arms over her chest and watched him a long moment. "Well?" she asked. "You wanted to talk. Here we are. Talk."

James wasn't sure where to start. "I think you're the one with some explaining to do."

"After the way you stomped off last night, *you* have some explaining to do."

He squinted. "Because I needed time to process you having my baby *two years ago,* I'm the one who has the explaining to do?"

"Technically, I had him fourteen months ago. We haven't spoken in two years."

"This is really the way you want to handle it? Me the pretend bad guy so you can be the Virgin Mary with the surprise baby?"

An expression he couldn't read flashed over her face. Mara bent to pick up the baby blanket and began folding it into smaller and smaller squares. "You aren't the bad guy. There is no bad guy in this scenario." James harrumphed. "Okay, maybe I was a little bit of a bad girl. I was scared."

"Of what?"

She put the blanket down and held her hands out at her sides. "Everything? I didn't know how to be a mother. We only had one real conversation. Every dinner we started ended up in doggie bags and eaten cold because we would run back to whatever hotel we were staying in. I don't consider cold meals actual dates. Then I was pregnant. It was too much, and I freaked out, and I cut myself off from everything."

Mara picked the blanket up again and put it into a bag. She tossed the T-Rex in, too, and then took a suitcase from beneath the bed. She pulled open drawers and began to pack. James grabbed a handful of lacy garments and put them back in the drawer.

"No, you don't get to tell me I have a kid and then pack up to leave. I don't care how scared you are." His gaze landed on a picture frame on the bedside table. Big brown eyes stared at him from the frame. The same brown hair, the same nose. Same smile. The jaw was different, but there were enough similarities between himself and the baby in the picture that James forgot to breathe for a long moment. He picked up the picture, lightly tracing the lines of the chubby face with his fingers.

"I'm not leaving," she said. "I'm moving my things to the orchard."

"But you told me it would be more convenient to stay in town because of the grocery store job."

"I did." Mara put the things he'd tossed into the drawers in the suitcase and shrugged. "Staying here was never about convenience. I wasn't sure how Gran or Collin or Amanda would take the baby news. Having the suite here meant I had a good reason not to stay there if they didn't want me and the baby around."

"So, they didn't know?" She shook her head. That, at least, was a relief. She may have lied by omission, but his best friend hadn't lied either outright or by omission.

"Well, that's a relief." She shot him a questioning glance. "Collin doesn't share his secrets much better than you do, but I was afraid... I'm glad he wasn't keeping the secret, too, is all I meant."

"I'm sorry," she said after a moment. "For not telling you then. For making you think one of your best friends was being dishonest with you. I know how much honesty and integrity is to you." She pulled a few pairs of jeans and some shirts from the bureau, adding them to the suitcase. "The baby looks like you, you know. Same hair and eyes, same smile. I don't expect you to forgive me—"

"But you want me to?"

She grinned sheepishly. "It would make things easier."

"I need to be a little mad at you." Except he was already feeling himself caving in on the anger thing. He could push his feelings about her keeping the kid from him into the background. They could make this work. Somehow. The baby was a real person, not a figment of some bad dream. James's baby. He couldn't turn away from that—it wasn't possible.

"I figured."

"Smart woman."

"I did skip the tenth grade."

"I remember. You went from freshman to junior. Col was not impressed to have you as a classmate *and* sister." This lighthearted banter was better than the serious conversation they needed to have. Easier and so much more familiar to him—at least where Mara was concerned. In every other aspect of his life, James always did the responsible, mature thing. With Mara, however, responsible and mature always turned into simple and easy.

"He was just mad that I made better grades than he did." Finished packing, she zipped the suitcase closed. "I don't expect you to forgive me," she said again. "And I didn't come here to dump this news on you and, I don't know, try to make our lives look like a really bad made-for-TV romantic comedy. Two hapless singles thrown into parenthood or something. I don't want anything from you. I don't need child support or insurance or even a hand changing middle-of-the-night diapers—"

"You have a nanny for that."

"Yesterday was her last day, actually. She left this morning. Also, he sleeps through the night no matter what horrifying things come out of his body. That doesn't matter. What I meant—what I mean is I'm the mom and you're the dad. You can be as involved or you can bc as uninvolved as you want. It's your choice."

His choice. As if being a father was a "check yes or no" decision. The anger he kept pushing away came roaring to the surface. Being a father wasn't an in-or-out choice, not for him. This baby, no matter what challenges he brought, was his family, and hc wouldn't turn his back on family.

Carefully he put the picture on the bed-side table. "It isn't a choice. He's my respon-siblity."

Mara reached for him, taking his hands in hers, and the sizzle that always accompanied her touch raced along his nerve endings. Stupid chemistry, anyway. James pulled away from her.

"That's what I'm trying to tell you," she said. "This isn't a responsibility you have to take on. No one knows you're the father, and no one has to know. You can continue on with your perfect life in your perfect town where you can be the perfect sheriff just like your father was—"

"And live a perfect lie by not taking part in my son's life? I don't think so."

"I'm not asking you to lie. You had a right to know, and now you know, but you don't have a responsibility here. He'll be fine. I can handle it. He'll have a large extended family—an uncle who is going to adore him, a great-grandmother who dotes on him. Amanda's a teenager, so her response will be largely dependent on whatever else is going on in her life, but if she isn't thrilled, I can deal with that, too."

"And what about college? Orthodontic bills? His first car?"

"I have a good job with great benefits and a flexible schedule."

"You have this whole thing planned out, don't you?" he said, keeping his voice soft. He shoved his hands in his pockets. She didn't need him.

From the first time they met up together, he had wondered where he stood in her life. Now he knew. Mara didn't need him. Why did that hurt?

Mara worried her bottom lip between her teeth. "I'm just saying that we were never serious. Our relationship wasn't intended to be long-term for either of us. We were just..."

"Filling a physical desire?" he asked.

She nodded enthusiastically. "Exactly the right phrase. I fulfilled a desire for you, and you did the same for me. It wasn't serious. We weren't making plans. My getting pregnant was an accident, but it doesn't have to ruin your future or mine."

"Because I can just walk away."

"Right."

"Because we were never serious."

"Exactly."

He wanted to ram his fist through the wall, and if she used another *yes* synonym, he was going to do just that. No, the relationship between them wasn't serious, at least in her mind. But he'd bought her a ring. He almost proposed that first day in Nashville, but decided to figure out some extravagant proposal scenario like on social media. He'd wanted to surprise her, to give her an amazing memory. She might have been playing around, but he for damn sure had feelings for her. She was his friend, his buddy. His confidant. She made him feel things—not just physical things—that no one else did.

None of that mattered, not now. Because she might insist they weren't serious about one another two years ago, but the situation had changed. They had a baby and, like it or not, he was now in her life and she was in his. She was still talking, but James couldn't focus on the words as he watched her. Everything blurred out of focus until he saw only her. Those big blue eyes. The curves that hadn't been there two years ago. The voice that still sent shivers along his spine. She was the mother of his child. She was exactly the wrong person to be in his life right now.

He didn't need her kind of complication, not at all. He was the Interim Sheriff of Wall County, and soon he would have to start actual campaigning for the permanent position. People would expect him to make the right decisions, to do the right things. Walking away from his family wasn't a right decision, not by a long shot.

"It *is* serious, Mara. You don't just get to wave some magic wand to make my part in this disappear."

"I can handle the discipline, the education. He won't want for any—"

James cupped his hands around her neck, pulling her to him. Mara squeaked as he laid his lips on hers, silencing her before she could say, for the fifteenth time, that she could be everything for the little boy in the picture. That James could walk away and never feel guilty about it. As if that would ever happen.

Her mouth was soft against his, and she opened to him, her tongue tangling with his. She tasted like banana, and her hair was silky against the back of his hand. James wrapped the length around his fist, holding her in place so that his mouth could plunder hers. Mara wrapped her arms around his neck in response, rising on tiptoe and slanting her head.

This they could do and it would be simple and easy. Just like it had been right up until Nashville. Kissing Mara was the easiest thing in the world for James. It was coming home while also having an adventure—familiar but exciting at the same time.

She made a low sound in her throat, pressing her body against his. Her breasts were fuller than he remembered. He reached to cup her rear with his hand. Her hips were rounder, sexier. She wove her fingers through the short hair at the back of his head, sending another shiver of awareness through his body. Then she pushed her hips against his.

God, he knew what she would feel like beneath him. He knew what to do to make that low sound come from her throat. How to kiss her so that she was weak with wanting. He knew that she liked to be ravished, but that she liked to do the ravishing from time to time, too.

And she wasn't serious about him. Didn't want him in her life. Was giving him an out to continue on with the life that had been planned for him since the day he was born.

He wanted that familiar, planned-out life.

James broke the kiss and rested his forehead against hers for a long moment.

He also wanted the unfamiliar, unplanned life that came with accepting responsibility for the baby they made in Nashville.

He wanted her to admit that while they hadn't exactly been making plans during their weekends-only relationship, it still had been a relationship. And it had been serious enough that they'd both gone out of their way to pretend that it was just about the sex.

"Is that serious enough for you?" he asked. He stepped away from her, putting his hand on the doorknob at his back. "Because if you keep telling people to walk out of your life, that's exactly what they're going to do." He waited for her to say something, anything, for a long moment. Mara only stared at him. James opened the door and walked into the hall.

FOR A LONG MOMENT, Mara stood staring at the door. Fingers touching her lips. Rooted to the spot. And then the anger kicked in.

This was twice he'd walked out on her. Twice in less than twenty-four hours. Yes, she'd been incredibly selfish and allowed her fears about, well, everything, to rule her. But she was trying to be better. Trying not to pack up her things and run off into the night as she'd done after high school, and again two years ago.

Things had been different with James that weekend. She had shared a little of her past with him. She didn't tell him about her career plans, but the things from her past, those were so much more personal than her work.

He'd talked about becoming sheriff—not just for his father, but for himself.

They'd made it through not one but three different meals without a single doggie bag or rushed sex.

The conversations, the changes in their routine, scared her, the similarities between what James said he wanted and the things she wanted for herself—a home, a family, a career. Living out of a suitcase had begun feeling old. She missed her family. Missed having a space of her own.

Mara held no illusions that Slippery Rock would be where she finally put down her adult roots, but she'd considered it. Had lain awake beside him that Saturday night two years ago thinking about it. Wondering if Slippery Rock could be her place, too. Wondering if the attraction and chemistry between them could grow into something more. The possibilities sent her running away from that hotel because, while the thought of living her life with James was exciting, it was also terrifying. What would happen if things didn't work out? There would be no more stolen weekends. Trips to the orchard would be tense and uncomfortable because he would always be in the back of her mind.

She'd been unwilling to take the risk, especially when he'd said zero about her being part of the life he talked about. So she ran, and wound up causing this entire mess in the process.

Well, she had to deal with it now, whether she liked it or not. And uncomfortable as it would be, they needed to talk without him storming off.

Mara followed him into the hallway and outside, catching up as he started the Jeep. She put her hands on the door.

"What the hell was that?" Not the question she'd intended to ask, but a good one, she decided. He'd never kissed her like that, with anger and passion and that little kick of what had to be excitement. The passion and excitement had been there, but the anger gave the kiss an extra jolt. She wanted to feel that jolt again.

She shouldn't want to, but she did. Mara would deal with that later.

"A mistake," he said.

And just like that, the jumpy, skittish feeling in her stomach melted into something that left her feeling cold, so very cold. She rubbed her hands against her arms despite the heat of the summer afternoon.

"Mistake? Right, well, sure. We don't kiss anymore. Haven't for two years. I meant the slamming out of the door," she said, because he didn't need to know that the kiss had thrown her. He could credit the question to her being angry that he'd walked out on her again. "We can't keep walking away from each other when we're angry." Not that anger had driven her away from him before. That was straight-up fear. Maybe they could get to that later, when he wasn't so annoyed that he wore his cop face and tapped his fingers against his steering wheel in staccato beats.

"I'm not angry. I'm pissed off."

"Like there's a difference."

"It's subtle, but it's there. Anger has reason. Pissed off is pure emotion." He looked at her for the first time. "Why does it matter?"

"Because when we continually hold on to the anger, it makes it easy not to look at the deeper issues, the uncomfortable feelings."

James continued to watch her for a long moment, his brown eyes unreadable. "You sound like a therapist."

Yeah, well, a little more than a year in therapy could do that to a person. Mara swallowed.

"I started seeing a therapist just before Zeke was born. I didn't want to repeat the cycle my parents started when I was little. Therapy seemed like a good option."

"Instead of telling me I had a kid, you went into therapy?" His eyes widened. Then he shook his head. When he finally spoke again, mockery was heavy in his tone. "Wouldn't it have been simpler to be honest with me?"

"I didn't start therapy because of you. I did

it because of me, for me. For Zeke." He had to understand. Therapy wasn't a way of avoiding James; it was a way for Mara to confront her past, to be the kind of mother that Zeke deserved.

"And that isn't supposed to piss me off? That I didn't even enter into your little plan? God, Mara, we have a kid together. A kid you didn't tell me about for nearly two years. I get to feel whatever I want to feel about that, and you don't get to turn those feelings into your excuse for keeping him a secret." His knuckles were white against the gray of the steering wheel. "That rates a little more than a five-minute announcement followed by you writing me out of your lives. When are you going to grow up?"

"I grew up two years ago. Quickly," she said. But he was right. Her therapist would agree. James could feel angry and confused and anything else about what she did. "His name is Zeke—Zeke Tyler Calhoun. I did put your name on the birth certificate. He's happy and active. He doesn't talk much, but I can tell sometimes that he has a lot going on in his mind. I have a feeling when he does start talking, he'll never stop." She took a deep breath. "I'm sorry, James, I am. I got scared in Nashville, and by the time I figured out I was pregnant, I convinced myself I'd let too much time pass. I knew there were things from my past that were going to be bad, for me and for him, and that's when I started therapy. And one more time, I convinced myself not to tell you until I felt I was healthy enough to deal with whatever you could dish out."

He pursed his lips and looked ready to rebut that statement.

"But the truth is that I was afraid. Afraid to be a mom. Afraid to be without my family. Afraid to be without the best friend I've ever had, whom I also happened to be hooking up with periodically. You can be mad at me for all of that. If I learned one thing in therapy, it's that we're allowed to feel what we feel."

"I'm not—" he began, but then stopped. "It isn't just—" James blew out a breath. "I'm angry, yes. And confused. And…this changes everything."

"That's what I'm trying to tell you. Zeke doesn't have to change anything for you. You can still run for sheriff. I think you'd make a great one. You don't have to worry about supporting us, not on a county sheriff's salary, because I have a great job with good benefits—"

James shut off the engine and got out of

the Jeep, slamming the door shut behind him. Mara took a few steps back. "If you tell me one more time that I have no responsibilities where this baby is concerned, I just might throttle *you* instead of the tackling dummy I tried to put through my basement wall this morning." He advanced on her, pointing his finger at her chest. "I'm not going to walk away and pretend I don't know I have a kid in this world. So we're going to figure out custody and child support and insurance and scheduling and all the other things that go along with being a two-parent family. We're going to do those things because they are the *responsible* things to do. But we aren't going to figure this out in a five-minute conversation that begins with you telling me I got you pregnant and ends with you telling me I don't have to take responsibility for it."

"I only want to give you options."

James shook his head. "Of course that's what you want. Because me walking away would make things easy for you. Just like you walking away in Nashville was the easy thing. Just like you not telling me you were pregnant was the easy thing. Just like you letting everyone believe you were responsible for the prank in the bus garage after graduation was the easy thing."

"I did that to protect you." It was the one selfless thing she had done in her life, and she'd done it to protect her best friend.

"No, you used what I did as your excuse to walk away from here."

"You could have come clean at any time."

Guilt flashed across his face. Then that calm, cool, detached facade was back, and Mara decided she must have imagined the guilty look. "And that is on me." He checked his watch. "My shift starts in ten minutes. We can talk more after."

Mara nodded—it was all she could do. She couldn't keep bludgeoning him with the I-don't-need-you routine, not when she knew now that it was a lie. Mara hadn't expected him to fall on his knee to propose. That would have been preposterous. But she had expected to see more flashes of the James who had been her best friend throughout high school, who had been her lover—God, she hated that word. It sounded so…old. Clinical.

James got in the Jeep, started it up and drove away, leaving her standing in the B and B parking lot.

She'd run from him because she'd been falling in love with him, and the two years without him hadn't dimmed the feelings. If anything, that kiss had brought them roaring right back to life.

Now she would really have to deal with her feelings for James Calhoun because he wanted to be in Zeke's life, and that made a little piece of her heart happy. It also left a big, empty place where the rest of her heart should have been. While James wanted to be in Zeke's life, he didn't want to be in hers.

CHAPTER SIX

FRIDAY EVENING, JAMES slid the sheriff's department SUV to a stop on the western side of Water Street. At one time, the street had been shaded by a line of oak, maple and honey locust trees. A few of the trees remained, but there were more stumps than trunks.

From where he stood, he could see the marina, which used to be filled with sport fishing and pontoon boats. These days there were more empty slips at the marina than boats on the water. One section of the marina still had drunken pilings and dock moorings connected by only a few locks. Now that the farmers' market was nearly rebuilt, maybe a few residents could band together to fix that wrecked section of marina.

A couple of blocks away, his small house overlooked the lake. That section of Water Street had been virtually untouched. It was strange how tornadoes would wreak destruction in one block and leave the next free from damage.

Kind of like how Mara had whipped back into his life. Professionally, nothing had spun out of control—yet. Personally, he wasn't sure where to start cleaning up the debris.

He could hear the hum of saws and the ring of hammers hitting nails from a few blocks farther down, where volunteers and construction crews worked to repair buildings damaged by the tornado. Days ago the sounds were soothing, reminding him that no matter what happened, his town would survive. Now the sounds grated, and he couldn't help wondering how much more damage the tornado could do. Mara hadn't said it, but the tornado had to be part of the reason she'd decided this was the time to come home. To tell him he had a child.

God, he had a kid. James felt completely unprepared for this particular occurrence. A tornado flattening portions of his town? No problem. But Mara and the baby were something else entirely. The impact that would come when people found out about them would ripple everywhere. His work. His friendships. His family.

James got out of the SUV. There were only a few other cars on the street, very little foot traffic to the cafés and tourist shops that would normally be packed on a sunny day in June. Next weekend, fireworks would light up the lake basin, and he hoped the promise of the regular event would bring both locals and tourists to the lake to fill the shore and the marina.

Having things this quiet, despite the ring of hammers and the whir of saws, was just odd. He didn't like it.

James rolled his shoulders and, taking a deep breath, pushed through the wobbly chain link fence of the house on his call sheet. Wilson DeVries had been a curmudgeonly old man for as long as James could remember. But since the tornado had taken down his maple trees, ruined the roof of his shed and crushed parts of his old fence, he'd been more bad-tempered than ever. James knocked on the screen door of the house.

Through the screen, he could see everything in its place. A line of remote controls sat on the coffee table next to a stack of *Rural Missouri* and *Grit* magazines. The floors appeared to be freshly polished, and there was a steaming cup of coffee sitting on the table beside an olive-green recliner that had to be at least thirty years old.

"Coming," a gravelly voice called from deeper within the house. Then James heard the shuffling of Wilson's slipper socks against the hardwood floor. The old man wore a white T-shirt with Slippery Rock Sailor, the school mascot, emblazoned on the chest. The few strands of gray hair he had left were combed over the top of his head. When he got closer to the door, he eyed James warily. "You here to arrest me?"

"You done anything that would warrant an arrest lately?" James asked.

Wilson pushed open the screen, which moaned a little in protest, and said, "Not that I can recall. You here for a well-check, then? I'm well enough."

James walked into the house, put his aviator sunglasses on top of his head and looked around. The rest of the house was just as spotless as the portion of the living room he'd seen from the porch.

"I'm here because your lawn is breaking the town ordinance against nuisance vegetation." He handed the notice to Wilson, who shoved his hands in his pockets. James put the piece of paper on the entry table beside the door.

"There ain't nothin' wrong with my yard," the old man said, a stubborn set to his jaw. "Just mowed it yesterday."

James glanced behind him. The grass did, indeed, look freshly mown. "The problem isn't the grass. It's the two maples you lost in the tornado that are now lying across your yard, along with the foot-long weeds growing up around them."

The old man rocked back on his heels. "I'll cut up the trunk and the limbs as I need 'em for firewood this winter."

"You won't be able to reach them for the thicket of grass and weeds by winter. They need to go now. You can have the local tree service take care of the cutting for you. They'll probably even stack the wood nicely in the backyard."

"I don't need those yahoos cutting up my trees." Wilson put his hands behind his back and rocked some more. "Had them trim one of the maples last summer. Ended up looking like a lollipop, and no maple should ever look like that."

Now the old man was just being stubborn, which James should have expected since he'd already been here twice with warnings that Wilson had summarily ignored. "Your trees are already down, and if you don't take care of it, you'll have a family of raccoons or skunks or opossums living there before the Fourth."

"It's my yard."

"Yes, it is, but it's inside the city limits, so

you have to live by the city ordinances. You have fifteen days to dispose of the downed tree, and fix the fence, or the city will have to take action."

Wilson crossed his arms over his chest and continued to rock. "Ordinances," he said as if it were the dirtiest word in the English language. "Don't people know a tornado come through here?"

"Yeah, it did. Nearly a month ago. Most of the other downed trees have been taken care of, and a lot of the buildings downtown are taking shape again. The community has banded together."

"Not here."

"Because you stood at your fence with your twenty-gauge on your shoulder, practically daring the volunteer crew to set foot in your yard. I know that's what you did because I was part of that volunteer crew, and I thought I was going to have to tackle you and your twenty-gauge to keep you from using us as targets." The thought still gave him chills. James had no qualms about facing off with a shooter bent on destruction, but taking down an old man who still attended high school football games and bought rolls of holiday wrapping paper from whichever class was selling it was another thing entirely. He was trained to use force, but using force against an eighty-year-old man who wanted to prove he could do things on his own felt wrong.

"I wouldn't've shot nobody. I got better aim than that," he said and pushed his eyebrows together. "I don't need help to take care of my own affairs."

"Everybody needs somebody."

"Well, you ain't my somebody, and I don't need you quoting song lyrics as you handcuff me and put me in your squad car."

James inhaled a steady breath. *Eighty years old, James*, he reminded himself. Eighty and alone and persnickety. "One, I'm not hand-cuffing you. I'm handing you a notice to clean up. Two, it's not a squad car. It's a squad SUV."

"You know, your daddy was a better sher-iff than you are."

"Yes, he was." Jonathan Calhoun was the most respected sheriff Wall County had ever had. He knew the ins and outs of the law, was tough but fair, and never, not a single time, did anything reckless. Somehow James had to find a way to live up to that reputation. "But the tornado put him on the sidelines. I'm what you've got."

"You're not much," Wilson said, eyeing

James as if he might try some kind of evasive maneuver.

James shook his head and held in a sigh. He knew that all too well. "I'm just the messenger, but I won't be for long. Read the ordinance and warning. If you want the volunteers back, all you have to do is call."

He left the house, taking the three narrow steps leading to the cracked concrete walkway in a single bound.

"I'll clean up when I'm darn good and ready," Wilson yelled through the open door.

James waved. "As long as you're darn good and ready within fifteen days, we won't have a problem," he said as he got into the department SUV.

He checked his call sheet. Wilson was his last call before his shift was over. The street was still quiet as James pointed the SUV toward the sheriff's office downtown. Being the interim sheriff came with a lot more paperwork than he was used to as a deputy, but in an area as small as Wall County, it amounted to only an extra hour or so of work. Being single meant no one waiting for him to come home from the office, no domestic schedules. He'd taken to working one of the patrol routes in the morning and using the afternoon to help one volunteer crew or another, then finishing his shift at night. The county commissioners didn't mind his split shift, and he figured setting himself up as a law enforcement officer who did more than carry a gun would help when the general election came around in the fall.

With Mara back in town, he'd have to pull a regular shift if he had any hope of getting to know his son.

He'd always planned on becoming the next Wall County sheriff, but he hadn't figured on that happening before he turned thirty. The tornado had changed a lot of things in his town.

James turned off Water Street and onto Oak, then pulled the SUV into one of the department spaces to the side of the Wall County courthouse. This close to downtown, he could smell the freshly cut wood, and the ring of hammers was more a pounding sound.

He waved to the deputies coming on shift as they exited the building, heading to their cruisers or SUVs, then strode through the front door. The sheriff's office took up most of the three-story building across the street from the courthouse. The tiled vestibule held a few plastic-backed chairs and a small table with out-of-date magazines. Danny Kennedy, who took a desk job the year before, sat behind the bulletproof glass, phone to his ear. He buzzed James into the bullpen filled with cubicles. A couple of deputies heading off shift sat at their desks, finishing paperwork. Despite the late morning hour, the room was quiet.

Jonathan, his father, wheeled himself into the bullpen where the deputies' desks and cubicles were located. "Patrols are still out from the morning runs. You have some payroll files to go over when you come back on shift as well as the usual paperwork. We're still trying to figure out who's behind the street vandalism from before the tornado, but it's been quiet."

Jonathan's leg, broken in three places, stuck out from the wheelchair, and his arm, still in a sling from a separated shoulder, was held close to his chest. His brown hair was a bit longer than usual, but he was clean-shaven, and his gaze was sharp. Deeper lines were etched around his mouth and eyes. He'd be fifty in a couple weeks. Before the tornado he could have passed for forty, but to James he now looked closer to the sixty mark. His injuries had taken a toll.

"You aren't supposed to be here, Dad."

Jonathan sat a bit straighter in the wheelchair. "It's still my office."

"You're still on bed rest."

Jonathan rolled his hazel eyes and shook his head. He wore the county uniform. James had no idea how his mother had managed to get his father into his dress blues. "Only because my surgeon is a worrywart."

"Technically, she is the head of orthopedics at the best hospital in Springfield. She has a degree from Harvard." Not that his father cared. He'd done one of these "surprise" inspections of the sheriff's office so often that James was no longer shocked to see him wheeling his way around the cubicles. James might want his father to be home recuperating, but he also knew he would heal faster, at least mentally, if he came to work from time to time. "Everything quiet?"

"Got another nuisance call about Wilson DeVries's tree. And the morning patrols thought they saw some illegal fishing on the south side of the lake, but the Fish and Wildlife guys were too late to catch them."

"I'll have a couple guys swing by Bud's. He'll know if anyone's been on the lake who shouldn't."

"Don't want to discourage the fishing too much. We still need the Bass Nationals to feel comfortable setting that new tournament here."

"I don't think anyone associated with their organization would be illegally poaching walleye or crappie. Probably some city guys down from Springfield or Tulsa." Together the two men headed down the hall leading to the private offices. James considered telling his father about Zeke but quickly dismissed the idea. He needed to get things straight with Mara first. Jonathan was a man who liked a clear plan of action. "I'm headed to the farmers' market to work with the volunteers for a while," James said. "Want me to drive you home first?"

"I managed to get myself here in one piece. I think I can get myself home." Jonathan paused at the office that used to be his. "Have an appointment with that young doctor on Friday."

"She's forty, Dad, not fourteen," James said, but Jonathan ignored him.

He patted his arm in the gray sling. "If it all checks out, I'll have the use of both my arms again. Maybe I can get out of this chair and on crutches."

"It's going to check out." James picked up a folder of paperwork from the desk.

"You bored with the quiet yet?" his father asked, and James felt as if he were missing something. Like there was a subtext to the conversation that he wasn't getting. He didn't like the feeling.

"I like quiet." Quiet meant everyone in his town was safe, that things were getting back to normal.

"We all do. Looks like that's one of the things that hasn't changed about Slippery Rock. We might have fewer trees, and our marina might still look like a drunk plowed into the docks, but we're still a quiet town." Jonathan pushed a button, and the wheelchair motor turned the chair in a half circle. "You eat lunch yet?"

"I'll pick something up at Bud's before I hit the market," he said, his mind turning to the paperwork in the folder. Just needed a few signatures—he could take fifteen minutes for that, then spend the afternoon with the construction crews before finishing his split shift. If he wasn't exhausted by then, he'd try to go out to the orchard to see Mara. To meet his son.

That would mean a conversation with Collin.

Maybe James would simply call her. James still didn't know if the rest of the Tylers knew about his connection to the baby.

"You could have dinner at the house," his

father said, and that note was back in his voice. "If you wanted."

James watched his father closely for a moment. Something wasn't right. Couldn't be the baby thing. There was no way he would know. Wrinkles James had never noticed on his father's face now seemed as if they had been etched there with a marker. The hazel color of his eyes seemed a little less vibrant, his perpetual frown a bit more pronounced. James could have dinner with his parents instead of dealing with the Mara situation. He'd already missed fourteen months of his son's life. One more evening wouldn't have a huge impact on the relationship he had yet to build with Zeke. Tomorrow was soon enough to start wearing the dad hat.

"I can make dinner. Six?"

Jonathan nodded, then left. The sound of the wheelchair motor faded down the hallway. James sat behind the desk his mother had picked out when Jonathan was first elected twenty years before. It felt strange to think that in a few months, this could be his office. Jonathan desperately wanted to return to the department, and that was probably what the subtext was about, how the injuries he'd sustained in the tornado prevented his work in law enforcement. Perhaps his regular visits to the station helped him cope with that knowledge. James thought he probably needed a little time to let go of the man he had been before the tornado trapped him in the patrol car under two-and-a-half tons of downed tree.

Pictures of his father and grandfather, who was the sheriff before Jonathan had been elected, hung on the walls. Pictures of James and the football team stood on the shelf under the side window. Everywhere in this room, he was surrounded by his past. Surrounded by his father.

With all the things that didn't change in Slippery Rock, James was going to make sure having a Calhoun as sheriff was one of them. He could be a father and a cop; his own father had shown him how to fulfill both roles for years.

SATURDAY MORNING, MARA put the last of her things in the bureau of the bedroom where she'd spent her teenage years. Lavender-checked curtains still hung at the windows, the walls were the same robin's egg blue and the clouds Granddad had painted on her ceiling were still visible.

The Pack 'n Play in the corner was a new addition, and it seemed to bring the room into the present. She'd never hung posters on her walls, never won any ribbons or trophies to speak of, so the shelves were lined with ceramic figures she'd collected over the years. Some were Christmas ornaments, some from trips the five of them had gone on during summer vacation. She especially liked the owl she'd picked up in a coastal Alabama town the year she turned sixteen. Mara ran her finger over the smooth porcelain, tracing the thin blue, yellow and red stripes and markings. Amanda had come home from that trip with a stuffed dolphin and Collin with driftwood he'd been convinced he could carve into an apple tree sculpture. He'd given up after a week.

James hadn't called. Realistically, Mara understood that it hadn't even been twenty-four hours since their argument at the B and B and that kiss. It wasn't as if years had gone by. Still, he'd said he wanted to be involved somehow, and he hadn't called. Well, she had other things to figure out right now, like how to make her childhood room work for herself and the baby.

She put her hands on her hips, surveying the room. She could use the bureau top as a changing table if she removed the paraphernalia of her teenage self—cheap perfume, an old jewelry box filled with junk and a set of antique brushes she found at an estate sale. She put the items in a box she found in the closet, then folded a soft flannel blanket that could work as a table pad until she found something better.

If she found something better, she reminded herself, as she set a stack of diapers and packages of wipes and powder and diaper cream to one side. For the first time, her professional future wasn't set. She was here for the next four weeks because of the contract with Mallard's. After that, there were no new contracts. There could be, but she'd intentionally left her calendar open. Not because she expected to be here for the long term—she held no illusions about Slippery Rock welcoming her back after all this time—but because she'd hoped she might have more than four weeks with her family. With James.

Mara put the suitcase under the bed and hung Zeke's diaper bag over the rocker in the corner.

If she decided to stay longer than the contract lasted, she would think about getting actual baby furniture.

Downstairs, she found Gran sitting on the sofa with Zeke. The little boy slouched against the overstuffed cushions with two of his favorite toys, a squeaky owl and a board book with bright pictures. Gran pointed to one of the pictures.

"Ball," she said. Mara leaned her shoulder against the doorjamb to watch. "Ba-a-ll," she said again, drawing out the syllables. Just as she'd done when Amanda was a baby, Mara remembered.

"Blob-ball," Zeke said, pointing to the same picture.

"Ball," Gran corrected him, and Zeke smiled happily.

"Baall," he repeated, and squeezed the owl. He grabbed the corner of the board page and turned it over to see an oversize moon drawn to look like a wheel of cheese. "M-m-ooo," he said.

"Moon," Gran corrected him again, and squeezed the owl as she pushed it gently into his face. Zeke giggled happily and kept turning pages.

"It's like time turned back fifteen years. You used to read with Amanda like that."

Zeke scooted off the sofa, and when his little feet hit the hardwood, he curved his toes against the wood as if he could turn his foot into a fist. Then, holding on to the sofa with one hand, he inched his way toward the pile of toys Mara had left on the floor earlier. Stuffed animals and hard plastic dinosaurs tumbled about. He picked a neon purple pterodactyl and the stuffed lemur he usually slept with.

"Blob ball mmmoo," he said to the toys as he sat in the middle of the pile.

"Some of my favorite memories are baby memories. Amanda as a toddler, your father. I wish I'd had you and Collin as babies, too." Gran started to get up, but Mara motioned for her to stay and took the chair beside her. She didn't get to watch Zeke play often enough, and she was going to enjoy the heck out of this particular moment.

No distraction about James or work or what might happen a few weeks down the road. Just her, Gran and Zeke.

"You know, you don't have to worry about getting a babysitter while you're here," Gran said. "You said with Cheryl gone you'd want to find someone. I'm your someone."

"Gran, you don't want to take care of him for the next four weeks. What about—" Mara stopped. Did Gran play bridge in town? Have a quilting club? A book club? She wasn't working at the farmers' market or the road-side stand this summer—Mara knew that much—but she had no clue how her grand-mother spent her days.

"My physical therapy is finished, but your brother insists I'm not strong enough to work the market or help out at the stand. I like canning and jelly making, but a woman needs more in her life than a sweltering kitchen and counters filled with pies. Adding playtime with my great-grandson isn't a bother." Her words were matter-of-fact, as most things were with Gran.

She drove Collin crazy with her late night TV-shopping habit, but considering some of the things Mara and Collin had gotten up to in their teens, Mara figured they both deserved anything Gran could dish out now.

"I don't want to impose," Mara said. "Staying out here, adding two more mouths to feed, busying up the bathroom and laundry schedules. It's summer. You should be—I don't know—having lunches with the church ladies or something."

Gran rolled her eyes. "Butter Bean, having lunch with the church ladies is worse than sitting in that sanctuary without air-conditioning in the middle of July. You know sooner or later someone is going to keel over in a heat-induced holy moment, but it seems to take forever just for the excitement to hit." She picked up Zeke's book and paged through it. "I don't mind looking after him for you."

"I can afford help. If someone else is here—"

"You think I can't do it." There was hurt in

Gran's voice. "I broke my hip, young lady, not my brain and not my common sense. Caring for a fourteen-month-old doesn't take a college degree, and there is no age limit."

Mara blinked. "Of course I think you can do it, but I don't want to impose on you. Any of you—"

"If you didn't want to impose, you'd have stayed at the B and B." Amanda stood in the doorway, arms crossed over her chest. Her white-blond hair was pulled into a ponytail, and her blue eyes glared in Mara's direction. She wore cutoff jeans, a yellow tank top, mismatched socks and worn Nikes. A flannel shirt was tied around her waist. "You don't live here, you know."

"I know that, Amanda." The last time she'd been home, Amanda had been at least three inches shorter. Now her younger sister was nearly as tall as Mara, and seemed just as angry as Mara had been at her age. "I'm not here to impose."

"Then why are you here?"

"I asked her to stay," Gran said, her voice placating. "She's family."

Amanda snorted. That got Zeke's attention. He turned toward the adults and began babbling with the lemur in one hand and the dinosaur in the other.

"I am *not* changing dirty diapers, and I'm not babysitting for free." Amanda scowled at the little boy. At least she was acknowledging his presence now. On Friday she had walked into the kitchen, seen them and immediately returned outside. Mara had no idea what to say to make things alright between the two of them.

Before the tornado, Collin had been worried about their little sister. She'd been acting out, rebellious. Mara thought things had changed, but obviously not very much. Not that she could blame Amanda.

When she was turning eighteen, the last thing she would have wanted was a family member to show up at the orchard with a baby in tow.

"*Family* doesn't ignore family," Amanda said, then whirled around. She stomped down the hall and up the stairs.

"Well, I guess Amanda isn't thrilled that we're here."

Gran reached across the space between them and squeezed Mara's hand. "She'll soften up. People coming and going is hard on her. It was hard on all three of you, but I think in some ways, it's worse for her."

"Why?"

Gran's smile was watery. "Because, in her

experience, people who leave don't come back. Your parents haven't been here in years. No calls, no cards. Your grandfather died. You left for college."

"But—" Mara started to protest, although she knew Gran was right. She'd abandoned her family when she left for college, and she had pushed them further away when she became pregnant. She couldn't expect Amanda to jump for joy to have her absentee sister show up with a baby on her hip. "Yeah. I did."

"You're here now, and none of us blame you for going." There wasn't a hint of disdain or censure in Gran's voice, just more of the no-nonsense that Mara had missed from the moment she left. "So, you're back, and we're happy, and I'm your babysitter. No arguments."

"Gran, you don't—" Mara stopped herself. Gran never did anything she didn't want to do. If she wanted to spend time with Zeke, Mara wouldn't stand in her way. "Okay."

"Good. Now, while I'm watching Zeke, why don't you go see if there is anything missing from our cupboards? As long as you're here, you might as well have a few favorites in the kitchen. If we have everything you need, you could start prepping dinner. I was thinking meat loaf and veggies for tonight."

"It's not even noon, why worry about dinner right now? Besides, I'm a guest." A guest who hadn't gone willingly into a kitchen in ten years.

"You're family, and we all share kitchen duties here."

Mara chuckled. "I totally get it now. You didn't want us to stay out here because you missed us. You wanted extra time off from the kitchen."

Gran slid her index finger along her nose and winked. It was her silly way of implying that something said sarcastically was true. "You were always the smart one."

"Does the cook still get the night off from cleanup?"

Gran nodded.

"Then I'll check the cabinets and I'll prep the meat loaf, but only because I don't want to deal with the aftermath of pots and pans."

Mara crossed the room, picked up Zeke and placed a noisy kiss on his cheek. The baby chortled and said, "Maa baall."

"I don't understand what you're saying, but I love you," she told him. "Gran's going to play with you while I search the cabinets, and prep dinner. And then, I'll make you something quick for lunch. Because I'm Super Mom." She put him down, and he continued chattering to his toys on the floor. "I have no idea why I just told him that."

"Because you want him to know you'll be here. Same reason I used to tell you kids where I'd be when you were in here playing and watching TV." Gran picked a book off the coffee table and took a seat closer to Zeke. "We'll be fine. Go."

Mara watched her son a few more moments. He was happy. Healthy. Gran was happy. Healthy. She glanced up the stairs. She'd figure out a way to reach Amanda, and she would figure out how to share her son with his father. First, though, she had to make a grocery list, and figure out how to create a meat loaf from whatever Gran had in the fridge.

Taking her phone from her pocket, she tapped a few letters and began looking for an easy recipe.

CHAPTER SEVEN

JAMES PULLED INTO his parents' driveway Saturday morning, feeling a little hungover despite the fact that he hadn't had anything to drink. After spending Friday afternoon at the farmers' market, he'd returned to the second half of his patrol shift which turned into a double thanks to one of the other deputies calling in sick. He'd spent the rest of the night into the wee hours patrolling the county, and stopping a handful of Slope patrons from driving tipsy.

He'd missed dinner and was hoping to pacify his parents with a quick lunch before calling Mara. He shut off the engine and stepped into the thick air.

There was no breeze this morning to sway the marigolds and black-eyed Susans in his mother's flowerbeds, and even the New Guinea impatiens that she swore were more resistant to hot summer temperatures seemed to droop. James took the two steps leading to the wide front porch of their Victorian home and sighed when he stepped into the cool foyer. He dropped his keys in the Depression glass bowl on the table by the door.

"Anybody home?" he called but didn't wait for an answer. They would be in the kitchen. He continued through the butler's pantry converted into a small office, with shelves full of his father's law enforcement awards and James's old football trophies. His sneakers made little noise on the hardwood floors.

In the kitchen with its miles of countertops and a large butcher-block island, his mother, Anna, pulled a roast from the oven and wiped her forehead.

"Hi, sweetheart. I think we should have grilled. I'm never going to get this house cooled down from the roast," she said. James kissed her cheek as he passed and grabbed a cold beer from the fridge.

"Trust me, we don't want to be standing over a barbecue grill in this heat. Sorry I had to cancel last night." Anna shrugged, not seeming too upset that he'd canceled. He took a long drink from the bottle. "Anything I can do to help?"

"Go entertain your father. He's making me crazy," Anna said. She hooked a strand of hair behind her ear with one hand and turned off the oven with the other. "We'll eat in the formal dining room. I am not eating in this hot kitchen," she said, more to herself than him. She reached for plates and glasses.

Jonathan wasn't in the living room, so James wandered the ground floor of the big house, looking for him. He was in the solarium, reading. He'd situated the wheelchair under a potted palm, and a box fan blew cool air on his feet. This room, too, had been renovated. Now, while sunlight poured through the tinted windows, the AC unit kept the room cool and comfortable.

"Hey, Dad."

"I didn't hear you come in, boy," Jonathan said, setting aside the Stephen King novel he'd been reading.

"You having hot flashes or something?" he asked, motioning to the fan. He handed a second beer to his father. "Man-o-pause, I think they call it?"

Jonathan harrumphed at that. "Not hardly. This damn cast keeps my foot and leg heated to about a hundred degrees. The fan prevents me from combusting."

"Mom says we're eating in the dining room instead of the kitchen. It's a little ripe in there, thanks to a pot roast and whatever else she's got going."

"I told her not to go to that kind of trouble. Isn't like you're company."

"Just your only son, who lives alone and eats mostly frozen dinners and pizza." James sat in a wicker chair that made him feel like a giant. His mother was crazy about wicker but had confined most of her pieces to this one room, her favorite. Scattered around the hanging ferns, potted palms and a few other tropical plants were a white wicker sofa, two rockers and the chair James occupied.

"You know what I meant."

James did. He'd never thought much about how Collin and Mara had grown up, not until the recent trouble with their younger sister. Now that Mara was back and he knew she'd been in therapy for the past year or so, he looked at their upbringing differently. What had seemed, when they were teens, like the perfect, permanent vacation from parental rules and restrictions now looked quite different. It made him view his own parents differently.

Not that her upbringing excused her keeping his son from him. But maybe he could stop being such a hard-ass about it.

He was twenty-eight and had been on friendly terms with Jonathan and Anna since graduating from college. Deep in his soul he knew if he needed them, they would be by his side in an instant. Mara didn't have that, at least not from her parents. Sure, she had Gladys and, before he'd died, she'd had her grandfather, Zeke, but was that the same thing?

Anna called them into the dining room. James grabbed the handles of Jonathan's chair and wheeled him into the room with a table big enough to seat twelve people. Only three places were set with his mother's favorite quilted placemats and the everyday stoneware plates—not the fancier dishes she brought out for their annual holiday parties. The roast still bubbled in the pan, smelling like all the good parts of his childhood.

He pushed Jonathan to the table, and since his father couldn't stand to cut, James took over. After they'd filled their plates, Jonathan asked, "How'd it go at the market yesterday?"

"Most of the west wall is back up. We'll be able to start on the roof and install the new windows next week. It's a good roast, Mom," he said around a bite of food.

Anna glowed at the compliment. Her blond hair was pulled back in a low ponytail, and she wore a gauzy pink shirt and those pants that cut off at the knee. Compared to his father's athletic shorts and T-shirt and James's own cargos and T-shirt, she looked like she might be headed out to play bridge or attend a hospital board meeting. She always looked like that. Along with keeping her home in pristine condition, cooking meals from scratch and puttering in her garden, Anna liked to look polished. "Thank you. I just threw it together after your dad said you were coming for lunch. We haven't seen enough of you lately. This new schedule is running you in circles."

"The work has to be done." He took another bite. "I'm going to stop the split shifts, though."

"Of course. It's too much to work your job and help the rebuilding crews," Anna said.

"You've put in more than your fair share of time," Jonathan agreed.

James felt as if the ten years he'd been out of high school dropped away, and his parents were patting his back for playing a good game or passing a test. Their approval of how he spent his time was nice to have, but he didn't need it. He'd pitched in because this was his town. His help might be missed, but now he had more than the town to think of. He couldn't work sixteen hours a day and have time to get to know Zeke. Starting today, he would let more time go by on that front.

"The reconstruction is coming along, but I'm stopping the splits for a different reason." Throat dry, James took a drink of water, then cleared his throat. It wasn't as if he were eighteen, and still needed his parents' approval. He was established in his job, had a house, was a responsible adult. Why was he so nervous about telling his parents he had a kid?

"Well, sure, have to get ready for the election," Jonathan said. "Get the paperwork angle figured out, think about promotions for the deputies, staffing. People will want to know your plans for the—"

"It isn't about the election, either, although I will start to lay out my plans soon. It's, ah, did you know Mara Tyler's back in town?"

Jonathan sighed. "I knew she wouldn't stay away indefinitely. At coffee this morning they were talking about her getting caught shoplifting."

"The girls at bridge were talking about it, too. Margery Harris, you remember Adam's mother-in-law? Well, she was telling me it was something silly, like cookies and milk. What kind of grown woman shoplifts cookies?" Anna shook her head. "Seriously, who over the age of ten tries to steal cookies and milk?"

"She wasn't stealing anything," James said.

"She's working on a new security system for Mallard's. She set off the alarm on purpose." Which was more or less true. She was testing to see if there was some kind of anti-theft alert for goods being taken from the store. When nothing happened on her way out, she'd planned to go straight to Mike Mallard with her findings; getting caught on the way back in caught her off guard. CarlaAnn's penchant for gossip and vengeance took things from there. He wanted to dispute her version of events loudly, but if he'd learned anything from their teenage pranks, it was that gossip slowed if he just didn't talk about it.

"You sure about that, son?" Jonathan asked, cocking an eyebrow. "You know the girl was out of control when you kids were still in school."

"Kids' pranks don't put her on the track to the penitentiary." And this conversation was quickly going in the wrong direction. His parents didn't have to like Mara, but judging her based on who she was at seventeen wasn't fair, either. "She's a securities and tech specialist for a big company in Tulsa. Travels all over setting up new systems."

"Sounds like you're getting reacquainted with her really quick," Anna said.

Jonathan pushed his half-eaten plate of

food away. "You got all this from the fifteen minutes you were questioning her in Mike Mallard's office?"

Yep, the Slippery Rock gossip mill was definitely in fine shape. James shook his head.

"Actually, I started picking it up a few years ago when we were both in the same city for a security and law enforcement conference." James knew he should rip off the having-a-child-with-Mara bandage quickly, but he couldn't. Not when Jonathan and Anna still thought of her as a teenager on the verge of a criminal record. "We started hanging out whenever we were in the same cities."

"I didn't realize you were using that paid time for anything other than work," Jonathan said.

"Speaking to my boss, I attended every conference workshop and lecture during those trips." James took one last bite, chewed and swallowed. "Speaking to my father, I spent what little free time I had on those trips with an old friend. And now that old friend and I have a child together."

Anna's fork clattered to her plate, and her jaw dropped. Jonathan set his mouth in a thin line and shook his head. "That isn't funny,

James," he said in the same lecturing voice he'd used when James was a child.

"It isn't a joke. Zeke is fourteen months old, happy and healthy, and he's in town with Mara. I thought you'd like to know."

Anna looked from her husband to her son, then shook her head. "We've been grandparents for over a year and you didn't bother to tell us?"

And now came the sticky part. How to reveal he hadn't known about Zeke without that information turning them against Mara for life. Despite James's inability to keep his lips off hers, he didn't see a future of wedded bliss for the two of them. Still, having contentious almost-in-laws was not the way to create a stable family for their son.

"We left things on a bad note before Mara knew she was pregnant," James said, deciding the truth was the best option in this instance. He didn't want to lie, not to anyone, about Zeke. There were some bits of the relationship with Mara that he would keep to himself, though. Like the diamond ring collecting dust in his roll-top desk. "The point is that we're working through all of that, and Zeke is here, and I thought you would like to meet him at some point."

"Of course we want to meet him," Anna said. Jonathan remained quiet.

"I'll figure out a plan with Mara and let you know what works."

The three of them were quiet for a long moment. James wasn't sure what more to say. He was an adult, yet he felt like a kid lying to his parents—not the most mature move in the world, but keeping the explanation simple would be best for all of them, Mara included. His parents didn't need to know she had walked out on him, they didn't need to know she'd undergone therapy, and they didn't need to know that he and Mara hadn't completely worked things out between them.

Hell, until yesterday morning, he didn't know she'd left Nashville because their relationship scared her. He needed to work out how he felt about that little bombshell for himself before sharing it with anyone else.

Anna stacked the plates and began clearing the table. Jonathan kept a sharp eye on James, making him feel like a fish on his father's hook.

"Zeke and Gladys did the best they could," Jonathan finally said, "and how Mara turned out the way she did when Collin has always been such an upstanding citizen, I can't guess. But Mara Tyler has never been good for you."

"She's a friend, Dad, and I'm an adult who can choose whom and what he allows in his life."

"She uses you."

"She's not using me, not now and not back then." If anything, he had been the user. James could have ignored every prank, but a part of him wanted the excuse to be a rebel. Like Mara. He could have pushed her on the relationship front, too, but a part of him liked sneaking around. Having part of his life that wasn't dictated by the family legacy.

"Of course she is, and of course she was. You think it's a coincidence that a destructive girl like her befriends the sheriff's son?"

"Technically, I was Collin's friend. She just tagged along with us."

"And led you all astray."

"We weren't sheep. We knew exactly what we were doing, just like all the other teenagers in this town have known what they were doing. I love this place, but it isn't the most interesting way to grow up. Sometimes we needed a little excitement."

"She painted another girl's phone number on the water tower."

"Because that girl dumped Aiden in a very cruel way. That, incidentally, was Adam's idea. Mara just figured out how to do it without getting caught. Well, until your cruiser made an unexpected patrol through the park."

"And I suppose the computer tricks were part of her planning for her future career as a security tech?"

"Actually, yeah. We boys saw something similar on an old movie and couldn't figure out how to do it. She figured it out."

"And now she needs a father for her child, and you're just going to step right into that role?"

"He's my son, Dad. Your grandson." Now, he was getting annoyed. James wadded the napkin in his hand. He wouldn't raise his voice. He wouldn't slam his hand against the table. He would be calm. Rational.

He would win this debate with his father.

"Says who?"

"Says his mother. The timing fits. His baby picture is almost a replica of mine—"

"You haven't even met this kid yet?"

"She's been in town less than a week."

"But she's had plenty of time to plan a grocery store heist and get you right back in her web."

James shook his head and stood. He put his hands on the table and leaned forward. "It's my child, Dad, and you can be a grandfather or not, but you won't talk about Mara like this. She made a few mistakes as a kid. We all did—"

"She's the only one who ran out of town ahead of the law."

That stopped James short. He knew from the start that the rumor mill almost immediately attached Mara's name to the school bus incident—it was part of the reason she left so early for college—but he hadn't known his father planned to arrest her.

"She wasn't responsible for that."

"Of course she was. Letting the air out of those bus tires was exactly a Mara Tyler thing to do, and she used you to do it." Jonathan folded his arms across his chest as if that statement was the end of it.

That stopped James for a moment. How much did his father know about that night? Although Jonathan was a straight-arrowed officer, to James's knowledge, his father had also been a fair officer. If Jonathan knew he was in the bus garage that night, though... Could he have been part of the reason so much of the talk about that prank turned to Mara? Was that why, when she left town, the case went cold? So that, in accusing Mara Tyler, Jonathan could protect his own son?

"Dad—" he began, but Jonathan cut him off.

"That's it, son. We're going in circles. It's time to end this."

They were nowhere near the end, and it was time for his father to stop treating James as if he had no idea how to make a decision. He'd done everything his parents wanted as a kid. Played football, got the grades, won a scholarship, went into law enforcement. "You know?"

Jonathan turned his attention to the tablecloth, picking at something James couldn't see on the fabric.

"I did it voluntarily."

Jonathan shook his head. "You were a kid—"

"I was eighteen, a year older than her. If I was a kid, what was she?" James paced to the end of the table and back.

"Trouble."

"She had nothing to do with the tires, Dad. That was all me."

Jonathan slammed his fist against the table. "She had everything to do with it. Without her there would have been no water tower, no misconnected computers—"

"All she wanted to do was leave the lights on to run down the batteries so the buses wouldn't start. No buses, no bus routes, no school. Instead of the underclass students finishing their last week of classes after graduation, they'd be out early, along with the actual graduating." James still couldn't put into words exactly why he'd taken things further.

Why it had seemed, standing in the dark parking lot with Mara, that if at that moment he didn't do one thing that was absolutely against the rules, he would lose himself. He'd needed a single moment when he wasn't the heir apparent to the Slippery Rock Sheriff's Department, when he wasn't on his way to college as the only one in their group who didn't drink, didn't smoke and didn't skip school. He'd gone along with the other pranks without truly taking part, and when Levi, Collin, Adam and Aiden skipped their graduation night plans, he'd felt as if he was losing something. He'd wanted, once before he turned himself into the law-abiding citizen who would become sheriff, to be like every other teenager in the world.

And so when Mara turned on the bus lights, he started letting the air out of the tires, not realizing the bus weight would ruin the tire rims. He'd deflated only three of those big tires when Mara stopped him and dragged him out of the parking lot. If she hadn't, the school would have lost all fifteen of the buses instead of only two.

"Well, that isn't what she did, is it?"

"Actually, the lights are exactly what she did. The tires were all on me."

Jonathan clenched his jaw. "No."

"Yes. I did it. I'm not proud of it, but I'm also not going to let you blame Mara for something she didn't do. We both made mistakes when we were younger, but we're adults now, and we have a baby, and we're going to do whatever we have to do to make sure that child has a good life with two parents. If you're on board with that, welcome to the party. If you aren't, it's really a shame."

James walked out of the house feeling as if a weight had been lifted from his shoulders. He loved his family, but what was going on between him and Mara was only between them.

A BELL TINKLED over the entrance of The Good Cuppa as Mara pushed open the door and stepped inside. At just after noon on Saturday morning, the coffee shop clientele was more a trickle than a bustle, but then, most people were playing on the lake by now or running whatever errands brought them into town. She'd been after good coffee. After searching Gran's pantry shelves, she'd found a handful of items that she would like to have on hand. A bag of coffee beans and a grinder were two of those items because, after only a day at the orchard, she knew ground and canned coffee from the grocery store was not going to be enough. With the meat loaf and veggies prepped for dinner, she'd taken the quick trip into town.

She surveyed the old bookshelf filled with whole bags of different roasts, finally deciding on a Brazilian blend. For all of Collin's interest in farm-to-table foods, he hadn't yet caught on that coffee in a can on a grocery store shelf was mildly flavored hot water rather than real coffee.

At the counter, a petite teenager operated the cash register. She had dark hair and eyes, and her name tag read Copper.

"I'll have an iced caramel coffee, extra ice. And this, too," she said, putting the bag of coffee on the counter.

"Watch her," said a man with a gravelly voice from behind her. "I hear she's already been in trouble with the law."

Mara whirled, ready to take on whoever was there, but stopped short. The man sitting at the little table near the fireplace had filled out from high school. His shoulders seemed broader and the voice was definitely deeper, but those hazel eyes could only belong to a Buchanan. And there was only one Buchanan man under the age of thirty in town.

"Adam," she said, smiling. "I thought you were still in the hospital."

"Yeah, well, I tortured the doctors and nurses enough that they kicked me out early." He tapped his hands against the arms of the wheelchair. "I just didn't get far before they threw me in one of these."

The barista passed Mara her cup. She took it and the bag of coffee, and went to Adam's table in the corner. She put her arms around his shoulders and hugged him tightly.

"It's so good to see you."

He didn't hug her back, and that was unlike Adam. He'd always been the touchy-feely type. It threw her off, and Mara stepped back.

"Do you want to sit?" Mara shook her head. "I mean, you're sitting, but do you want me to sit with you?"

Adam smiled, but the grin didn't quite reach his eyes. "Sure, I can spare a few minutes."

"I don't want to keep you—"

"It was a joke," he said and shrugged. "A bad one. I don't have anywhere to be, and a little company would be better than sitting here and staring at the walls while I wait for Jenny to finish up at Shanna's Dress Shop. She's helping her mom pick out a dress for the second marriage of one of the bridge ladies."

"Margery is still playing with the Tuesday night bridge ladies?"

"And they've expanded to Sunday afternoons, Saturday mornings and Thursday afternoons." Adam rolled his eyes, and for the first time seemed like the man she remembered. "How long are you in town?"

"A few weeks, maybe. I'm working on the new security system at Mallard's, and after that…" She shrugged. "We'll see."

They fell silent. Mara watched as the clock on the wall counted off the slowest minute of her life. What could she say to Adam? She hadn't seen him since high school. She knew he was injured but didn't realize he was in a wheelchair. Did that mean he was paralyzed? Sheriff Calhoun used a wheelchair because of broken bones, but Adam didn't appear to have a cast on either leg. Should she ask him about the chair? Talk as if it was normal? She settled for taking another drink of the iced coffee.

"You can ask," he said, and she thought she caught a bit of defiance in his voice.

"I wasn't sure you'd want to talk about it."

"It's kind of the elephant in the room at this point—or it will be until I get out of the chair."

"How long are you in the chair? I mean, is it permanent?"

"Depends on how long it takes to get the dog."

Mara felt as if she were missing something. "What does a dog have to do with paralysis?"

"I'm not paralyzed. I have the chair because my hip and knee need surgery, but until they get my head figured out, I'm not a candidate."

"What's wrong with your head?"

"Traumatic brain injury. Bricks from the old Methodist church bell tower hit me during the tornado. I had three seizures in the hospital, so they tell me I'm now epileptic." Adam circled his index fingers on the vinyl of his chair. "I'm on the wait list for a service dog. They supposedly detect abnormal brain activity like seizures so I can get to a safe place before I collapse. Once the dog gets here, and once the docs are confident in the medication regimen to control the seizures, I'll have the surgeries on my leg and be out of the chair."

"I didn't know," Mara said, and the words felt woefully inadequate.

"Could be worse. The bricks could have severed my spine instead of just putting me on the seizures list."

She reached across the table, taking his hand in hers. "I'm so sorry."

Adam nodded, and she thought it might have been the saddest nod she had ever seen. "Me, too."

The bell over the door tinkled again, and Mara saw James enter. He wore cargo shorts, a T-shirt and old Nikes. The uniform she'd seen him in earlier in the week made his shoulders appear wider and his hips leaner, but the casual clothes brought out the country boy in him. She'd always found that country boy to be irresistible.

James pushed his aviator sunglasses on top of his head and looked around. He spotted her with Adam and frowned. Then he took a closer look, and Mara thought his face paled a bit. With his attention on their table, he crossed to the counter and placed his order— black coffee—and waited for the teen to pour it into a travel cup.

"Still you and James, huh?" Adam asked, dragging her attention off the cop at the counter and back to the man at her table.

"Still?" she asked, and hated the squeak in her voice.

"We might have been idiot teenage boys, but we weren't blind idiot teenage boys. Other than Collin, I think we all knew you and James were hung up on each other."

Mara blinked. "I wasn't." He'd been her friend back then. The attraction started later.

"You turned down every guy in school."

"That doesn't make me hung up on him," she said, motioning toward James with her thumb.

"It does when you spent all those date nights with James watching old movies or swimming at the lake."

Mara started to protest but then stopped. From the time the school accelerated her ahead a grade when she was fourteen, she had spent a lot of time with James and without the other guys. Collin hadn't dated, but he'd spent most of his time working the orchard with Granddad. Adam and his brother, Aiden, had both had a string of girlfriends, as had Levi. It had seemed normal to spend time with James. But looking back on it now, after they'd spent three years having a long-distance, fling-style relationship, maybe that hadn't been so normal.

"We were just friends." Then. And now

they weren't friends, but they were parents. Parents who didn't have a future together, and one of whom couldn't stop thinking about the other's hot mouth. Probably just residual attraction from not sleeping together for two years; they'd always done the sleeping-together thing well. She had no doubt James had been practicing his skills on someone since Nashville, but she hadn't. Two years was a long time to go with no sex. She sat a bit straighter in her chair when James turned toward them.

Adam shrugged and, when James approached, made room for him at the small table.

"When did they release you?" James asked.

"Yesterday evening," Adam said.

James sat between them, and the hair on her arms prickled. He smelled good, like soap and sunshine, and although he sat a few inches from her, she swore she could feel his heat. He sipped his coffee and looked out the window. Adam fiddled with his empty mug. Mara watched the two of them, who always had so much to say to one another when they'd all been kids. Strain etched a line between James's eyebrows. Adam bit his lower lip.

"The Cardinals are playing like crap," James said after a long moment.

"Royals, too," Adam replied.

Neither mentioned the chair in which Adam sat. Mara knew she hadn't handled the wheelchair thing well, but at least she had addressed it. Considering his father's injuries, James should have been used to wheelchairs, albeit not seeing one of his best friends in one. It wasn't as if mentioning the chair could cause James to need one, too.

"At least the weather is hot and miserable," Mara said sarcastically, hoping to pull them into more normal conversation.

"Hottest summer on record, at least so far," James agreed, still keeping his attention focused outside the coffee shop rather than at their table.

"Need rain or the farmers won't have a good harvest," Adam added. Then he turned his attention to Mara. "How are the new trees at the orchard holding up under the heat?"

Mara blinked. "Are you kidding me?"

"What?" they said in unison.

She focused her attention on Adam. "Not five minutes ago you told me it was the elephant in the room."

"What's the elephant in the room?" James asked, as if he had no idea what she was talking about. Mara didn't buy that for a second, not when he was looking everywhere except at Adam.

Before she could answer, a woman Mara didn't recognize walked into the coffee shop. She had long, curly brown hair pulled back into a ponytail and wore lime-green capris and a white-and-green polka-dot tank top. She spotted their table and made a beeline in their direction.

"Hey, James," she said when she reached them. "Or is it Sheriff Calhoun already?"

"Acting, only. Until the election," he said, "Hey, Jenny."

She grasped the handles of Adam's wheelchair. So this was Jenny. She was the perfect match for Adam, Mara thought, or at least the Adam she remembered. The boy she'd known was happy-go-lucky, and this woman's open expression, her bouncy walk, and the way she spoke to James, was bubbly.

"I'm Mara," she said, reaching across the table to shake Jenny's hand. "Mara Tyler."

"Oh, I know who you are," she said with a smile that lit up her face. "I was a year behind you in school. Well, until you accelerated, and then it was two. We didn't have any classes together, though."

Mara tried to place Jenny in the halls of

Slippery Rock High but couldn't. "I don't remember."

"Why would you? You were busy with the Sailor Five," she said, mentioning the nickname the local media used for James, Adam, Aiden, Collin and Levi. "The rest of us were just background noise." But she didn't sound angry or annoyed at that.

"It was hard to keep them in line," Mara joked.

"I can imagine. This one," she said, tapping Adam's shoulder, "keeps me running 24/7. Even now." She shot a look at the wheelchair, and a flicker of sadness showed on her face for a moment. "Speaking of, we're supposed to be at your mother's for lunch and still have to pick up the boys from swim practice. See you all later?" she asked, but she was already pulling the wheelchair away from the table.

"I can manage," Adam said, and his voice wasn't bubbly or even moderately friendly. It was straight-up annoyed.

"I was only trying to help," Jenny said, knitting her eyebrows. Adam pushed the wheels and rocketed the chair forward, not waiting for her. Jenny watched him for a moment, then offered a half wave to Mara and

James as she hurried after him. "We'll see you later," she said at the door. She held it open while Adam wheeled through it, and the two of them disappeared down the street.

"That was uncomfortable," James said after a long minute.

"Ya think?" Mara asked. "What was with all the avoidance?"

"I wasn't avoiding anything."

"You barely said ten words to a guy who, until a few weeks ago, you had a standing weekly dart game with. A guy you grew up with. One of the Sailor Five."

James sipped his coffee. "He barely said ten words to me." His voice was all defensive and wounded pride.

Mara shook her head. "He was sitting in a wheelchair, not on top of a bomb."

"I didn't know he was out of the hospital or that he'd be here."

"Because if you had, you wouldn't have spoken to him like you might catch whatever it is that landed him in the chair? Newsflash, James. Wheelchairs aren't contagious. Neither is the traumatic brain injury that put him, for now, in that chair."

"He's not paralyzed, though, right? I've asked Jenny fifty times, but she always skips over the question. His parents are holding things together at the cabinet shop but they're not talking about it, either."

"Traumatic brain injury, causing epilepsy. And a hip and knee that are going to need surgery."

The relief that flooded James's face annoyed Mara even more.

"For once the town grapevine didn't get the story right," he said.

She put her hand on his arm, and that was a mistake, because the little flame of attraction she'd been trying to ignore since he walked in the coffee shop flared into a full-blown wildfire. Mara moved her hand away. "There's something going on there. Seizures and surgery aren't paralysis, and that's wonderful, but that man isn't the Adam I remember."

"Yeah. It's not the Adam I played darts with a few weeks ago, either." James sipped his coffee, still looking uncomfortable. "What are you doing in town?"

"Getting groceries for Gran and real coffee for me." She gently shook the to-go cup in her hand.

"Do you want to walk for a bit?" He angled his head toward the barista, who was paying more attention to the nail file in her hands than their conversation. "Copper isn't part of the gossip mill, but you never know who might walk in. We could talk. About Zeke."

Mara nodded. Outside, she put the bag of coffee into the front seat of her SUV, then walked down the street with James. She could hear hammering and sawing from the crews working on the building that housed Buchanan Cabinetry a couple of buildings away. James turned them toward the marina, taking her hand as they crossed the street. Once they were back on the sidewalk, he released her. Mara wanted his hand back. She shook her head. It was silly, missing the feel of his hand when there were so many bigger issues between them.

"Why aren't you on duty?"

"Pulled a double last night. I'm off until Monday morning, when my call sheet will hopefully not include another call to Wilson DeVries." She shot him a questioning look. "You remember the old guy who attends all the football games?"

"He always bought wrapping paper from me."

"You and every other kid who knocked on his door. One of his maples fell in the tornado. So far, he's being, ah, persnickety about clean up."

"Persnickety?" Mara giggled at his use of

the word, which did seem to fit the older gentleman who hooted and hollered at football games, but who was very particular about the kind of wrapping paper he purchased.

"It's an official cop word. Like 'bamboozle' or 'heist.'"

"And 'cockamamie'?" she asked.

"That one, too. Anyway, I'm off duty and I was going to head out to the orchard. So we can talk."

"If you were on duty right now, would you be walking with me?"

"Depends. Where would we be walking from and why?" He said the words lightly, but still Mara wondered.

"Some people would say, no matter what was happening in town, walking with me would be part of your job." James tilted his head as she spoke. "So you can ensure that I don't make off with one of these boats, for instance."

"You never stole a boat."

"But I did steal milk and cookies."

"I thought you said that was a test."

"What I say and what people say about me are usually two very different things." They stepped from the cobblestone sidewalk to the wood of the marina dock. Not that she wanted to talk about what people said about her. For the most part, she didn't care. She'd realized long ago that certain people in town liked gossip. And if they had to embellish a bit to make it more salacious, so be it. For a while, she had done her damnedest to keep people talking about the present so they wouldn't be tempted to speculate about the Tyler kids' past.

As long as the people who cared about her knew the difference, she was okay. She shot a glance at James. Until a few days ago, she'd hoped he might be one of those people. Now she wasn't as certain. And it was completely her fault.

"I'm sorry. For everything I've done where you're concerned over these past two years. If I could do it all again..." Part of her wanted to say she would do it differently, but that wasn't necessarily true. She had needed to confront all those demons surrounding her childhood. If she had told James about her pregnancy immediately, she probably would have kept shoving all that stuff into the deep recesses of her mind, insisting to herself that the past didn't matter. "What I did was selfish, and it hurt you, and I'm sorry for that."

James was quiet for a long moment. Together they turned down a long section of dock, this one leading farther out into the lake. Their footsteps were quiet along the wooden boards, the water lapping gently against the pilings, and a few boats skimmed across the water farther out. A light breeze blew across the water, making the heat bearable, and the sky was the clearest blue, reflecting in the still water farther out. She had missed the quiet beauty of Slippery Rock. The back of her hand brushed against his. She had missed him. So very much.

"You know, I've seen both oceans, the Rocky Mountains, all of the Great Lakes. Nothing is quite as beautiful to me as this man-made lake."

"Because this is home," he said, and it was as if his voice touched her. The hairs on the back of her neck stood up, and a shiver ran down her spine. "I get it," he said, and she knew he wasn't talking about the lake. "I told my parents about Zeke at lunch today, and it was as if the past ten years hadn't happened. I was eighteen again, telling them I was—I don't know—failing chemistry or something."

"You were never failing chemistry."

James chuckled and bumped his shoulder against hers. "You know what I mean. Maybe I'm an idiot, but I don't want to be mad at you. Not now. We were friends for a long time before we were…anything else. We're adults now, and we have a child, but we can be friends again."

Mara swallowed. Friends. Not when the friendliest of touches between them made her senses go into overdrive. "What about—" She'd been on the verge of mentioning the kissing, but James spoke before she could say it.

"Zeke? I want to meet him. Get to know him." They turned another corner and walked toward the shoreline. "You said you didn't need money from me, but you know me. I need to help out that way, so we'll figure out custody and holidays and child support. We can figure out the co-parenting thing as we go along."

"Right, right." Mara forced the words from her throat. "We're friends. We'll figure it out." The words tasted bad in her mouth, and she sipped her iced coffee, hoping it would drown out the bitterness of the word *friend*. The drink, too, left a bitter taste in her mouth. She tossed the cup in a trash can bungee-tied to one of the dock pilings.

"I'd like to come by the orchard this afternoon, if that's alright?"

Which meant dropping another bombshell on her family this afternoon. Well, Amanda might not be talking to her right now, but Collin and Gran had been accepting of the baby news. It stood to reason they would accept the fact that James was the baby daddy. This way they'd know she hadn't procreated with a drugged-out rock star or something. She'd procreated with the most responsible man in all of Wall County. Possibly all of Missouri. A man who always took his responsibilities seriously.

"Sure," she said. "Why don't you come for supper, around five thirty?"

They'd reached the edge of the dock. James held her hand again as she crossed onto the cobblestone sidewalk. Mara ordered her hand not to shake at his touch and her insides to stop flopping around like the fish people caught on lazy Sunday afternoons.

James nodded and offered a wave as he turned toward his Jeep.

"Well, I guess that went well," she said to no one. He hadn't kissed her in anger or exasperation. He'd told her they could be friends. He wanted to take responsibility for his child.

So why did it feel as if she had lost something important between holding his hand as they crossed the street earlier and him walking away now that they were back on solid ground?

CHAPTER EIGHT

"BUT HE'S ARRESTED ME. Twice." Amanda stopped short. She and Mara were walking up the orchard drive from the roadside stand. Amanda's summer job was working the orchard's roadside stand. Several patrons had stopped earlier, but for the past hour the stand had been dead, so despite the fact that it wasn't quite four o'clock on Saturday afternoon, she convinced Amanda to head toward the house.

Mara needed to start dinner, and she wanted to shower before James arrived. She also needed to tell Gran. And Collin. She'd started with Amanda, hoping the news might break the glacier between the two of them.

It hadn't.

"Did you deserve to be arrested?" Mara asked. "And were you ever actually jailed or did he just take you into the station house?"

Amanda pressed her lips together and began walking again. "No. And no," she said after a long moment.

"Really?"

"What? Are you my mother now?"

Mara supposed she deserved that. She'd been using her mom voice on Amanda all afternoon, trying to get the teen to open up. To talk about anything. She should have stayed away from the James conversation, but at least she hadn't mentioned the *F* word yet. As far as Amanda knew, he was only coming to dinner.

"No, I'm your older sister. I'm staying in your house, and an old friend is coming to dinner. He won't arrest you or question you."

They cut across the lawn instead of taking the crook in the driveway that wound toward the big, red barn. The farmhouse was just ahead.

"He'll come up with something," Amanda insisted and hurried her pace.

Mara shook her head. Usually, the gingerbread trim and crisp white walls soothed Mara's mind, but not today. Gran sat on the porch swing with Zeke, looking comfortable despite the heat of the late afternoon. Amanda started up the steps.

"Wait a second," Mara said. Amanda paused, her hand on the doorknob. Mara looked around, but Collin was nowhere to be seen. Probably in the barn office or off somewhere with Savannah; Mara had yet to meet Collin's girlfriend, although she remembered her vaguely from high school. "We're having a guest for dinner," she said to her grandmother, who nodded absently and continued playing with Zeke. He waved a dinosaur in her direction, and she waved a stuffed owl back at him.

"He isn't a guest," Amanda said. "He's a rigid cop."

"Technically, he's the acting sheriff, but I suppose he could be described as rigid." Mara pushed the image of James in bed from her mind. That was not the kind of rigid Amanda was talking about, and it wasn't anything that Mara should have been thinking about, either.

"How nice. We haven't seen James around much since the tornado. What's the occasion?" Gran asked.

"Probably wants to put me on probation," Amanda muttered.

"I saw him at the coffee shop." *And regularly for most of the time since I started grad school*, she thought but didn't say. "He's, ah, coming out to meet Zeke." Mara felt her cheeks heat. She straightened her shoulders. Gran shot her a look. Mara nodded, and Gran focused her attention on Zeke again.

She ran her thin hand over the little boy's

hair, gazed into his eyes and seemed to catch her breath. "Oh."

Amanda pushed open the door. "I'll just be in my room, planning my prison wardrobe," she said dramatically.

"They don't let you take clothes to prison, Amanda," Gran said. Amanda muttered something Mara couldn't understand and slammed the door behind her. Mara watched through the glass as the girl stomped up the stairs.

Mara turned to Gran. "James is—"

"I picked that up, Butter Bean," Gran said, holding up a hand to stop Mara from talking. "I didn't realize the two of you had stayed in touch."

"He had a law enforcement seminar in the same town where I was working a few years ago. Things just kind of started. The first few times, it was just friends hanging out, and then…things changed," she ended lamely. Gran was quiet for a long time. "Gran?" she finally asked.

Gran batted the lemur toward Zeke, and the little boy giggled. "I thought there wasn't a father in the picture. Like, maybe he had walked away or you'd gone to a fertility clinic or something."

"Neither of those things."

"Are the two of you—"

Mara shook her head. "No, no, we're not. We haven't been that for a long time." *Because you walked away.* Mara told the voice in her head to shut up. "We're just friends now. Friends with a baby."

"How long has he known?"

"About as long as you," Mara admitted, and Gran's eyes widened to the size of quarters. The stuffed lemur in her hand dropped to the porch floor, and Zeke lunged for it. She grabbed him in her arms, and Mara snatched the lemur to put it on the swing cushion near him. Zeke picked up the lemur and the dinosaur and began to make fighting noises.

"I didn't know I was pregnant for a while, and we, ah, *I* left things badly with him the last time we'd seen each other." Mara sat down heavily in the rocker near the swing. "I didn't know how to tell him, and I didn't know how to be a mother, and I convinced myself that until I got things figured out on my end, it was better he didn't know."

"I'll bet that went over well with him."

She offered Gran a small smile. "We've agreed not to keep going down the Mara-was-an-idiot road, for his sake." She motioned to Zeke. "And we're going to figure out the co-parenting thing."

"Does that mean you're staying indefinitely?" Gran asked, unable to mask the hopefulness in her voice. "You keep saying you're here for this one job."

"I don't know," Mara said. "Part of me wants to be here. Part of me isn't sure how being here works, not in the long run. I travel a lot—"

"Zeke could stay here on shorter trips. I could go along on longer ones," Gran offered. "Amanda doesn't start school again for a couple of months. Collin and I could work out some kind of schedule to make sure she's taken care of, too."

"I'm not turning you into my at-home or traveling nanny service. We have plenty of time to figure it out. All of it. Nannies and work and custody and visitation." Mara breathed heavily. It seemed like a lot to figure out in the four weeks she was scheduled to be on the Mallard's job. "Right now I want to get showered, and then I'll throw the meat loaf in the oven."

Gran put her hand on Mara's arm. "And Collin and Amanda and I will get out of your hair for the night—"

"That isn't fair to you," Mara said, beginning to panic because what if James and Zeke didn't click? What if she annoyed him so much he started kissing her again? Or, God, what if she couldn't keep her hands off him? It had been hard at the coffee shop and then the marina. With more people around maybe she wouldn't get all hot and fidgety and start thinking about him naked. The family would be the perfect buffer, for her and for Zeke.

"Nonsense." Gran waved her hand in the air. "Dinner out isn't exactly unfair, and the three of you don't need an audience as you get acquainted. It will be stressful enough without us sitting in the next room or around the same dinner table."

"But—"

Gran cut her off. "No *buts*. There will be plenty of opportunities for big family dinners while you're here. Tonight you can introduce James to this handsome little fella," she said, picking Zeke up to rub her nose against his. The little boy laughed and put his hands to her cheeks so she couldn't move.

Gran set Zeke on his feet and then, still holding on to his little hand, went inside. Mara pushed her foot against the porch floor, setting the rocker in motion, and sighed. She could do this. She'd handled even the most obnoxious executives on jobs for Cannon. She could handle one county sheriff, no matter how handsome he was.

JAMES SAT IN his Jeep, watching the front door of the Tyler farmhouse. He'd been here a thousand times in his life. Picking up Collin for football practice, the five of them going hunting, working for Zeke Tyler during harvest season.

James wasn't sure what to expect, coming here as Mara's ex-something and the father of her child. He couldn't lay claim to the term *boyfriend*. He didn't think the term *lover* fit, either, because although they'd had a lot of sex, there was very little emotion attached to what they'd been doing. No pillow talk. No declarations of feelings. Just a series of hookups, at least until Nashville.

That trip had been different.

That trip had ended whatever it was that he'd had with Mara.

He hated Nashville.

Collin, Gran and Amanda came down the porch steps. Gran held on to Collin's arm as they got into Collin's truck. Collin waved as they passed, but James couldn't make out his expression. Didn't matter. James was going inside the house, and his best friend would have to deal with what had happened between James and his sister.

James was going to have to deal with it, too. He held no illusions about his friendship with Collin; it was strong, but family outweighed even the deepest of friendships.

He got out of the car and strode to the front door. Knocked. And forgot to breathe for a second when Mara answered.

She'd pulled her blond hair up into a pony-tail that brushed the delicate line of her neck. She smiled at a little boy with hair the same color as James's and eyes that had just a touch of green mixed in with the brown. "Hi," she said, and the smile she'd been offering their son was turned on James.

She wore blue athletic shorts and a match-ing tank that showed off curves she hadn't had before Zeke. Something fluttered low in his belly. Then his whole body seemed to heat. Had to be a weird trick of the weather. The temperatures still hovered around the ninety-degree mark.

"Hi," he said. He focused on the little boy. "Hello," James said, and the toddler turned his face into his mother's neck.

"He's shy with new people," Mara said, mo-tioning James inside. She closed the door be-hind him and took him into the living room. The same comfortable, overstuffed furniture he remembered. She handed him a goofy-looking stuffed purple dinosaur.

"What's this for?"

"Playing," Mara said, and sat on the floor with Zeke in her lap. She picked up another animal, this one with a long tail, and wiggled it in her hands. The boy grabbed at it and laughed.

James sat on the floor and wiggled the dinosaur around. The boy didn't giggle at him. He just watched solemnly. Mara shoved her stuffed animal in the face of James's stuffed animal, making the little boy giggle again.

"Zeke, this is your Daddy," she said, her voice gentle despite the attacking motions of the stuffed animal in her hand. "You have to play back," she told James, and he realized he was sitting on the floor, doing nothing.

He pushed his stuffed animal against hers, trying to ignore the brush of her fingertips against his and the jolt of electricity it sent through his body. Mara tossed her stuffed animal in the air. It landed on Zeke's head, and he grabbed at it with his chubby hands. When it fell to the floor, she picked it up and twisted it gently against his face and neck.

Well, James could sit here and watch her play with their son, or he could join in. Zeke giggled and grabbed the stuffed animal from Mara's hands. He pushed it toward her face, making giggly-growling noises. James pushed the purple dinosaur toward Mara, too, and tried to imitate the noises Zeke was making.

The little boy stopped playing and looked at James for a long moment, then dropped the stuffed animal and snuggled closer to Mara. James mimicked Mara's earlier toss, but instead of grabbing at the dinosaur, Zeke just sat on Mara's bent knee. Mara picked up the animal he dropped, but he didn't play with her, either. He just watched as if trying to figure out what James was doing.

"I don't think he enjoys our game," James said, a bit intimidated by the little guy who obviously didn't like him.

"I think he's not used to anyone monster-attacking me except him," Mara said. She put both stuffed animals on the floor in front of Zeke. He kicked at them with his feet but didn't pick them up.

"You told him I was his father."

"Well, you are, and at fourteen months, it isn't exactly a trauma for him to learn he has one. The key is to present it naturally, not to overload him, and make this as normal as possible. He's had a lot of introductions this week. Great-grandmother, uncle, aunt. Now dad."

James picked up the purple dinosaur, tossing it absently from hand to hand. "It felt weird, you introducing me so nonchalantly."

"You expected a presentation with slide-shows and engraved cards?" she asked.

Zeke scooted his body toward her bent knee, edging closer to the stuffed animal on the floor.

"No, I... I'm not sure what I expected."

Mara ran her hands over the little boy's hair. "To be honest, I've been trying to fig-ure out all day how to introduce you. Seeing you at the door, I decided just to be straight-forward about it."

"Thanks." James couldn't pinpoint ex-actly what the *thanks* was for—her introduc-ing him normally or her introducing him at all. Either way, the word seemed inadequate. He tossed the dinosaur once more. "So, what happens now?"

"We have dinner. We play a little more, then put this guy to bed. Another night we do it all again, as often as you want."

James nodded.

Zeke lunged for the dinosaur, startling James. The boy fell to his knees, clutching the dinosaur to his chest. James froze, un-sure whether to offer comfort or not. Mara held her hand up, stopping him from reach-ing for Zeke. The little boy rolled over onto his back, the dinosaur still clutched to his chest, and made a roaring sound as he got to his feet. He grabbed the other stuffed animal and high-stepped his way toward the sofa, both animals faux-attacking one another as he crashed against the soft cushions.

James watched, mesmerized, as Zeke happily mounted some kind of attack with the stuffed animals against the sofa. He mumbled something James couldn't quite understand. "What did he say?"

Mara shrugged. "I have no idea. The only two words he really has down are *dog* and *ball*, but he chatters a lot."

"Is that normal?"

"All babies develop their words differently, but the books say his vocabulary will sky-rocket over the next six months or so."

"Books?"

"Baby books, development books. I think I've read every one printed in the past ten years. He has good hand-eye coordination, and he's walking more and more. He's in good shape."

"Could I borrow one of those books?"

Mara nodded. "Of course."

James couldn't take his eyes off his son, playing attack-the-couch with the stuffed animals in his hands. "He's amazing."

"I think so," she said, and her voice was soft. Mara turned to watch Zeke for a moment. "Zeke," she said, and his head swiveled in her direction. "Are you hungry?" she asked, moving her hands as she spoke. Zeke mimicked the hand movement and started in their direction.

"What was that?"

"Baby sign. We do the signs for *tired* and *hungry* and *more* and *full*." Mara stood, and Zeke wobbled closer. James stood, too. "It gives him a bit more autonomy, makes it simpler for me to understand him."

"Can you teach me?"

"Definitely," she said. "We'll work on it at dinner. I'll just run upstairs to grab that book for you."

Before James could stop her, Mara had hurried up the stairs. He expected her to reappear a moment later, but there was no sound from upstairs. He looked at the baby, who looked back at him. James waited, but Mara didn't return. There was no noise from the kitchen. The lack of familiar faces didn't seem to bother Zeke, though, who turned to his stuffed animals and resumed his fake-attacking play.

Was it a test, then? James scooted a little closer to the couch, but Zeke stayed focused on his toys. The baby hadn't liked it when James joined in the attack-mommy game a few minutes ago, so maybe he should try something else. There was a stack of blocks of different sizes near the recliner. James picked up a few and began building a tower, one of his favorite things to do as a kid.

He'd built entire cities with interlocking blocks and had practically lined his room with models of log cabins, and once had managed to stack a bunch of blocks nearly to the ceiling before the structure came tumbling down. There were only five of these blocks, but he could do something with them.

He took his time stacking the blocks, making sure Zeke had a clear view. Largest on the bottom, smallest on the top. Zeke turned, watching him, the stuffed animals lying still on the couch. James waited, but the little boy only watched. Okay, new approach. Smallest to largest. Balancing the blocks took a bit of maneuvering, but James managed.

Zeke tilted his head, then put his hands in the air and kept bending as if trying to figure out what was going on with the blocks. He tumbled over onto his back and giggled. James held out his hand, and after a moment, Zeke put his pudgy baby hand in his. James couldn't breathe for a second.

He didn't think he had ever held anything so tiny and soft, and it made him wonder just how tiny and soft the little boy had been as an infant. He'd missed it. He'd missed the late-night feedings and the fifteen-times-a-day diaper changes and the first bath and... Pain hit his chest with the force of a sledgehammer, knocking the wind out of him.

He'd missed it, and he couldn't completely blame it on Mara. Yes, she should have told him, but what about his personal responsibility? He'd been half in love with Mara Tyler in high school, and after the first time they ran into one another, in Jefferson City at that law enforcement workshop, that half-in-love feeling had put him in way over his head.

He'd kept seeing her, telling himself that it didn't matter how he felt or how she felt. He'd been convinced that she might eventually come around, that she might feel about him the way he felt about her. But he'd never told her how he felt—not even in Nashville when she had been so different. She'd been softer, more vulnerable, had talked more about Slippery Rock. He could have told her then how he felt. And maybe if he had, things would have been different. Maybe she wouldn't have run.

Or maybe she still would have run, but

when she'd discovered she was pregnant, she would have at least called him.

There were a thousand maybes in his brain, and not a single one of them mattered more than holding his little boy's hand.

Zeke stood on wobbly legs and high-stepped to the inverted tower of blocks. He poked one finger at the middle block, and the tower all came tumbling down around him. For the first time, he looked at James and smiled.

Whatever mistakes James had made with Mara, he wasn't going to make the same mistakes now. Two years was long enough. He had a son and he had a town that depended on him. He wouldn't let either of them down.

MARA SAT AT the head of the stairs, watching through the pickets while her son played with his father. She swiped away a tear as Zeke put his hand in James's.

She had been so wrong to keep the two of them apart. So very, very wrong, and she had no idea how to make things right. She couldn't turn back time, no matter how much she wished, at this moment, that she could.

Zeke began stacking the blocks, and when James added one to the new tower, Zeke knocked them over. He put his chubby hand over his mouth and giggled. Mara smiled in response. He was such a sweetheart. God, she had had no idea she could love someone as much as she loved her son.

James restacked Zeke's uneven tower, explaining about sizing and connections as he moved each block into position. He was using his cop voice, which Mara found hilarious. Only James would talk to a fourteen-month-old baby building a tower as if he was a fifteen-year-old teen out on a joyride. The man was nuts. And possibly the sweetest person she had ever known. Mara put her hand over her heart and sighed. God, she could love a man who spoke to a child as if he were an equal. It was how Granddad always talked to Mara and her siblings when they were small.

She traced her fingers over the embossed lettering of the book next to her. This was her favorite parenting book because it was written tongue-in-cheek with real-world examples, compared with the dry books written by psychology professors that read like…well, textbooks. None of the books she had read, though, had prepared her for this moment.

When she'd left Tulsa for Slippery Rock, she'd thought she was ready. She had put whatever came over her in Nashville firmly in the past; she knew she and James weren't good for one another in the long run. He wanted things she didn't, such as a life in Slippery Rock. He came from a place she didn't, with two parents who were steady and caring and could have been the poster family for those old sitcoms she'd devoured when she was home sick from school. She came from two adults who were so hell-bent on never being adults that they'd left their children alone for days on end while they partied, and who ultimately abandoned their children to their grandparents.

That was the one selfless thing Samson and Maddie had done, and for that one act, Mara refused to hate her parents. Looking at Zeke, she couldn't begin to understand why they had done the things they had, but she couldn't hate them.

The kitchen timer sounded. She jumped from her perch and descended the stairs.

"Dinner in five," she called over her shoulder, putting as much breeziness in her voice as she could. James had restacked the blocks into a perfectly straight tower. Zeke reached for one of the middle blocks, and as she crossed into the kitchen, she heard the tower tumble down. Mara chuckled.

In the kitchen, she grabbed quilted pot holders with orange, green and purple foxes on them, then pulled the meat loaf and the vegetable casserole from the oven. She set the hot dishes on the built-in counter trivets to cool, filled a sippy cup for Zeke, and grabbed two more glasses as well as plates and flatware.

"This might be the most domestic thing you've ever done in your life, Mara Tyler," she said to herself.

"You're kind of cute when you're being domestic," James said from the doorway. Mara whirled, putting her hand to her chest.

"I didn't realize you'd followed me in." He crossed to the counter and picked up the plates. "I can do that."

"I know how to set a table, although I've never actually done it."

Mara wasn't sure how to respond to that, so she changed the subject. "Iced tea?"

"Real sugar, not one of those substitutes?"

She straightened her shoulders, cocked an eyebrow and put as much starch in her voice as she could muster. "Would any self-respecting Missouri girl put anything but real sugar in her iced tea?"

"Technically you've been living in Tulsa and a hundred other cities or states, but I'll take that as a yes to the sugar, and you can take that as a yes to the glass. Thanks."

Mara filled the glasses. "You were looking pretty comfortable out there."

"So it was a test." It wasn't a question, and he'd used his überserious cop voice.

"Not a test, per se, just… I felt like the two of you might get along a little better without me for a minute." She put the glasses on the table and picked up the flatware to finish the table settings. She had wanted—no—she had *needed* to see how the two of them would act together. Sooner or later, James would have visitation, and he would be alone with Zeke. She needed to know he wouldn't tune the toddler out.

James was an only child, and while he'd always been nice to Amanda when they were kids, there was a big difference between being nice to a child and being a responsible adult and parent for a child.

"Also, I needed to get that book for you." She pointed to the sideboard where she'd dropped the book when she entered the kitchen. "Why don't you sit? I'll grab the little man, and we can eat."

He put his hand on her arm, stopping her. That familiar sizzle sped along her skin. "It was a test."

Mara shook her head, then sighed. "You

would have done it differently. You'd have done it perfectly."

"Mara." His voice was quiet, and the sound of her name on his lips made the sizzle burn a little hotter. She froze, needing to keep the heat between them under control, but wanting it to burst out like a wildfire. His mouth hit hers, but instead of the anger that had fueled that kiss outside the B and B, the contact was slow. Smooth. And it nearly undid her. His mouth was strong against hers, familiar, and yet it was as if he had never kissed her before.

Which was ridiculous because he'd kissed her at least a thousand times over the past five years. Kissed her and held her and made her scream in another thousand different ways. All of those ways were fast, urgent, and filled with pounding heartbeats and maybe a fumble or two because they were always on borrowed time. He had to leave or she did. His work called or hers did.

This was different, as if they had all the time in the world. As if nothing could interrupt them or stop them. As if there was nothing left to get in their way. No job that kept her on the road. No small town holding on to him. No checkered past, no teenage pranks.

His lips continued to move over hers in a light caress, teasing her lips apart. His hand slid to her nape as his tongue finally dipped into her mouth. Mara locked her hands behind his head, wanting to hold him in place, wanting the moment to continue. She'd missed him. Missed her best friend. Missed her lover. Even knowing he wasn't right for her or, more accurately, she wasn't right for him, she had missed how his body felt against hers. How he made her feel deep inside. As if she was loved.

As if she was lovable.

James's hand caressed her neck, and her hunger kicked into a higher gear. When his fingers walked past her shoulder and over her ribs, she forgot to breathe, and when his hand cupped her breast, Mara's knees buckled.

James. He was what she had been missing for the past two years. She'd kept herself busy with work, committed herself to the therapy sessions with her doctor and showered all the love she had on Zeke. But under all that busyness, she'd been hollow. Felt incomplete.

Mara pushed the thought away. She was not the kind of woman who needed a man to feel complete. She was independent, in all the best senses of the word. And yet…there was something about this man that made her feel as if she could be even more.

It was a scary thought. Almost as scary

as the thought of never having his lips on hers again.

Something brushed against her leg, and it snapped Mara back to her grandmother's kitchen. Kissing James.

God, this was so not the point of this evening. The point of this evening wasn't to rekindle the lust-fest the two of them had going two years ago, it was...

She drew away from him. "That shouldn't have happened."

Zeke patted her leg again. He thrust one of the blocks up toward her. Mara took it, then gathered the little boy into her arms.

"This isn't about us anymore. It's about him," she said and buckled him into the high chair. "We have to think of him first."

CHAPTER NINE

IT SHOULDN'T HAVE BEEN this hard not to touch him.

Mara shoved her hands in the pockets of her shorts. She and James were walking in the orchard with Zeke. It was Sunday morning, less than twelve hours since he'd met his son for the first time, and it was as if he'd been a father for years.

When Zeke was born, it had taken her a couple of months to get to that comfort level with the little boy. Being a first time, single mom and being a buddy to a toddler weren't exactly the same things, but it still pained her that James and Zeke seemed to be adjusting to one another without any problems at all.

It was sickening how quickly he had adapted to being a father. Sickening and sexy, and that was trouble on a whole other level.

The sexy thing was flat-out unfair. New mothers got bags under their eyes and stretch marks and sagging skin. Her breasts had gotten bigger, but so had her hips, and so far no amount of sit-ups or yoga poses had flattened her stomach. The changes to her body didn't bother her, not really. But the fact that nothing about parenting seemed to be bugging James did.

As a new father, James had broad shoulders, washboard abs, and a voice that still sent prickles up and down her spine. After those few minutes together on the living room floor when she'd left to get the book, it was as if the two of them had always known one another. Zeke accepted his new playmate; James seemed to accept his new daddy role.

He had to be angry with her, but he hid the mad well. Other than that moment when he kissed her out of anger. He needed to get really mad. Not just grab her and kiss her mad, but really angry. Yelling mad. Shutting her out of his life mad. She could deal with outrage. She was prepared for anger. His reaction so far was throwing off her game.

He picked Zeke up and settled the boy on his shoulders as if he weren't also carrying a backpack. They crossed from the peach trees to the apples, and it was as if they crossed a line. The peach trees were fully grown and bearing fruit. Many of what would have been fully grown apple trees were stumps, and saplings were now planted where the bigger trees once stood. The tornado did significant damage here, and it was hard to see, to know that their grandparents' work was destroyed. But Collin, dedicated man that he was, was fixing the situation.

"I think this is a good spot," she said when they reached an area filled with bigger trees to offer shade from the summer sunshine.

James set Zeke on the ground, and the little boy squatted to run his hands through the thick carpet of grass. James took the backpack—full of picnic foods and a blanket—from his shoulders. Mara spread the oversize blanket under a tree. It was all just…too domestic, as though they'd been an actual couple with a child from the beginning.

He rested his back against a tree, watching their son as he explored the area around them. Zeke followed a white butterfly for a moment, until it went too high in the sky. Then he bent as if looking for another in the grass at his feet.

"How do you do it?" His question caught her off guard.

"Gran made the sandwiches. I just put the fruit in plastic baggies."

James rolled his eyes at her. "You know what I mean. Single mom, full-time job."

"You met my nanny. I wasn't exactly alone.

Cheryl traveled with us from that first job after maternity leave. She made it easy for me to do my job and be a parent."

"Still, you never had a break."

She sat on the blanket, watching Zeke for a long moment. Not once had she second-guessed her decision to have him. Oh, there had been moments—like when he cut his first tooth—when it would have been nice to have a partner. But for the most part, he was an easy, agreeable child, and she loved that he made her look at life differently.

Pre-Zeke, things had been all about her. The kind of life she wanted to lead, the kind of work she wanted to do. With Zeke, life was about more than a job or a paycheck. It was about the family she was creating, the family she had never really had despite Gran and Granddad's best efforts. They had been great stand-in parents, but not even Ezekiel and Gladys could take the place of the parents who refused to make room in their lives for Mara or her siblings.

A smile stole across her face as she thought about the ways Zeke had changed her. "Who needs a break when you have someone like him?" she asked, pointing in his direction.

"I have to admit, I never pictured you as a mom."

"Neither did I. I'd convinced myself I was too self-centered to be a parent." Her gaze connected with his and for a moment, she wished things between them could have been different. That he wanted more than Slippery Rock or she wanted less than travel and new cities. She wasn't a small-town girl, though, not really. She was the Tyler with itchy feet, like her parents. She couldn't be happy here, not in the long run.

"What changed?"

"Him. It's hard to think only about yourself when there is a helpless infant who's depending on you for feedings and diaper changes, and who needs you to sing his favorite song when he's not feeling well."

"He has a favorite song?"

She nodded. "The one from *Dumbo*."

"You hate that movie. In speech class, you refused to watch it because—"

"And the first time he cried, it was the one song that seemed appropriate." Mara put her hands behind her, leaning back a little to keep Zeke in her line of sight while he continued his exploration of the apple orchard. The sun was high in the sky, burning off the last of the cooler morning. Before long, the orchard would be stifling, but right now it was perfect with a light breeze blowing through the leaves, and enough shade to keep the heat at bay. "It calmed him, and I may not watch that movie, but I do like that 'Baby Mine' song."

James took a bottle of water from the back-pack and drank. "I'll have to remember that."

"Just don't watch the clip on YouTube. It'll tear your heart out." It had torn out hers. See-ing Mrs. Jumbo trying to get to her child, but being unable to reach him… Mara shook her head. She didn't want to go down that road, not now. There were more important things to talk about, and this seemed as good a time as any. They were alone. Zeke was distracted with the clover in the grass and the butterflies in the air.

"Why aren't you angrier with me?" she asked.

"Who says I'm not angry and just covering it up well? I did walk away from you. Twice."

"And you came back. Twice."

He plucked a stalk of grass from under the tree where he sat. "Why do you want me to be angry with you?" he said after a moment.

Mara shook her head. "James, I don't want you to be angry, but anger is how most peo-ple would react."

"Why do you need me to be like most peo-ple?"

"Why are you answering my question with other questions?"

He was quiet for so long, she thought he wouldn't answer at all. Then he folded his arms over his chest. "I don't see the point in getting angry about something I can't change. I can be angry with you, but what does that solve? You made a decision. Now we both have to live with it. But raking you over the coals about it for the foreseeable future? What does that really solve?"

"But you haven't been angry at all." That wasn't normal. It couldn't be normal, not even for a well-adjusted, possessing-two-parents man who had been voted most likely to succeed their senior year. And probably again during his years in college and at the police academy.

"What does anger solve? It won't change the fact that you had our baby and didn't tell me about him. It won't change the fact that you disappeared out of our Nashville hotel room in the middle of the night—"

"Technically it was five in the morning."

"Five in the morning," he agreed. "I can get angry if you want me to, but what will that solve?"

It would make him more human, for one thing. It would give her something to focus on other than the more sticky emotions he made her feel. If he got angry, she could get

angry. Then the uncomfortable emotions—
the ones that told her a hundred times a day
what an idiot she was for walking away from
him—would be quieted. If she'd told him the
truth about how she was feeling, she might
have been with him when she learned about
the pregnancy instead of in Florida. If she'd
called or come home to tell him about the
pregnancy… But she hadn't. She'd been too
confused and scared about what loving him
meant.

"You sound like one of those internet memes,"
she said. "'What doesn't kill us makes us stronger.'"

"'Except bears, bears will kill you dead,'"
James quoted. "I like that meme."

"You would."

"Are you trying to piss me off? Because
I'm not mad at you about something real and
tangible?"

Mara started to object but bit back the
words. Because she had been poking at him.
Not hard, sharp pokes, but little ones. As if
he were the bear and she had to make sure
he was dead before he made her dead, like
the meme.

"I would be furious," she said, keeping her
voice quiet even though there was no one
around to hear them except Zeke. The little

boy couldn't have cared less what they were talking about; he was busy wandering after another white butterfly. "I would be filing papers and coming up with new and devious ways to get back at you."

"That would only drive a wedge between the two most important people in his life right now. I don't want to hate you, Mar. Once, I thought—" James snapped his mouth closed. He hadn't used his nickname for her since he caught her in the revolving door at the grocery store, and it sent a shiver up her spine. Mara leaned toward him, but he kept those full lips pressed together.

Once he thought…what? Before she could ask, Zeke toddled toward them, making the sign for *hungry* with his little hands. *Way to go, Mara. Get distracted talking to James and forget to feed your son.*

That judgment wasn't one hundred percent fair to her. It was just after noon, so the kid wasn't starving by any stretch of the imagination. Still, they'd come out here for a picnic, not to dissect the feelings James had—or didn't have—about the secret she had been keeping for the past year and a half. His feelings were his. Wasn't that the first rule she'd learned in therapy? Not to project her feelings onto other people and not to project the feelings she assumed people had about her onto herself.

She wasn't to blame for the way Samson and Maddie treated her siblings or her. James wasn't wrong for refusing to be angry with her. It was strange and she didn't understand it, but those were his feelings, not hers.

She put bottles of water and plastic containers with fruits, cheeses and bite-size portions of ham on the blanket, along with plates, napkins and cutlery. Then she settled Zeke with a plate. She handed another to James and waited while he filled it.

"I'm sorry," she began, but he made an impatient gesture.

"I already told you, I don't need any more apologizes about Zeke."

"No, I'm sorry I keep pushing you to share your anger or mistrust or whatever it is you're feeling. Those are your private emotions, and you don't have to tell me about any of them." She selected a bunch of grapes, a banana and a few cubes of Colby-Jack cheese. She offered the cube of cheese to Zeke before popping a grape in her mouth. She chewed and swallowed before speaking. "In therapy, I worked a lot on misplaced emotions, on self-esteem and on confronting the whole past, not just my interpretation of the past. I'm not your therapist, though." She gave a small, self-conscious laugh. "I'm not a therapist at all, and I shouldn't have tried to act like one."

After a while, he nodded. "For what it's worth, I was angry. When you first told me. I learned a long time ago not to rest on angry because it hides the most important emotions, the ones I'm still dealing with. I'm not angry that you kept Zeke a secret, Mar. I'm hurt that you thought you had to, that you thought I wouldn't understand or couldn't. But I'm not angry."

"I didn't mean to hurt you. I was just so afraid of what having a baby meant." Hurting James had been the last thing on her mind. Protecting Zeke, making sure he had a stable upbringing and a parent who was focused on him—those had been her priorities. "I had a plan for my life, and it didn't involve kids, and it didn't involve long-term relationships— working or romantic. Finding out I was pregnant, it kind of changed all those plans."

"And now?"

She smiled. "Now I'm finding that learning a new city every few weeks can be tiring, and it's a pain in the butt to pack and unpack all our belongings every few weeks. I'm realizing how much I've missed my family, and even this town. I never thought I'd miss Slippery Rock."

"It kind of grows on you."

"Like moss." Mara decided to go all the way. If she wanted honesty from James about his feelings, she might as well be honest with him about hers. Most of them, anyway. "My parents never had room in their lives for us. There was room only for Samson and Maddie, and we were the accessories they couldn't get rid of. For a long time, I blamed myself for that. I got sick a lot as a kid, and I thought all the attention I needed was the reason they would leave for long periods. I thought I was too much."

"It wasn't you," James said. He fisted his hands, the knuckles turning white.

"I know that now. Therapy helped me come to terms with their narcissism and my own self-esteem issues. But before that, when I found out about the pregnancy, all I could think about was how they'd neglected us. That trip to Nashville…you and I were supposed to stay for only two days, and a week later we were still in that same hotel room. Still getting lost in conversation over dinner. How many times did our servers have to tell us they were closing?" She shook her head. "That bubble we were in scared me at the time—it was too much like Samson and Maddie, and I had to leave. When I found out I was pregnant, I was terrified. It felt like I was repeating the cycle." She ruffled Zeke's hair. "I hadn't met him yet, but I knew I couldn't let him believe he wasn't wanted, that he was too much. So I decided to keep it quiet. To fix the things that were wrong with me, and then, when I was stronger, let you in. But the longer I kept quiet, the harder it was to say anything."

"And so you didn't."

"Not until the tornado. The senseless and instant destruction proved how precious time is and reminded me we have no guarantees of tomorrow. I was so scared that I'd waited too long. That you would be hurt, or someone in my family. I had to come home to face all of you." Mara pushed her plate, the food half-eaten, away. "I can deal with you hating me, James. I deserve it. But don't let that turn your emotions against him, too. Please."

She could handle whatever he wanted to dish out, for herself. But Zeke was innocent in this situation. He deserved better. This little boy who had helped her finally grow up deserved the absolute best.

"I don't hate him, Mar. And I don't hate you.

You were my best friend for a long time. Based on that history alone, I couldn't hate you."

"Okay, then. We'll figure the rest out." And maybe while they were figuring out how to be co-parents to their child, she could find a way to get over the attraction she still felt for him.

GOD, HE WAS such a liar. Such an idiot.

He didn't hate her. He truly didn't. But what he did feel when he was around Mara was much worse. He was still attracted to her, and that was so far from okay he couldn't even see the *okay* target he was aiming for. How could he still be attracted to her after she walked out on him and kept his child from him?

Sure, they had a friendship-based history, but damn. Friendship didn't mean he had to forget she had never felt about him the way that he felt about her, Nashville or no Nashville. Whatever she'd been feeling had made her walk away. He hadn't walked away, despite realizing he loved her. Was in love with her.

Mara chased Zeke behind a tree. The little boy giggled and laughed when she peeked her head around the trunk and roared like a dinosaur.

Two years ago, he had been ready to propose something deeper than an every-few-months booty call. He had been ready to suggest that she come back to Missouri. Not Slippery Rock. As much as he loved the place, there was very little call for her kind of work here. But she could have found a job in Springfield or Joplin. Long commutes to work weren't ideal, but they could have made it work. If she had only stayed.

She didn't stay. She wasn't staying now. He had to keep that in mind. It didn't matter that they'd been friends for more than half their lives. It didn't even matter that for three of those years they'd been lovers. What mattered was the fact that they now shared a child who deserved better than living in hotel rooms or short-term apartments. He could give Zeke a solid, steady life in Slippery Rock.

James popped a grape in his mouth as he watched Mara and the little boy chasing one another around the trees. She was so carefree here. Why couldn't she see how good Slippery Rock would be for Zeke?

He rose, then snuck behind one tree, making his way around Zeke, who was trying to catch Mara. Her attention was focused on the little boy, leaving her open to James's attack. James lunged from behind the tree, catching her around the waist and bringing her to the ground with him.

"Got her, Zeke," he said in triumph.

She was breathing heavily, and her breasts pressed against his chest. Those big blue eyes darkened, and her pink tongue darted out of her mouth to moisten her lips. A flash of electricity seemed to spark between them, igniting a fire deep in his belly.

You don't have her, James reminded himself. *She isn't yours. She was never yours before, and she can't be yours now. There is too much at stake.*

He had Zeke to consider. He deserved parents who weren't on-again, off-again.

There was the election, too. When it became public knowledge that James had fathered a child with Mara, her past reputation would influence his bid for sheriff. And he knew that for certain townspeople, her past would outweigh the smart, capable woman she was now. It wasn't fair, but it was the way things were. There was a real possibility his campaign wouldn't be about his ability to serve this community but about how hooking up with Mara called his morality into question.

He dipped his head toward hers, wanting the feel of her mouth against his, and unable to deny himself. He wanted to taste her, not out of frustration and not with anger.

And that was quite possibly the dumbest thought he'd had in the past few days. Hell, it hadn't been a week since she came back to town, and already she was taking up most of his time. James didn't want to be angry with Mara, but it was a long step between not being angry and letting the chemistry between them determine his actions.

Her lids drooped, and her head lifted slightly off the ground.

At least his wasn't the only body that still wanted.

Zeke pounced on the two of them, roaring like Mara had a little while before. He giggled as he slid off their two-person pile, settling against Mara's side. James slid off Mara to the other side. This wasn't the time; there could never be a time. Not now.

Not because of what she had done, but because of who she was, and who he was. He was the man who would stay in Slippery Rock. His adventures would be had wearing the sheriff's department uniform and, maybe, with the title of Sheriff on a nameplate on the desk his mother had picked out for his father decades ago.

Mara was the woman who couldn't stay.

Her adventures would be everywhere, and they wouldn't include family heirlooms like desks.

"Sorry," he said, shaking his head slowly. "I shouldn't have done that."

She sat up. "No worries." She stood, brushing her hands over the seat of her shorts. She turned her attention to their son, reaching out her hand. The two of them started playing the chase game again, but this time James stayed out.

It would be better if he kept things clearly separated in his mind, because there was no future to be made between him and Mara.

CHAPTER TEN

STRONG HANDS CARESSED her belly, and a deep voice whispered something she didn't quite catch in her ear. The something was enough to make her stomach do an excited little flip-flop and the hairs on her nape stir in anticipation. He was warm beside her, smelling of sandalwood with just a hint of something spicy. His arms and back were smooth to her touch, warm and hard, and she couldn't get enough of running her hands over him.

It was all so familiar. God, she had missed this. She arched her back, wanting his touch on her breasts. Oh, and he needed to do more than whisper sweet nothings in her ear.

Mara stretched her arms over her head, and the feel of the cold iron bed frame against her hands jolted her quickly out of the dream. The images were slow to leave. She and James had been entwined on silken sheets, and the headboard had been a rich, smooth wood with intricately carved spindles instead of the iron of her childhood bed.

The coverlet rich and velvety like that bed in the suite in Nashville instead of the soft cotton of one of her grandmother's quilts.

Entwined like they'd been in Nashville.

Nothing at all like what was going on now in Slippery Rock, where James just wanted to be her friend. Where James wanted to be Zeke's dad, and her friend. Where Mara couldn't stop reacting to the sound of his voice or the *friendly* brush of his hand against hers, and where that angry kiss they'd shared when she'd first arrived threw her into dreams she hadn't had for the better part of eight months.

She shot a glance toward the Pack 'n Play in the corner. Zeke still rested peacefully. She sat up, shook her head and slid her legs over the side of the bed, letting her toes squeeze the thickly piled lavender shag rug. Sunlight streamed through the windows, the gauzy lavender-checked curtains she'd insisted on for her senior year in high school doing little to dissipate the strong light. Lavender-and-blue flowers were painted just above the headboard, and her favorite owls, again in lavender and blue, sat on the bedside table. She'd found them in a wedding store and convinced Gran she needed them.

The familiarity was nice, if a bit weird. Most of her assignments for Cannon Security entailed staying in blandly furnished apartments. The bits of blue and lavender were a nice change from the taupe palettes she'd been living with for the past few years.

Robins and larks chirped in the trees outside her window, another nice change. Usually she was wakened by the sound of freeway traffic or inadvertently triggered car alarms. All in all, it was nice to be home.

She just needed to wrap her head around the fact that, for James, their past was exactly that. The past. He was Zeke's dad, not her lover. Not any longer.

She grabbed clean clothes and headed for the bathroom down the hall. Once she was showered and dressed—denim capris, a light green tank top and flip-flops, leaving her long blond hair to dry around her shoulders—she felt ready to face her actual job at Mallard's. Mike was back from vacation, and today was the day for full diagnostics of the old system so she could begin building the new. Daydreams and night dreams about James would have to wait.

Zeke turned over onto his tummy, his little hand beginning to rub against the mesh of the Pack 'n Play. She picked him up, his body still a bit limp from sleep, and cooed while she started his diaper change. He smiled at her and farted when she removed the diaper. Mara waved her hand in front of her face.

"Nice, kid, nice. You've gotta save some of that for your dad, okay?" Zeke grinned at that. She'd read all the baby books but still wondered for the millionth time just how much of what she said to him the child understood, and how much he just liked the sound of her voice.

She put a pair of shorts and a lightweight T-shirt on him and started down the stairs.

Gran and Amanda were seated at the kitchen table when she entered. Collin must already have been in the orchard for the day.

"Good morning," she said, making her voice sound chirpier than she felt. Nearly a week of waking up halfway to sexual satisfaction from a dream about James had that effect on her. At least, that's what she thought it was. Mara couldn't remember ever having this many sex dreams, at least not back-to-back-to-back.

Amanda waved her spoon in Mara's direction, then gathered her cereal bowl and Gran's empty plate. "Need to check the berry garden. See ya later," she called over her shoulder as she rushed out the door. Mara checked the dishes in the sink. Cereal bowl mostly full. Again. She set Zeke in the high chair Collin had brought down from the attic over the weekend. He waved his hands and started talking in his usual gibberish. Mara put a few pieces of cereal on his tray and filled a sippy cup with milk from Walters Ranch.

"Do you think they'll ever stop using glass bottles?" she asked, not expecting an answer.

"Bennett says milk tastes better from glass than plastic. I agree," Gran said, referring to Levi's father and his penchant for old-fashioned milk bottles instead of the plastic jugs most stores carried.

Mara filled a cup with orange juice. "I'll have to take your word for it, but Zeke definitely likes it." And Mara liked that he hadn't inherited her intolerance for milk. She gestured toward the sink, then the back door. "You think she's ever going to stop running out of the room when I come in?" she asked.

Gran shrugged as she rose. "She's not sure what to think about you being back, that's all. She's especially not sure what to think about you being back with a baby. Want some eggs?"

"Just juice and toast," she said, taking what she needed from the refrigerator. While she waited for the toast to pop up, she asked, "Why does it bug her that I'm back?"

Gran sipped coffee from an orchard mug.

"I don't think it bothers her. You haven't shared your plans with her. Like I said, it's harder on her when people leave than it was on you. You and Collin always bounced back from those visits with your parents, from their coming and going, especially around her age. Amanda doesn't bounce, and since you graduated, you've never been here more than a day at a time. Put that with the tornado and the volunteer construction work Collin's taken on, and she's not quite sure what to think."

"I'm her sister. I'm here for a job."

Gran raised an eyebrow. "That's part of the problem."

The toast was ready, and Mara spread on a thin layer of apple jam made by Levi's mother, Mama Hazel. She bit in and closed her eyes as the sweetness of the jam slid over her taste buds.

"How long *are* you here?" Gran asked pointedly. "You don't have just yourself to think about now. There's Zeke, too. At some point, he'll need preschool, a regular address—"

"He's barely talking, and you're planning for his education already?" Mara teased her grandmother, but the thought of leaving wasn't quite as exciting as it usually was, and that bothered her more than she was ready to admit, even to Gran. She didn't want to leave, not just yet, maybe not ever. But staying here, so close to James, and being only his friend? She didn't think she could survive that.

"I'd like nothing more than for you to stay, but only if that is what you want. You're the one who says you have itchy feet."

That was not a reminder Mara liked. Yes, she knew it was true, but that didn't make hearing it any easier. She finished her toast and downed the glass of juice. "I'll go back to the B and B if it's that inconvenient for Amanda to have me here."

"There's nothing wrong with being like your father. There is a kind of beauty in always wondering what is around the next corner, and being brave enough to take that next turn. He makes me absolutely crazy, and I hate what he's put you kids through, but he is my son. I wouldn't have the three of you if it weren't for him." Gran made Samson Tyler sound like some unique, noble combination of a hippie and an adventurer.

The truth for Mara was that Samson was an inconsiderate, immature man who had no interest in taking responsibility for anyone but himself. He'd dragged their mother along on his "adventures" for nearly thirty years. Not that Maddie Tyler complained about the quick moves, job changes or any of the rest of it. She simply smiled, packed their things and headed off in his ancient VW Beetle.

Gran was still talking. "You'll stay here, of course. Amanda will get used to you and Zeke. You need a babysitter while you're working on the Mallard's contract. We all want you here. Some of us are just better at expressing that."

Mara could relate to not expressing her feelings. That fear of rejection had made her run away from James in Nashville, and it had kept her away from home for too long. If she'd had a bit more strength all along, Amanda wouldn't be running away from her now. James would know his son. Mara shook off the guilt settling over her shoulders.

"Well, if I'm going to prove to my sister that I'm at least a little bit reliable, I'd better get this inspection done quickly. When she ventures back in, tell her I'll be home after lunch. We can work the roadside stand together this afternoon. We'll take Zeke with us."

"I'M GLAD THE news crews covering the tornado damage left before this reconstruction project started. Although I hear they're going to do some kind of six-month reminder of what happened. How we recovered," a low voice with a bit of a twang said from behind Mara. She turned to see a woman with a mass of long, thin braids, light caramel-colored skin and deep brown eyes behind her. "Mara, right?"

The voice and the look rang a bell, but Mara couldn't put a name to either the face or the voice. "Yeah, but I don't think—"

"I was a year behind you and the guys in school. Savannah Walters. Levi's sister."

"And Collin's girlfriend. You're the one he keeps sneaking away from the house to see."

Mara had walked downtown to get a break from Mallard's. While most of the workers, and Mike Mallard himself, were perfectly nice to her, she'd felt the glowering gaze of CarlaAnn from the moment she arrived at the store. During quiet moments at the register, the clerk had made it her mission to tell whoever was around about the so-called shoplifting incident.

"And I'll bet you've had just about enough of CarlaAnn, haven't you? Don't worry, she kept the town talking about me not so long ago. It'll pass." Savannah grinned. "And in Collin's defense, I keep sneaking away from my house, too. This grown-up relationship thing when you're living with parents is weird."

"I can imagine."

Savannah held out her hand, and Mara shook it. Savannah sat beside Mara on the bench facing what used to be the farmers' market. The roof had been torn off in the tornado, and one wall collapsed. The big plate glass window had blown out. Along with a crew of construction workers, Collin had helped to reinforce the walls. Today, he'd joined Levi and the rest of the volunteers working on the back side of the roof.

"Why don't you like the news crews coming around?"

Savannah shivered. "Bad memories."

And then everything clicked. Savannah had been on a talent show and had a big hit on country radio before a scandal rocked her career around the time the tornado rocked Slippery Rock.

"You were on that benefit concert show, right?" Mara asked. "The one that raised funds for the reconstruction." The other woman grimaced and then nodded. "You were good."

"I'm glad I'm not in that spotlight now."

Mara wasn't sure what else to say. She didn't know Savannah Walters, not even from

Collin. That was another aspect of being back that was different. There was a time in their lives when she and Collin told one another everything. She remembered that expression on his face when she'd told him that James was Zeke's father. He'd looked betrayed…and hurt. That hurt ran deep, and it was because of her. Because she had shut so much of her life out of his. She needed to fix that.

She needed to fix a lot of things. "What *are* you still doing in Slippery Rock? I mean, I love my brother, but you had a Nashville record deal."

"It turned out I hated singing on stage. Crowds and me," she said with a shake of her head, "not simpatico." A smile lit Savannah's face, and her eyes seemed to fasten on Collin's broad, muscular back. "Now I'm back here and figuring out who I am for the first time in life. I know, I know, that sounds—"

Mara held up a hand. "I totally get it. I've been doing the same thing for the past couple years."

"With Zeke?"

She nodded. "Zeke changed a lot of things." She watched the men working on the farmers' market for a long moment. "Slippery Rock tends to change things, too."

"I'm going to build a camp for foster kids,"

Savannah said, and Mara's attention snapped back to the woman sitting beside her. "Still in the planning stages, but as you said, Slippery Rock tends to change things for people. Foster kids need a place to just be. I figure if Slippery Rock could change things for me, it can change things for them."

"I think that's amazing. My brother and this town are lucky to have you."

"Thanks." Savannah's focus turned to Collin, and she sighed.

Mara recognized the look on Savannah's face. Territorial. In love. She'd seen a similar expression in the mirror in Nashville. She'd seen it again in the mirror after her argument with James at the B and B. Lord, but she was in trouble.

"Do you think they realize they're basically giving the women of Slippery Rock a free show?" she asked. "All that tanned skin and muscle and sweat?"

Savannah cocked her head to the side as if inspecting the crew of workers. "You know, I think this oblivious thing they have going is a total act. They definitely know."

Mara chuckled. Another man joined the men working on the market, and her mouth went dry. James wore a blue department polo and khakis, and his face was shaded by the bill of a ball cap. He wore black sneakers instead of the combat-type boots he'd worn last week. His shoulders seemed almost as broad as the nearly demolished door he walked through as he greeted the rest of the crew.

He didn't ask where to join in, just picked up a hammer and helped Collin's crew setting the studs for the new wall.

"Wow." She couldn't stop the single syllable from escaping her mouth. Mara clapped her hand over her mouth. "Ignore me," she said through her fingers.

Savannah grinned. "He does make you look twice, doesn't he?" She elbowed Mara. "And lucky you, you get to claim him as the father of your baby."

Of course Collin had told Savannah. Mara shouldn't have been surprised. Still, she wasn't sure just how public James wanted his parental status to be.

"Does everyone know?" she asked, and her chest seemed to tighten. Which was silly. He was the father of her child, and people were going to find out. There was little either of them could do about that.

"I haven't heard any gossip, if that's what you mean. But I'm not really on any of the phone trees in town."

"We, ah, aren't really telling people. Not

until we get it all figured out between the two of us, I mean."

"Sure. The last thing you want to do in Slippery Rock is tell anyone part of any story. Before you know it, the story will be finished and will end in the one way you definitely don't want it to end." Savannah stood. "I have an appointment with my mom and a jam recipe. See you around?"

Mara nodded. "We should have lunch sometime while I'm still here."

"I'll call you."

She walked away, leaving Mara alone on the bench across the street from the market. She watched the men working. James never looked in her direction, which she supposed was a good thing. It meant he was over whatever had been between them. He was over it; she'd already walked away from it. The sooner she got those facts through to her hormones, the better. And yet she remained on the bench, just watching.

Mara clasped her hands in her lap. Crossed and uncrossed her legs. He was completely oblivious to her. It wasn't fair.

It was also hotter than Hades out here. She left the bench and crossed the street to Bud's, where she ordered a large soda. At the end of the sandwich counter sat a huge cooler filled with fish bait, and Mara shivered. Why Bud made his sandwiches so close to fish bait remained a mystery to her. A gross mystery.

Bud, his steel-gray hair in a familiar buzz cut, gave her the drink but didn't stay to chat. He was distracted with a few fishermen at the other end of the counter, which was just as well. Mara didn't feel much like small talk. Back in her SUV, she hit the button to close the moonroof, then rolled up the window, filling the hot car with cool air-conditioning.

She drove out of the downtown area, past Mallard's, and turned onto the highway that would lead her to the orchard. She'd come here to rebuild her relationship with her family, not with James. She wanted to help him build a relationship with Zeke, but that didn't need to have anything to do with her.

Slippery Rock was the home she wanted to love but had never quite been able to. The place where she'd taught herself code and spent much of her time with her head buried in a book. The place where she'd learned that practically nothing would cover words painted in John Deere green on a town water tower, and that the best friend she would ever have would be the one person she had treated absolutely worst.

What she felt when he was around was simply residual attraction. She would get over it.
She had to.

"YOU KNOW, IT doesn't take two adults and a toddler to run this stand. Not on a ninety-eight-degree afternoon." Amanda scraped her hair toward the top of her head, then twisted it into a bun. She held it there for a long minute, and Mara realized she must not have an elastic with her. She pulled one from Zeke's bag and handed it to her. "Thanks," Amanda grumbled. She secured the bun and crossed her arms over her chest.

"You're welcome. And you aren't an adult."

"Yes, I am. I'm—"

"Seventeen," Mara said. She gathered her hair in her hand and flapped it, hoping the slight motion would cool her neck. It didn't work.

"I'm going to graduate high school by Christmas. That makes me an adult."

"No, that makes you a seventeen-year-old almost high school graduate. When you hit eighteen, we'll talk about you being an adult."

Amanda grumbled something Mara couldn't understand. The sniping, which had been going on since she'd returned to the orchard just after one o'clock, had to stop. If she was going to start a good relationship with her sister—and Mara truly wanted this—she had to be the adult.

Zeke rolled his ball across the plywood floor of the stand. It bumped against Mara's foot, and she rolled it back to him. Zeke seemed as thrilled as Amanda to be cooped up in the little stand. All of two cars had passed in the hour they'd been here, and neither had slowed.

Mara stood. "Come on," she said, motioning Amanda to join her. What her sister needed—what they both needed—was a little free time. They couldn't get reacquainted if they were both so miserable they couldn't have a decent conversation.

"What now? Are we going to flag people down as they drive past?" Amanda asked, but she followed Mara outside.

"What people? You're right. Everyone is inside in the air-conditioning. Grab that side," she said, pointing to the other side of the stand. When the stand was open, the plywood that covered the counter area was held up with a pulley system. It offered a bit more shade without blocking the breeze. When there was a breeze. Today the air was still. Amanda released the pulley from her side and Mara released hers, closing the covering.

"What are you doing?" Amanda asked. "We're supposed to be here until five. It's barely two."

"We're playing hooky."

Zeke had made his way to the open side door, and Mara held her hand out to him. Zeke put his hand in hers.

"Grab the diaper bag, would you?" Mara called over her shoulder as she locked Zeke in the car seat Collin had installed in one of the orchard's utility vehicles. Amanda got into the vehicle while Mara locked the side door of the stand and hung the Closed sign on the front.

"Collin isn't going to like this."

"What's he going to do, fire us?"

"We don't even get paid."

"See what I mean? He can't fire us if he doesn't pay us." Although Mara was one hundred percent certain that Collin would disagree with that statement. She would have to do some fancy explaining when he found out they'd ditched their post.

"I don't think Collin's going to see it that way. He likes to tell me idle hands are the devil's playthings." Amanda rolled her eyes. "As if any of us ever had idle hands around here."

Mara put the vehicle in gear and started

down the lane, but instead of driving past the house, she turned onto a narrow path that would lead to the lake. Just in case Collin was paying attention, she'd keep them out of his direct sight.

"That was one of Granddad's favorite sayings. He used it on us—well, on me—a lot."

"I remember. Kind of. I was little when you lived here before." Amanda sighed. "Did he tell that to you as often as Collin uses it on me?"

"I'm not sure. About how many times have you heard it in, say, the past month?"

"At least fifteen."

"I'd say that's about how often Granddad would say it to me." Amanda heaved another sigh that seemed to come up all the way from her feet. Mara patted Amanda's arm sympathetically. "You don't like the comparison?"

"I just don't think it's fair, is all. I'm practically on track to be Mother Theresa next to the things you did."

"The things I did?" She knew her childhood crimes—she couldn't get away from them, not even as an adult. Still, it would be nice to know exactly how she measured up where her sister was concerned.

"You wrote on water towers, messed up computer systems."

"You gave pointers to kids planning to tamper with the Memorial Day fireworks display. Pointers that wound up starting a fire."

"Because they didn't properly follow my directions. *You* and the guys all brought dogs to school on the same day."

"You yarn-bombed an old man's yard after the tornado. And have been painting the sidewalks downtown."

"I was only trying to hide those ugly weeds. And the yarn disintegrated with the first rainstorm." Amanda shot her gaze toward Mara. "How do you know all this?"

"Who else would paint antilittering slogans on sidewalks and storm drains?" She paused. "Also, Collin was worried about you. He told me when I called after the tornado."

"Oh." The thought of Collin worrying about her rather than just being annoyed with her seemed to stop Amanda for a moment. "Well, I worry about the environment. People should be more careful with their trash. Those drains empty out into the lake. It's…it's…unsanitary. And I used water-soluble and environmentally safe paint, so the next good storm will wash away the paintings." Amanda folded her arms across her chest. "They say you destroyed a whole fleet of buses—"

"Technically only two, the third bus's tires

didn't completely deflate," Mara clarified. She didn't bother to tell Amanda the bus thing wasn't her fault. It wouldn't matter, and the whole truth could be bad for James.

"You ran away rather than face up to what you did. You don't care about anyone in this family. You're a liar."

Mara winced. "Ouch."

"You didn't even come home for Granddad's funeral."

She'd been seven months pregnant when Granddad died. Seven months pregnant and in a remote area of Alaska. She hadn't gotten Collin's phone calls or emails until the day of the funeral, and the pain of not being there for her family was still strong.

"No, I didn't. I've been an awful person. To you and to Gran and to Collin. I've been especially horrible to James. None of you deserved any of the things I did or didn't do because I was always gone." She turned off the dirt track through the plum orchard and onto the gravel road leading to the lake. "I'm here now to fix the things I did wrong."

"Until you leave again."

"I have a job, Mand—"

"Don't call me that. Only my family calls me that."

Mara winced again. "Double ouch." The

terrain changed, and she navigated from the gravel road down to the swimming area they'd used as kids. "I want things to be different. I want things to be better, and I'm here to try to make them better. I'm not your mother. I'm not an aunt or even a trusted family friend. I'm the sister who ran away, who left you behind, and I'm sorry."

She parked the utility vehicle under a huge oak, set the emergency brake and unbuckled her seat belt.

"Do you think we could maybe start from there?" she asked.

Amanda stared straight ahead for so long that Mara turned away. She released Zeke's safety harness and began to slather sunscreen over his exposed face, arms and legs. She put a floppy hat over his head, and the little boy kicked his legs in protest. He hated the floppy hat, but the sun was so brutal today that it was necessary. Mara grabbed a toddler-size life jacket from the bin in the cargo area and slid it over his torso. Then she rubbed sunscreen on her own face and arms.

Amanda finally left the front seat. She held out a hand for sunscreen, and Mara dropped a dollop into her palm.

"You're going to get bored here and leave again," Amanda said, the words flat.

Mara capped the sunscreen and handed the bottle to her sister. "Kiddo, boredom had nothing to do with me leaving ten years ago, and so far life in Slippery Rock is promising to be anything but boring moving forward."

Boredom had never been the problem. Mara wanted to see things, to have experiences that she couldn't have in Slippery Rock. There was very little call for a computer programmer in a town of fewer than ten thousand people. And with her reputation, the school wouldn't have hired her as a janitor, much less as a computer tech for the district. Mara liked the black-and-white framework of the programming world, and she liked that even with those very strict rules, things still went buggy from time to time. Figuring out the bugs was like going on a little adventure right in her desk chair.

"Did you even miss us?" Amanda asked.

"All the time, kiddo. All the time." Mara let Zeke down from his seat, and he walked toward the crisp blue water. Mara followed, and Amanda fell into step beside her. "I missed taking you for mani-pedis when you turned sixteen. I missed the craziness of Collin teaching you to drive—I'm assuming that was as awful as it was when he tried to teach me."

"He acted as if I was going to drive straight into the lake when we were still in the driveway."

"Sounds about right." Mara put her arm around Amanda's shoulders, and for the first time, her sister didn't flinch away from the contact. That had to be progress, Mara thought. "I missed you starting high school, but I won't miss your graduation. I'd do a lot of things differently if I could do it all over."

She would start by not disappearing soon after graduation, even if she'd disappeared for the right reasons. James made one mistake that night; one mistake shouldn't derail his entire life. She had hoped that letting people assume she deflated the tires would somehow atone for the other things she'd done. Instead, running away made it easier to keep running, the way she'd run from her feelings for James in Nashville.

"Will you miss us when you leave again?"

Mara sat on the warm sand and dipped her toes into the cool water. Zeke picked up little stones and threw them into the lake, laughing as he splashed at the edge. Amanda sat beside her, stretching her legs farther out into the water.

Would she miss Slippery Rock when she left again? So very much, and she had been back in town for only a handful of days. She couldn't imagine her life, or Zeke's, without Gran in the kitchen or Amanda sulking in the living room or Collin wandering around with that stupid I'm-in-love expression on his face. Mara had four more weeks here, at least. How much harder would it be to leave then?

And then there was James. James, whom she'd fallen in love with somewhere between Jefferson City five years ago and Nashville two years ago. James, whose face she saw in her son's every day. James, who was serious about everything in his life, but who had never been serious about her. She could fall for him again, and he could fall for their son, but would he ever feel about her the way she felt about him? And did she want him to?

He had a bright future. Sheriff of Wall County. There had to be a thousand small-town women swooning over him, a thousand women who would want to stay at home and have kids and enter their baked goods in the county fair competitions.

She had a set future as a traveling computer programmer and security expert. Never in the same city for more than a few months. She didn't bake. She didn't want to be a stay-at-home mom, despite loving every minute she was able to spend with Zeke. There were ways to make a home base work, despite her traveling schedule, but not in Slippery Rock.

She had a reputation as a troublemaker.

He had a job and responsibility to arrest troublemakers.

It didn't matter how she'd felt about him before; it didn't even matter that she still had those feelings for him. Mara Tyler was not the right kind of woman for James Calhoun, despite the fact that she'd had his baby. There was nothing she could do about that.

Well, there was one thing. She could keep her love for him to herself. Because if James knew she was in love with him, he would do the responsible thing. He would try to marry the mother of his child, because that's what responsible people who had children did. They got married or stayed married for the sake of the children. Mara couldn't think of anything worse than loving James and being married to him when the child they shared was his only reason for being in the relationship.

She stared into the distance, at the sunlight glittering across the lake like a million diamonds. There was no way she could stay, no matter how badly she would like to, not when every touch from James made her insides do that flip-floppy thing.

"I'm going to miss everyone," she said after a long time. She bumped her shoulder against her sister's. "More than any of you can know."

CHAPTER ELEVEN

ADMIT IT, CALHOUN. You want her.

The problem isn't that I want her. It's that I shouldn't want her.

And now he was arguing with himself. Great.

This situation was so beyond messed up, he couldn't find the right words to describe it. She'd walked out on him two years ago. She'd marched right back in a week ago with a baby, and he couldn't be mad at her. He should have been furious. He should contact one of his father's judge friends and swear out a warrant for kidnapping or parental interference or something. Instead, he'd kissed her. Kissed her and thought about her and gotten all tied up in knots because of her.

James tossed a dart at the board on the wall, missing by at least five inches to the right. He'd been throwing for crap all evening, and it had nothing to do with the beer on the table behind him and everything to do with the woman no longer in his life. Except she was in his life. With his child. She just wasn't in his life in the way he'd once secretly hoped she would be. The way he shouldn't want her to be now, and yet he kept catching glimpses of what life could be with Mara fully in it. With Zeke. There would be more family dinners. There would be more kissing and touching. They'd always been good at the kissing and the touching parts of their relationship.

He tossed another dart at the board, but it fell to the floor a few inches shy of the wall.

God, how big an idiot did he have to be where Mara Tyler was concerned?

At least he was throwing darts alone on this Monday night rather than with Collin and Levi; he needed to shore himself up for their regular Wednesday game because the two of them would never let up if they knew how much of his brain power was consumed with Mara. And if Adam joined in now that he was home from the hospital…

Buck up, Calhoun, and stop obsessing about a woman who has never felt about you the way you feel about her.

"Get ya another, honey?" Juanita asked as she passed by.

"Just an ice water and the bill, thanks." He crossed to the wall, pulled his darts out of the board and picked up the last one off the floor before setting them into their holders to the side of the target.

Kissing Mara, touching Mara was still on his mind. He should maybe take a drive out to the orchard. It was only, he checked his watch, a little after eight. Maybe he could help her put Zeke to sleep, and then after maybe they could take a walk and—

Not gonna happen, Calhoun. The woman might be okay co-parenting with you, but she's already walked out on you once. Get that through your thick skull.

He pushed thoughts of Mara and her sexy mouth out of his head, grabbed a dart from the holder, and threw. The white-tipped dart hit the board in the lower right quadrant. Not bad. Now if he could just follow that up with another three or four decent throws, he could assure himself he was getting back to normal. He liked normal. He thrived on normal. Normal was everything he had wanted for his life for as long as he could remember. Mara being in town was messing with the normalcy he wanted.

He tossed another dart, and it went wide left.

She was making everything better than normal, and better than normal was danger-ous. Better than normal was when she disappeared on him in Nashville. And if she disappeared this time, it wouldn't be just her he'd miss. There would be Zeke to consider, too.

The three of them had spent a lot of time together over the weekend. A picnic at the lake, an outing to the park and a walk along one of the trails circling the forest near the lake. Things were progressing well. At least, things seemed to be progressing well.

Zeke laughed and giggled when James was around. They built block towers. The little boy had even handed over the purple dinosaur on Sunday afternoon so they could attack the cushions of the porch swing together.

The whole Tyler clan, along with Savannah, was coming to his house for a Fourth of July barbecue later in the week. That was a positive.

"James, just the deputy sheriff I wanted to see."

James stopped midthrow when Thom, the owner of the Slippery Rock Grill and the town mayor, called to him. He wore his usual summer outfit of khakis and a short-sleeved button-down shirt. The older man took off his straw fedora and ran one hand over his nearly bald head.

"What can I do for you, Mr. Mayor?"

"I heard you had some trouble at Mallard's last week."

James shook his head. He'd thought the gossip about Mara's shoplifting had died down. God, sometimes small towns sucked. "Not really, unless you count their malfunctioning doors a problem."

Thom put his hands in his pockets and rocked on his heels. "CarlaAnn mentioned a shoplifting incident. With Mara Tyler?" Thom whistled low through his teeth. "I thought that girl would have matured by now, like the rest of you."

"Mara's just fine." Better than fine, but he knew Thom didn't really care about Mara's mental health or maturity. Despite the minor nuisance of most of Mara's pranks, Thom had come down hard on the enforcement side. James often wondered if the man would have felt the same if Collin or Levi or one of the twins had been their ringleader. He frowned. "You should check your sources more carefully. Mara works for the security company that is revamping Mallard's old system and was conducting a security check."

"Oh." The older man seemed annoyed at the simple answer.

Not James's problem. He jostled the darts gently in his hand.

"I also heard you've been spending a lot of time at the orchard."

"Collin and Mara have been friends of mine for a long time. I'm not sure why it's suddenly hit the grapevine." He tossed a dart at the board and hit dead center.

Thom leaned in and whispered, "You know how these things can look. Favoritism, old boys' network, even if one of the 'boys' is a woman. If you want to win the election in a few months, you have to be conscious of how all this looks to the outside."

"How all what looks?" James asked, unable to keep the ice from his tone. He focused his attention on Thom, who shrugged his shoulders and refused to meet his gaze.

"The acting sheriff not conducting an investigation into a shoplifting incident."

James squeezed his hand around the darts. "There was no incident, and therefore no investigation. As to the election, I am running, and I do plan to be the next sheriff of Wall County. My record is clean and, if anything, my friendship with the entire Tyler family should serve as an indicator that I take my personal relationships just as seriously as I take my professional obligations."

Thom blinked. "Of course. You wouldn't be a Calhoun if you didn't take those things seriously. Your father is one of the best men I know. His legacy—your family legacy—is important to our whole town. We don't want anything or anyone to tarnish that legacy."

James put the darts on the table, picked up the glass of water and took a long drink. "Thanks for the tip," he said, tossing a ten on the table before walking out of the bar.

He had no intention of ruining the legacy his father, grandfather and great-grandfather had worked so hard to build at the sheriff's department, but he also had no intention of ruining the legacy of his only son. Somehow he would have to find a way to meld those two legacies into a life he was proud of living.

JAMES SAT ON a three-legged stool at the counter of Guy's Market. Bud was down at the end helping a couple of fishermen decide between minnows and crawfish for bait. James didn't recognize the men, but he recognized the type—old ball cap, old jeans, worn tennis shoes. In town for the Fourth of July fireworks, they'd probably begged out of shopping in Springfield with their wives in favor of spending the day in a rented boat, bass fishing for dinner.

Sunlight sparkled off the water. James would have liked to be going out with them.

He could have used a few hours of enforced silence with nothing to do but wait for a fish to latch on to his hook. All that nothing would give him the space to think and sort out what he was going to do about Mara.

He couldn't keep his mind off her, and in his mind she was not the woman who'd walked away from him. Not the woman who had kept his kid from him for more than a year. Nope, he kept skipping right over the difficult part of Mara, straight to thoughts of Mara the siren he remembered from all those weekends they'd spent together.

James shook his head. He had to stop skipping over the hard things and really figure out what he planned to do. And he needed to do it fast, because in a couple of hours, Mara and her entire family would be at his house for a Fourth of July barbecue and fireworks.

Bud finished with the fishermen and returned to James's end of the counter. "How's it going, Sheriff?"

"Deputy," James corrected him, "and it's going." Going straight to hell with confusion, but, hey what did that matter? He would know better how to react to Mara if he could convince himself she was playing some kind of game, and that she would get tired of it and leave.

The thing was, though, this didn't seem like a game. Not that they'd had any deep conversations about her past or his, her future or his, but there was something different. It wasn't just the more open way she discussed her actions and motivations for keeping Zeke a secret. And it wasn't just the changes that childbearing had brought to her body. There was a depth to her gaze. In the past, it always felt as if she was just out of his grasp, and maybe just out of the grasp of anyone else. And maybe she'd kept herself separate deliberately all those years ago. But now, she was more present in Slippery Rock.

Bud leaned against the counter. "Deep thoughts for noon on a Thursday," he said and put a large takeaway cup before James. "Coke, fully leaded."

"Thanks." James took a long drink, liking the feel of the carbonation against his throat.

"Need anything else?"

"Club on wheat, extra mustard." He motioned to the end of the counter where the fishermen had been. "Summer crowds seem to be coming back."

"Most of 'em have already forgotten about the tornado. Tourists have a way of ignoring things like tornadoes and hurricanes and earthquakes once the news stops running the pictures. That concert Savannah rigged up after, though, that helped, too. Showed people we were still alive down here." Bud slathered mustard over one side of the bun and began stacking turkey, ham and roast beef on the other. "You want a pickle?" He didn't wait for an answer, just stuck a big pickle spear in the middle and closed the sandwich. He put it on a paper plate and handed it to James. "Speaking of the tornado, how's the cleanup at the DeVries place going?"

James shook his head. "It isn't. Those trees are still there, and the weeds are getting higher. He's my last stop for this shift. Then I'm off for the night." James picked up the sandwich and took a big bite.

The bell over the door rang. Jonathan wheeled himself into the shop while Anna held the door for him. His arm was out of the sling, but he must not have gotten clearance to use the crutches yet. James hadn't spoken to either of his parents since that night at dinner, and he knew that was childish on his part. He should have called to check on them. Jonathan's reaction to the news about Zeke, to Mara, had stuck in James's craw, though, and he didn't want to be the one to make the first move.

Since he was a child, he was always the one who made the first move—who apologized for not making the game-winning touchdown, for being too loud at dinner. For having friends who didn't meet Jonathan's idea of perfection. One friend in particular. He'd never minded Collin, Adam, Aiden or Levi, but Mara had always been another story. Despite what she'd done with Zeke, she didn't deserve the kind of scrutiny and judgment Jonathan tended to dish out. Using her teenage angst and boredom against her as an adult was petty. Intimating that she was responsible for James's actions on graduation night was insulting.

He'd made his own decision that night, and he'd paid for it—literally—in the form of anonymous donations to the school district's transportation fund.

Anna wheeled Jonathan to the end of the counter.

"Usual?" Bud asked, looking from James in the middle of the counter to his parents at the other end. He didn't wait for an answer, just started making two more sandwiches—this time roast beef on rye.

"James," Jonathan said after a long moment.

"Dad." James took another bite of his sandwich, then a long drink from the cup.

Anna watched her husband and her son closely but didn't say anything. James took another bite and slowly chewed.

Let them wait. Sure, it was more childishness, and yeah, it was petty, but he wasn't in the wrong here. Zeke was his kid. Mara was his friend, despite what she'd done. This was his life, not Jonathan's and not Anna's.

Bud put their sandwiches on paper plates and poured two more sodas from the fountain.

Anna looked from Jonathan to James and back again. "Oh, would the two of you stop? You're both being ridiculous."

Bud grabbed a rag and began wiping down the sandwich prep area. Taking mental notes to gossip about later, James was sure. Well, it had to get out sooner or later.

"I'm sorry," Jonathan said, and James swiveled to look at his father. Straight shoulders. Annoyed expression. He hadn't touched his lunch. James let the words hang in the air for a minute as he sipped his soda and chomped on a chip.

"It is your life, and I shouldn't have said what I said about—" Jonathan paused "—her."

His words weren't a great apology, but they

were more than James had ever heard from his father. Maybe there was hope for him, for them, after all.

"I could have been less blunt about the way I told you," James said, because if Jonathan could give a little, so could he.

James finished his lunch while Bud continued his pretense of cleaning the prep area. His parents remained at the other end of the counter, eating their sandwiches.

"You got rid of the sling," James commented, not sure what else to say.

"Yesterday. Tomorrow we talk crutches, and then figure out when to schedule the next surgery."

"Thank goodness," Anna said. "I was running out of ways to entertain him. Now that he'll be more mobile, he can find his own pastimes." She elbowed her husband. Jonathan grinned.

"It was nice, you picking up after me," Jonathan said.

"Like I haven't been doing that for the past thirty-five years. This just slowed you down enough to notice." She turned her attention to James. "If you wanted, you could come by for dinner tonight, before the fireworks."

"The Tylers are coming to my place for a barbecue. The Walterses will probably show

up, too. You should drop by," James said before he could second-guess the invitation.
They had a right to meet their grandson, and
it would be nice for Jonathan, especially, to
see how much Mara had changed in the time
she'd been gone from Slippery Rock.

"We don't want to intrude," his mother
said. Jonathan said nothing.

"It's a family dinner. We're family, right?"

Bud turned at that nugget of information,
and James wanted to kick himself. The comment was innocuous enough, at least until
Mara started to be seen around town with
a baby. Mara, a baby and James's comment
about them all being family would start the
tongues wagging for sure. And once they
started talking about the present, the past
was sure to come up. He'd have to do something about that.

"Can I bring something?" Anna asked, but
her attention was focused on Jonathan.

"Just yourselves. Gladys is bringing pie,
and I've got kabobs ready to go."

"I'll bring my potato salad," she said, excitement evident in her voice.

"Sure, Mom."

"Steak and chicken?" Jonathan asked.

James nodded. "With fresh peppers and
cherry tomatoes and mushrooms."

Jonathan nodded. He'd finished his sandwich and threw his plate and cup in a nearby trash can. "We'll bring the potato salad, and maybe some sparklers or something, too. The Fourth is always better with sparklers."

"We're watching the big show over the lake after dinner. It's supposed to start around nine."

"Sounds like a fun night," his mother said, and she squeezed Jonathan's hand in hers.

Jonathan put a twenty-dollar bill on the counter before wheeling himself around to James. He clapped him on the back. "We'll see you in a few hours, then."

"I'll be home anytime after four."

Anna hugged him as she passed. The bell over the door tinkled as Anna pulled it open for Jonathan to maneuver through. When the two of them were gone, James breathed a sigh of relief. Crossing this hurdle with his family was a good start. If he could keep Jonathan thinking in the present instead of the past, maybe he could keep the rest of the town in the present, too.

"So you and Mara Tyler, hmm?" Bud asked.

"We're friends, always have been." *Friends* didn't seem like quite the right term to describe his relationship with her, but it was the best he had. They weren't more than friends, not anymore. They weren't enemies, either.

Bud whistled. "People are gonna talk about that. Sheriff James Calhoun and rebel Mara Tyler. People are definitely going to talk."

"I'm not the sheriff," James reminded Bud.

"Not yet."

"She isn't a rebel, either. The six of us were teenagers with too much time on our hands, that's all."

Bud nodded. "Sure, sure. For what it's worth, I always thought those pranks were genius, especially painting Simone's number on the water tower. That girl was a terror, and her mama never could see it. Still can't or she wouldn't have started the talk about Mara being a shoplifter."

"She wasn't shoplifting. She was conducting a security check." James shook his head. He'd had to correct the story only twice this week, but it was two times too many. Unfortunately, he had no cause to talk to CarlaAnn; it wasn't as if gossiping was illegal.

"I'll see if I can't get that added into the grapevine."

James watched the older man for a long moment. "I would appreciate that," he said and handed a twenty over for his lunch.

"Not necessary, Sheriff." Bud pushed the

money back toward James. "I always did like that girl. She had spirit."

"Still does."

Bud smiled, and it was the first genuine smile James had seen from the man since before the tornado. He waved at the older man as he left the store.

He'd go see Wilson DeVries about the downed trees in his yard, finish his paperwork, and look over schedules for the rest of the holiday week and still be home before four. The Methodist church bells sounded, signaling the top of the hour. But the clock in the old tower showed eleven as it had for as long as James could remember. Some things never changed.

Maybe adding Zeke into his ordered life, and having a tangible connection to Mara, wouldn't throw his well-ordered life into a tailspin.

CHAPTER TWELVE

MARA PULLED IN behind James's Jeep in the driveway of the little lake house. Like so many homes that were built before the engineers dammed the Slippery Rock River to create the lake, it didn't look like the waterfront homes she'd seen on either coast or even in Chicago. The front porch, which faced the street, was wide, with a porch swing to one side and a larger area behind it for eating. The peaked roof hinted at a second story, and the front door was painted a vibrant green that matched the shutters bracketing the windows. He didn't keep plants or other decorations on the porch, but a red, white and blue flowered wreath hung on the door.

Probably his mother's doing. From what Mara remembered, Anna Calhoun was the type to decorate for each season and holiday.

Even without the flowers, the place was inviting. A large maple provided shade, and rosebushes marched in straight lines along the sides of the house.

"Are we getting out or are we going to sit here?" Gran asked, and Mara realized she'd been staring at the house for too long.

"Going in. If you and Amanda can get the bags, I'll deal with Zeke and all his stuff."

Amanda sighed from the back seat, where she'd been pointedly ignoring Zeke for most of the ride into town. Mara had noticed she'd fallen into Zeke's usual game of dropsy, though, and she thought she caught the hint of a smile from her sister a time or two.

Mara tossed the keys in the oversize tote and unbuckled Zeke from his seat while Amanda and Gran grabbed bags of chips and bottles of lemonade and soda from the cargo area. James met them at the front door, looking a little too comfortable in cargo shorts, a navy T-shirt and flip-flops. Mara didn't think she'd ever seen him wearing anything on his feet but his department-issue boots or sneakers. She loved seeing him looking casual. And she was staring.

Pull it together, Mara.

She slipped past him into the living room. The dark mahogany floors gleamed. He had leather furniture facing a television in the corner and framed pictures of his family on the walls. On the fireplace mantel were pictures of him with the guys in their high school football uniforms.

Zeke wiggled in her arms, and she put him down to explore.

"What can we do to prep?" she asked.

"Everything's ready. Just waiting for the rest of the crew to get here."

"Rest of the crew?"

"I figured since Savannah was coming with Collin, it made sense to invite Levi and their parents, too. And my parents stopped by Bud's this afternoon."

"Oh. Your parents. Okay." A cold feeling filled Mara's stomach. She liked James's mother, but his father…made her nervous. As if he was just waiting for her to make a single misstep so that he could throw her in jail. Or maybe run her out of town.

"It'll be fine." James assured her, but his words only made her feel more unsteady. He put a hand at her lower back, and the unsteady feeling tripled as heat spread from the point of contact.

Not the time, Mar. Pull it together, already.

"Of course," she said, pushing as much happy energy as she could into her voice.

He reached out his free hand, and Zeke took it so that the three of them walked into the kitchen at the same time. She could see Amanda through the kitchen window, putting earbuds in her ears and settling into a reclining lawn chair. Gran grinned at them as she put bottles of soda in the fridge.

"Don't you three look just perfect together?"

Mara didn't need a mirror to know how they'd look. James was tall and tanned with brown hair. She was tall but not tanned with blond hair. Zeke was short and chunky as babies should be, with the brown hair from James but eyes that definitely came from her side of the family tree. Like the perfect combination of the two of them. Together they would look like a family. She had to remind herself that they weren't a family in the traditional sense.

She stepped away from James, needing the physical reminder that they would never be that family. Not having his hand at the small of her back seemed like a good first step.

"Gran, I'll do that. Why don't you go relax on the deck with Amanda?"

"Nonsense," she said, putting the last of the soda in the fridge. "We can all go out to enjoy the afternoon."

With nothing else to do, Mara followed them outside.

Chairs were set up along the deck and around a circular fire pit in the middle of the backyard, which ended at the shoreline. A couple of paddleboats and a canoe were upended on the thin ribbon of sand, and Zeke headed straight for them. Mara caught up with him just before his little feet hit the beach. He tried to wiggle away from her, but she held firm.

"Not until we get a life jacket on you," she said.

"No-no-no," he said, still struggling against her hold.

"Hey, he said that clearly," James said behind them. He held a neon-green life vest. "Good job, little man." He ran his hand over Zeke's hair, and the boy stilled.

"No-no-no," he repeated.

Mara shook her head. "It figures *no* would be one of his first clear and repeated words." She turned the boy so James could get the jacket on him, then set him on his feet to explore the sandy area between the yard and the lake. "You have a beautiful home," she said.

James looked around as if seeing it for the first time. "I like it," he said. "It beats living in an apartment or, worse, the trailer park on the other side of town."

"You could always live with your parents," she suggested, keeping her eyes focused on Zeke.

"No, thank you. As much as I love them, I like having my own place." He stood beside her, his shoulder nearly touching hers. The noncontact made the hair on her arms stand on end. It was weird. "You ever wish you had a place of your own?"

Sometimes. Not that she wanted to get into that. "I like moving around." It wasn't a lie, not exactly.

James nodded but didn't say anything else. "You mind if I take the kid out in a paddle-boat?"

"Guard him with your life."

She watched as James flipped over the paddle boat and pushed it out into the water. Then he returned to the sand and held his hands out for Zeke. The little boy went willingly into his arms, and Mara wasn't sure if she should feel glad that Zeke was so accepting of James or scared because he was going to be in the middle of the lake and she wouldn't be with him. Or jealous because, until this trip, she'd been the center of Zeke's life, and now he had her, a father, an uncle, an aunt and a great-grandmother.

"Nice image," Collin said beside her, startling her.

Mara put her hand to her heart. "Don't do that," she said, slapping at his arm. "I swear, for a guy as large as you are, you walk like you're a mouse." She spotted Savannah on the deck with Gran and Amanda. Levi exited the house, followed by his parents, Bennett and Mama Hazel. The two men made Collin look positively small, even from this distance. Gran hugged Mama Hazel, and the two of them sat at the table under an umbrella.

"The whole gang's here."

"Not all of us. Adam isn't coming, and Aiden hasn't been back to Slippery Rock for almost as long as you."

"I just saw Adam at The Good Cuppa the other day."

Collin shrugged. "Jenny called earlier, said they were spending the holiday at home."

That was odd. Adam always liked a party, at least from what Mara could remember. But then, a lot had changed in Slippery Rock since she'd been gone, not the least of which were the injuries that had put him temporarily in a wheelchair.

Giggling sounded from the lake, and she

turned her attention to the paddleboat and the man and boy in it. Zeke dragged his fingers through the water as James worked the bicycle-like pedals. The boat seemed to be going in circles rather than a straight line, probably because James was the only one pedaling.

"I meant to tell you, Savannah reintroduced herself to me the other day. She's a good fit for you."

"Yeah?" Collin had that goofy grin on his face again, the one he usually had whenever Savannah was mentioned.

"Yeah. Are you two considering…?" She watched Zeke try to get one of his legs over the side of the paddleboat. James had a hold on the life jacket strap, keeping him in the boat and, God, that really shouldn't have sent a stab of longing through her. It really shouldn't. He was just a man. A solidly built, handsome man, but just a man.

"Marriage?" Collin shrugged. "Maybe. Someday. We're not in a hurry. You and James?"

"We already have a kid, thanks."

Collin was quiet for a long moment, as if considering his next words. Not good. He had a tendency to say things that made her think too hard when he chose his words this carefully.

"I meant considering the future. Like what

happens when your job with Mallard's fin-
ishes up."

Exactly what she had been trying not to
consider. Mara didn't know what happened
when the job was over. Normally she would
pack her things and head for the next town,
the next job. Nothing about this situation was
normal, though. For the first time since she'd
brought Zeke home from the hospital, she had
no other jobs lined up. Didn't have a nanny to
care for him while she worked. Didn't have
the slightest semblance of a plan.

She needed a plan—one that didn't involve these messy feelings she was having
for James.

"Like staying together for the kid?" She
wanted to pull those words back as soon as
she said them, but they were out, and there
was nothing she could do about that. "We
aren't staying together because of Zeke. He
deserves better than that." For the first time,
she wasn't sure if the *he* in the sentence was
Zeke or James. Either way, it sent a swarm
of bees jostling into her belly. "I think I'll
go check on Gran. James seems to have the
paddleboat trip under control."

She walked slowly toward the deck and
said hello to the Walters family but didn't
stay. Instead she went inside. The picture on

the mantel was from the state football championship. Levi, James, Collin, Adam and Aiden stood in a semicircle, sweat on their faces, grinning like fools. They'd just won. Levi, Collin and the twins had cemented their scholarship offers, and a day or so later James would sign to play for a college in the northern part of the state. The five of them looked so young in the picture, so excited about the future.

Now Adam was in a wheelchair and Aiden was in California. An injury had ended Levi's career early. Collin had eventually turned down the scholarship to the larger school that could have landed him in the NFL with Levi in favor of a smaller school where he was able to come home on the weekends to work with Granddad.

And James…

He'd taken the big scholarship, gotten his law enforcement degree and come back to Slippery Rock. The way he'd always said he would. He had a pretty little house on the lake, and in another few weeks he would begin his run for sheriff. Just as he'd always dreamed.

She'd thrown a wrench into his plans; she knew that despite the happy look on his face while paddleboating with their son. The question now was, how big a wrench?

His yard was filled with people. James watched Savannah and Collin walk along the shore. His parents sat with Bennett, Mama Hazel and Gladys on the deck. Mara and Amanda were playing in the sand with Zeke.

"You put on a nice party," Levi said from behind him.

"How are the kabobs holding up?"

"My dad just finished the last of them. You're out of luck if you were thinking about having another."

James patted his stomach. "Nothing is going to fit in here except a beer. You want?" He grabbed two longnecks from the cooler on the corner of the deck, then sat in a free chair. Levi joined him. It was nearly eight, and the sun still hung above the trees, but soon the lightning bugs would be out, flitting around the backyard. He shut down the grill; everyone had had their fill of food, and sat in groups, either on the deck or closer to the beach. Then the fireworks would begin lighting up the night sky.

"So, you and Mara."

The question caught him off guard. Which was silly, considering this was Levi. He'd never been one to beat around the bush. When he wanted to know something, he asked.

"I should've caught on at darts that night when you wouldn't shut up about her staying at the B and B instead of the orchard."

"She's at the orchard now, if you're keeping score."

"Surprised she isn't staying here." Levi took a long drink, his Adam's apple sliding up and down his throat. "So you and the kid can get better acquainted."

The idea of Mara moving into his home sent a funny feeling ping-ponging through his belly. Seeing her every morning, every night…it was almost too familiar. Like all those weekends they'd met up in one city or another. Only then there hadn't been a child involved. A child he was quickly falling in love with. A child she would take with her when she left. And there was no question that she would leave.

There was nothing to hold her in Slippery Rock.

He wanted to find something that would hold her here, but if her family hadn't been enough pre-Zeke, then they wouldn't be enough now.

"We're taking it slow," he said finally.

"Smart move. Less trauma for the kid. He's cute."

James couldn't hold back the grin. "Yeah, he is."

"Looks like her, which is good for you."

"Ass."

Levi shrugged, but his brown eyes danced with laughter. "We could use a hand getting the last of the debris from the old church off the lot, if you've got the time. The day care that rented the building has plans to rebuild in the same location."

"I could take a day away from the sheriff's office." He'd been putting in so much double duty, the commissioners would probably like him to take a day off. "It'd be nice to have more of the town functional for Founder's Weekend at the end of the month. A lot of people come to town."

Levi nodded. "Parade and food trucks tend to bring them in. Once the debris is cleared, the construction crew can start on a foundation and the actual building."

"I'll be there by ten."

"What do you think about making tomorrow night a darts night?"

"It'd put a nice cap on the day, shooting darts with the three of you after all that sweaty work."

"I was thinking Savannah and Jenny and Mara, too. Might make things easier for Adam."

It might. And if it gave him more time with Mara, James was all for it. "You have a girl you're going to drop on us?"

"No," he said, and the word was hard. Levi finished his beer and stood. "I'm going to head out before the fireworks. See you in the morning."

James picked up the empty beer bottles. Levi strode across the lawn and disappeared around the side of the house. Collin and Savannah met James at the deck.

"We're going to head out before the fireworks," Collin said. It was as if there was an echo in the yard. "Early morning tomorrow."

Yeah, James would just bet the two of them were leaving to go to sleep. "I'll see you at the day care— Levi said you could use another pair of hands."

"Always can."

"He also said darts are on, with the ladies, for tomorrow night. We need to get Adam back into the swing of things."

"I'm in."

"Girls at darts? Interrupting such a manly pastime," Savannah teased. "Thanks for dinner, James." Savannah pressed a quick kiss to his cheek. "You guys sure Adam will be okay with all of us at guys' night?"

James wasn't sure about that at all, but he

also knew that Savannah wouldn't want to hurt Adam's feelings or make him uncomfortable.

"Are you coming to play?" he asked.

Savannah shook her head, and her long braids swung against her shoulders. "I don't dart, but I'll happily cheer you guys on."

"Then Adam won't mind."

Collin and Savannah said their goodbyes, and as the sun began to sink below the trees along the shore, James realized the older guests were clearing the deck table and putting away chairs.

"Thanks for dinner, James," Bennett said, raising his hand in a wave. "We're going to watch the fireworks from the marina."

"You can see them just fine from here."

"Bud's making homemade ice cream," his mother said. "Thank you for inviting us. The baby is—" she paused "—just perfect."

"We'll save you some seats," Mama Hazel said, and waved before she and Bennett walked away.

James had no reply to that. Mara and Amanda brought Zeke to the deck. The little boy laid his head on Mara's shoulder and, with his index finger, twirled a long strand of her hair.

"Let me get this sweet boy home," Gladys

said, taking him from Mara. "Amanda, would you grab his diaper bag for me?"

"The fireworks haven't even started," the girl protested.

Gladys shot her a look, and Amanda picked up the bag beside the sliding glass door. "We'll take the SUV," she said, and when Mara started to say something, she talked right over her. "You'll bring Mara out after the big show, James. Zeke will be fast asleep before we hit the city limits sign, and there's no need for all of us to miss the fun."

"Exactly," James's father joined in, and James shook his head to make sure he was hearing everything correctly. "It was a nice evening, but I'm sure there are things the two of you need to talk about without a toddler interrupting."

James looked at Mara, who seemed just as confused as he. James's parents hurried around the side of the house, following Bennett and Mama Hazel's path from a few moments before. Only he and Mara, Gladys, Amanda and Zeke were left on the deck.

"Gran, I'll drive," Mara began, and Gladys shook her head.

"I know how to drive, and you haven't had a fun night out since you came to town. Stay. Watch the fireworks. As much sun and sand

and food as Zeke's had today, he'll sleep the night through."

James didn't say anything at the obvious manipulation. The idea of spending some time with Mara alone was appealing. They did have things to talk about, and it would be simpler to talk without Zeke or his parents or her family around to overhear.

Mara looked at him, and James shrugged. She blew out a breath. Gran patted her cheek with her free hand.

"We'll see you in the morning. Good night, James," she said, and started around the corner of the house. Amanda slung the diaper bag over her shoulder and mumbled something James couldn't hear. When Mara hurried after them, he did, feeling a little silly that they were all making the trek to the front yard. Gladys was capable of driving, and so was Amanda. And Zeke was obviously nearly out for the night.

At the SUV, Gladys buckled the little boy into his seat. Zeke's eyes were heavy, and his hand reached for the plush puppy strapped to the side of the seat. Once behind the wheel, Gladys fastened her seat belt and waited for Amanda to do the same.

"You two have a nice evening," she said to

Mara, then rolled up the window before backing down the driveway.

Mara watched as the SUV disappeared down the street. "I think my son has been kidnapped."

"Our son. And I think that would technically be babysitter's interference, since that is your grandmother behind the wheel and you're staying at her house while you're here."

"Is that really a thing? Babysitter's interference?"

"No." James shook his head. "Mostly because parents don't usually balk at a grandmother babysitting for a couple of hours." He brushed his hand against her elbow. "And we could use the time to talk."

Mara glanced at the road, but the taillights of the SUV had disappeared. She followed him into the backyard. James pointed to one of the reclining lawn chairs, grabbed two bottles of water from the cooler and sat in the chair beside her. He'd have liked another beer, but he wanted to be sober for this conversation.

"I'm helping the crew clean up at the day care tomorrow. So that they can start on the new building next week."

"Collin mentioned that."

"After, we're meeting at the Slope. Wednesday night darts, but on Friday." The sun sank farther behind the trees, cooling the air nicely. A light breeze blew through the oak trees along his property line. Not too much longer and the fireworks would start. "You should come. With me." Why did he feel like he was seventeen again with those five little words?

That first weekend in Jefferson City, things had flowed naturally from surprise at seeing her to a quick drink that led to dinner, then to her hotel room.

Asking her to darts shouldn't have been a bigger deal than that night, but somehow it was. He took a long drink of water, but the liquid did nothing to calm the fire in his throat.

"Do you really think that is a smart idea? You know how the gossip mill works."

"Maybe I don't care how it works."

Mara fiddled with the label on her bottle, tearing one corner free, then gently working the rest of it off in one long sheet. "We can't do this."

"Play darts?"

"Fall into old patterns."

"We've never played darts before."

She turned to look at him, her blue eyes dark in the evening light. "You know what I mean."

"Yeah, I do." He just didn't care. He knew he should have cared. Two days ago he'd cared. Hell, earlier this morning he'd cared what people would think once the word got around about him and Mara. About Zeke. Somewhere between his conversation with his parents at Bud's and tonight with all their friends and family around, he'd stopped caring. He wanted to spend time with Zeke, definitely. But more than that, he wanted to be with her. "We aren't kids, Mara. What other people think of us doesn't matter. Not compared to what we *know* about the situation we're in."

"And what situation is that?"

He reached for her hand, rubbing his thumb across the smooth skin of her wrist. "We had clandestine weekends for three years. We have a son. We're now in the same town at the same time, and neither of us is attached to anyone else."

"You want to have an affair? In Slippery Rock?" Her jaw dropped. "That is not responsible. I'm leaving in—"

"And I'm not leaving. We both know where we stand."

"James." She shook her head. "That would be crazy."

"Maybe it's time I did something a little bit crazy."

"You don't do anything crazy."

"I did once." He wasn't proud of what he'd done on graduation night, but he'd paid his penance for it.

"And look what happened," she said.

"I sent anonymous checks to the school transportation fund. You left town."

"Because if I wasn't here, they would never think to ask you questions. Plausible deniability."

"I didn't ask you to do that."

"You didn't have to. I was leaving anyway. I just moved up the timetable. Wait, did you say you sent anonymous checks?"

"Of course. The school borrowed money to get the buses back into service quickly. I sent donations every quarter to pay them back."

Mara blinked at him. "When Cannon hired me, I got a signing bonus and sent the whole thing to the school. For the transportation fund." She laughed. "I should have known you would find a responsible way to right the situation."

She'd not only left town to take the spotlight off him but also repaid his debt. "I didn't ask you to do that, either."

"What else was I going to do? If I'd dropped

the whole senior prank thing, like my brother and the others tried to get me to do, you would never have gone with me. You wouldn't have gotten caught up in the moment."

"It wasn't your fault. Letting the air out of the tires was my idea. I wanted to do something crazy, just one crazy thing, before I lost my chance."

Mara linked her fingers with his. "See what impulsive gets you? You're the responsible one. I'm the impulsive one. Those are our roles. Meeting you guys at darts would be…switching roles. That didn't end so well last time."

"You think it was responsible to walk away in Nashville," he said.

"Of course."

"You switched the roles in Nashville. I'm switching them here."

A loud boom sounded in the distance, and the first firework lit up the sky in a shower of green and purple sparkles.

He'd convinced himself it was the responsible thing to do, letting her walk away in Nashville. Now, he could see that had been a rash, impulsive move. Made out of hurt and anger at her. James didn't like to make the same mistakes twice, but this time it was he who would switch the roles, and he wasn't doing it out of fear.

He was doing it because he couldn't imagine not being this close to Mara without being physically close to her, as well.

Another boom sounded, and the sky over the lake was lit brilliant white. Her blue eyes were worried, and there was a cute little line between her brows.

"I know you're leaving. You know I'm staying. What's the harm if we spend some time together before that happens?"

THE HARM WAS that she was already finding it hard to keep their roles separate, and they'd barely spent any time alone. There was Zeke to consider. There was her family to consider. There was James's future as the sheriff to consider.

For the first time in her life, Mara wanted to consider all the options. To weigh every potential consequence before acting. If she'd done that in Jefferson City or any other place they'd met before Nashville, things would be so different between them.

"The harm is to Zeke. The harm is to your career. What happens when people start to talk about us? This is small-town America, James, where people still salute the flag and go to church on Sundays and attend every parade. No one is going to elect a sheriff with ties to a criminal."

"You're no criminal."

"Not to you. Not to my family. But you know as well as I do that there are more CarlaAnns in Slippery Rock than there are Gladys Tylers or Mama Hazels. People like CarlaAnn are vindictive, and they have long memories. I can't be the reason you don't get elected."

"Wow, that's a little insulting."

"It's the truth." Another boom sounded, startling her. James watched her expression in the flashes of light, and she hoped he couldn't see through her bravado. Yes, she was worried about his career. More than that, she was worried about what it meant that she wanted to say yes. She wanted to say yes now more than any other time in her life.

"If the people in town are stupid enough to not elect me because of pranks from our high school days, I don't want to be their sheriff." His gut twisted as he said the words. He wanted to be sheriff—he wanted it for himself—but he wanted to get the position honestly, and hiding Mara or Zeke felt wrong. "We have a kid. We also have chemistry together, and I'm not saying this at all the right way, but as long as the town is going to talk, why shouldn't we give them something real to talk about?"

Mara sighed. "Sweet words, Calhoun. You're a real sweet talker."

"Well, as long as I'm on a roll, I'll say this. I like being with you. I like talking to you, and I like having sex with you. I don't plan on having that sex when Zeke is in the same room, so x him out of the equation. I don't plan on having sex with you in the middle of the courthouse square, either, or in the farmers' market or in the middle of the lake. People are going to talk one way or the other, so while the fireworks show is finishing up, why don't you think about how you'd like to spend the time you're in town? You want to spend it thinking about all the things we could be doing with one another or actually doing those things? Worrying about the people who are talking about you, about us, or telling them to screw off because you have your own life to live?"

He released her hand, but didn't leave the chair beside her. He was close enough that she could feel his heat, and it seemed hotter than usual. Maybe because of the annoyed speech he'd just made.

Mara folded her hands in her lap and tried

to focus on the display lighting the night sky. The blues and greens and purples and whites all blended into a kaleidoscope that hid the stars. It was beautiful.

James might be right that people would gossip no matter what the two of them were doing, but that didn't mean she had to fall right into bed with him. She needed to be responsible here.

She needed…

God, she needed him. Or she wanted him. Mara couldn't be sure which was the stronger emotion, and she thought maybe it didn't matter. James was right about the chemistry thing; the two of them had that working in their favor.

She tapped her foot against the grass. Chemistry was not responsible.

Paying her bills, that was responsible. Repaying the school, responsible. Walking away from him in Nashville had been fear-based but also responsible. She hadn't been ready for the feelings she felt for him. Hadn't been certain what, if anything, he felt for her. She had still been hiding from the feelings of abandonment by her parents.

The Mara she was today resulted because she had walked away from him in Nashville. She'd been responsible.

A series of booms sounded, signaling the end of the fireworks display.

Mara swallowed.

She didn't want him to drive her to the orchard, not just yet. It was selfish, but she wanted to stay here, sitting with him on the back lawn, watching the lake. She wanted to pretend, just for a little while, that this was where she belonged.

CHAPTER THIRTEEN

THE LAST OF the fireworks faded into the night sky, leaving the backyard in a blanket of darkness. In the distance, he could see smoke from the displays, but the breeze kept it moving toward the middle of the water instead of inland.

Mara hadn't said a word since he laid everything out for her. Hadn't moved a muscle since she folded her hands in her lap a few minutes before. He knew because, while she sat rigidly watching the end of the display, he had been watching her. Waiting for her to throw caution to the wind, the way she always did.

Then he could take her inside and feel her body against his again. He could feed the flames of attraction he'd been trying to ignore since he saw her between the revolving door at Mallard's. Responsible? Not even a little bit. And he didn't care.

"James? The absolutely most responsible thing we can do is drive out to the orchard."

Damn. James clenched his jaw, prepared to take his argument to another level. One that involved his lips on hers until she agreed with him. He would use any persuasion he had to until she admitted what she wanted.

Until she admitted that she still wanted him.

She was being stubborn and scared. Stubborn fit her, but scared didn't. Mara was one of the bravest people he knew.

"I don't want to be responsible." Her words were quiet amid the sound of the cicadas buzzing under the trees.

James's mouth went dry when she stood and pulled her loose tank top over her head. She kicked her navy flip-flops from her feet and unbuttoned the denim capris, sliding them over her hips. Under them, she wore a bright red bikini.

"I'm going for a midnight swim, if you'd like to join me," she said and started for the shoreline.

"It isn't midnight," he reminded her.

Mara shrugged. "Details."

James tossed his T-shirt to the side as he followed. At the water's edge, he slipped off his flip-flops. The water was shallow in this area, but it dropped off quickly. Mara dived beneath the still water and surfaced several yards from shore.

"The water's perfect," she said, moving her arms in half circles, treading water.

James splashed water in Mara's direction. He dived beneath the surface, swimming under the water until his fingers brushed against her legs. He surfaced and shook his head to get the water out of his eyes.

"This is not responsible," she said as if trying to remind him. Or maybe she was reminding herself. James couldn't be sure.

"Responsibility is overrated," he said, then wrapped his arms around her and pressed his mouth to hers as he pulled her to him.

The water was warm, surrounding them like the most comfortable of cocoons. He had Mara in his arms, really in his arms, for the first time in two years. That kiss outside the B and B didn't count because it had been fueled by anger. If he hadn't kissed her, he'd have throttled her.

Tonight all he wanted to do was kiss her, and so he did.

Their legs tangled together in the water.

"This isn't much of a swim," he said.

"Cardio is cardio. We'll just have to work a little harder to get our heart rates up." She was close to him, so close he could feel her heat in the water, and that familiar sizzle shot through his body.

Damn, but it was a good thing he could stop reminding himself that sizzling with Mara was off-limits.

"We're in about eight feet of water right now. We got cardio covered just staying above the surface."

Mara put her hand against his chest. "I'd rather not drown tonight, and if you kiss me again like that, drowning is definitely an option. We should head back in."

"Mara," he said as his legs brushed against hers, "until fifteen minutes ago, this was not part of my plan."

"Mine, either," she said as her arms circled his neck again. "If we both regret this in the morning, we can pretend it never happened."

James was absolutely positive he wouldn't regret sleeping with Mara in the morning, and there was no way he could pretend it never happened. "I've never regretted a single moment spent with you. That goes for before we were hooking up and after."

She smiled in the moonlight, and his chest squeezed. "Me, either."

James kissed her, gently at first, getting a feel for her. She tasted sweet, like the strawberry shortcake Mama Hazel had brought to dinner. The feelings the kiss brought, however, were anything but sweet. The air between them seemed to sizzle, her arms tightened around his neck, and James let go.

The other kisses had been a sampling, just a teaser to take the anger away. The way he'd always had a drink of apple juice after taking medicine as a kid. This wasn't a taste, and there was no burn of anger that he needed to destroy with sweetness. This was Mara, his Mara, and he wasn't going to let her go.

James let the slight current move them closer to shore, and then dropped to his knees, bringing Mara with him. With the small beach he'd created in his backyard behind them, he pulled Mara down on top of him. She sank over him, kissing his mouth, his jaw while her hands explored his torso.

James deepened the kiss, letting his tongue dip into her mouth. Enjoying the press of her breasts against his chest, and the slide of the water at their legs rippling gently in the night air. His thumb caressed her neck, and he could feel the unsteady beat, beat, beat of her carotid.

He cupped her breast in his hand, and her nipple pebbled beneath the silky fabric of her bikini top. He'd noticed with that first kiss, but being here with her now, the difference between her body in Nashville and now was definitely different. She would always be tall, and would likely always veer toward the willowy side of things, but she'd developed curves at her breast and hips that hadn't been there before. A slight roundness to her tummy.

The changes were small, but they made her even more beautiful to him. Because the changes were a physical reminder of the little boy they'd created together. James pushed the bikini cup aside, wanting to feel her skin in his hand, and Mara moaned.

"I'm not the same girl I was, James. Having a baby, it changes the female body—"

"I don't care." James buried his hands in her hair, wanting to keep her here, right here for the rest of his life. Who cared about work or location. As long as she was with him, everything would be alright. "You were a beautiful girl, and you grew into a beautiful woman, and you're more beautiful right here on this beach."

She laid her mouth on his, dipped her tongue inside his mouth. "You say exactly the right things," she said.

Mara slid down his chest, kissing her way to his sternum as her hands played with his flat nipples. She slid a little farther and he felt her hot tongue tracing along his abdomen. Her head was the only part of her within reach, so James buried his hands in the blonde strands. Her hands tugged at the waistband of his shorts, and then slipped inside to cup his length.

He was hard, but when her hand went around him, he felt himself harden even more. Her thumb found the small opening at the tip of his shaft and caressed gently.

"You have no idea what you're doing to me right now," he said, trying to hold it together so that this moment on the beach wasn't over too quickly.

She chuckled in the darkness. "Are you sure about that?"

"Not even remotely sure," he said, and then she took him in her mouth and James thought he might lose it. Her tongue replaced her finger, toying with his tip for a breathtaking moment. And then she was placing light kisses along his length, teasing him gently with her teeth. Her mouth on him was hot, the water at their feet hot. Hell, the whole damn beach felt like it might combust from their heat, and still he wanted more.

He loved the feel of her mouth on him, but he wanted his mouth on her. Wanted to give to her as much as she gave to him. With his hand still buried in her hair, he urged her back up, before flipping her onto her back.

"Was this all part of the plan?" she asked. "Invite me to a barbecue, have some kind of mind-reading conversation with my grandmother so that we're childless for a few hours and have your way with me?"

James grinned. "I already told you it wasn't."

"Ah, but you were always the responsible one, and even if you have a condom hidden away in a treasure box under the sand, this is still not the most responsible move either of us has made. Maybe, in addition to irresponsibility, you've turned into a liar."

"And what if I have turned into the biggest liar in Slippery Rock, Missouri?"

She put her hand in his. "Then I guess I'll just have to reform you."

"Oh, reform school sounds like fun." James pushed his knee between her thighs, and then tugged the strings of her bikini top, flicking it aside so he could look at her. Just look. With his index finger, he traced the swell of her breast, and felt her belly tremble against his. He drew a slow circle around the tight areola, liking the pebbly feel of this part of her. And then he dipped his head to place a feather-light kiss on her breast. "You could wear a nun's habit or a Catholic schoolgirl outfit and smack my ass with a ruler."

Mara laughed, the sound musical in the still night. "You've turned kinky over the past two years. I'm not sure I like this side of you."

"You're going to love this side of me," he said, his tongue nearly tripping over the word *love*. This wasn't about love. It was about lust. Lust and attraction and chemistry and having Mara in his life one more time. James had no idea what happened when the job with Mallard's was over; he didn't know how custody would work or visitation or any of the rest of it. He just knew that if he had only a couple more weeks with Mara, he was going to make the most of them.

"James," she said, the word echoing breathlessly in his mind. She traced her hands over his face, as if she could see him despite the dark night. "I've missed you. So much."

He kissed her forehead, the tip of her nose and then her mouth. "I've missed you, too," he said. He kissed down her neck, liking the erratic feel of her pulse beneath his lips. Felt her body tighten when he traced the contour of her collarbone with his tongue.

He couldn't tell what she wanted if he didn't have contact with her big blue eyes, even the disjointed contact skewed by moonlight. He needed to look into those eyes, into her, to make sure he was what she wanted. So he made himself stop kissing her, just for a minute.

"What is it that you want, Mar?"

"For the next couple weeks, until the job with Mallard's is over, I want everything. Something has been building between us for a long time, and it scared me. So much that I walked away and I kept walking until I couldn't any longer. The tornado, the therapy, the...missing you. All of those things worked together until coming back here seemed like the most natural thing I could do. I don't know where this leads, and I don't want either of us to get hurt, but I don't want to be alone. Not anymore."

"I don't want to be alone, either," he said, and although he wanted to add more to that thought, he stopped. This wasn't the moment, not yet. They both needed time to think about what they wanted, and maybe releasing some of the heat between them would help them come to a decision. Still, he had to give her one more out. "No matter what happens, I'll still be there for Zeke. I'll still be your friend. And I'll drive you home now if you want."

"I think that kiss kind of blew friendship right out of the water," she said. "And I always hoped you would be here for Zeke, from the beginning. Maybe it's the holiday. Maybe it's being back here that makes me want to be the rebel again—and, yes, sleeping with the sheriff is a rebel thing to do for a girl like me—but I don't want you to drive me home."

"I don't want to drive you home."

"Then don't."

"Who are you and what have you done with my best friend?"

Mara pressed her mouth to his, and none of the questions about the future that were still circling his mind seemed to matter.

"You will always be my best friend. Maybe, for a few days, we can see if there is something more."

"You're sure about this?"

She nodded. James's heart beat a little faster in his chest.

"You threw caution to the wind on the lawn chairs a while ago. Stop trying to get it back."

In the dark, he found the thin triangle of fabric covering her center and pulled it over her hips. He found the bundle of nerves hidden behind the lips of her vagina with his thumb and flicked gently. Her body tensed, and he felt her nails score his back. James sucked her nipple into his mouth, alternately teasing the tight bud and then soothing it with his tongue.

This wasn't enough. Touching her, feeling her body tense because of his hands wasn't enough. He wanted to be inside her. He wanted to feel her fall apart around him, and then he wanted to fall apart, too.

"I don't have protection," he said, his voice muffled as he tried to speak and kiss at the same time.

"What?"

"We need to go inside. I don't have protection on the beach." How they were going to make it inside the house he had no idea. He wasn't sure he could walk at this point, much less get Mara inside, too.

"I'm on the pill."

"You were on the pill and I used a condom in Nashville. And look where that got us."

She pressed a kiss to his chest. "I'm also not ovulating, and I'm not going to ovulate for at least another eight days."

"You know your ovulation cycle?" He leaned his weight on his elbow, while his free hand continued to tease its way across her abdomen, playing with the sensitive spot at her hip, and coming within a centimeter of her core. Mara shivered.

"Having a child, especially an unexpected

child, teaches you things." She pressed another kiss to his chest. "I don't want to go inside, James. I don't want to wait. I just want you. We're safe this time. I swear."

That was all he needed to hear. Mara wasn't a reckless woman. She was smart and careful. Besides he didn't think he could make it inside the house and up the stairs to his box of condoms, either.

James positioned himself over her, found her opening with his length and pressed inside.

She was warm and wet and velvety and hugged his length like a second skin. James found the rhythm he wanted, and Mara followed, her hands hot at his shoulders, and her legs tight around his waist.

Her body tightened around him, and her back bowed before he felt her go boneless beneath him. A sated smile spread across her face, and James followed her into oblivion.

MARA KEPT HER arms and legs wrapped around James in the darkness, not wanting to let the moment end. James kissed her collarbone, then rested his head beside hers. He eased from her body, rolling onto his back, but keeping her pressed firmly to his side. Before she could figure out what to say to him, she heard his soft snores beside her.

How could he sleep at a time like this?

Gradually her heartbeat slowed, and she pressed her hand to her heart. She could hear the night birds calling from the trees high above. In the distance, cars drove along the road that led out of Slippery Rock. Mara closed her eyes, willing the emotions washing over her to go away.

She opened her eyes, but nothing had changed. Her hand tremored against her chest, she felt tears welling in her eyes, and fear warred with the feeling of contentment that hadn't lasted nearly long enough.

She didn't want to leave. Not just his home, and not just tonight.

Mara bit her lip, listening to the gentle waves brush against the sandy shore. She didn't want to leave, at all.

"I want to stay," she whispered into the night. No one answered. James shifted slightly beside her, as if he might pull her body inside his while he slept.

She wanted to stay.

To forget her past and his future and just be with James. To raise their son together. To have barbecues with both their families and all their friends, and to make love with him after in the quiet of this beach, of their bedroom.

She wanted to wake up on a Sunday morning knowing she didn't have to pack her bags for a new assignment in a new city, and that scared her. Most of her adult life had been spent keeping herself intentionally apart from friends, from her family. Because if she didn't depend on anyone, no one could hurt her.

And then she'd had to go and fall in love with James Calhoun. Not once, but twice.

Cicadas buzzed in the yard, and somewhere in the distance a car door slammed. In the sky, stars twinkled as the smoke from the fireworks show finally dissipated. These were ordinary sounds, ordinary sights. Things she'd heard all of her life, on a thousand different nights.

Somehow, though, she knew nothing would ever be the same.

CHAPTER FOURTEEN

JAMES THOUGHT HIS body might combust beside Mara's. Which was ridiculous since he'd just combusted inside her.

He took off the condom and dropped it in the trash can beside the bed.

The two of them had dozed on the beach for a little while before making their way inside to make love in his shower as they cleaned the lake water and sand from their bodies.

A few minutes ago her hand on his hard length woke him from a dead sleep. And he didn't care.

Her breasts were as perfect in his mouth as he remembered. Her skin as soft under his hands. The muscles of her belly still shivered when he brushed his palm over her hip bone, and although the curve of her hip was wider and her belly was more rounded than he remembered, he didn't think he had ever seen a woman as stunning as Mara Tyler. The curve of her hips, the rounded area of her belly were results of her carrying his child. He was in awe of that.

She sighed beside him, her breasts pressing against his side. This was what he'd been missing. Not just the sex, but the closeness.

Mara knew things about him that no one else knew, and not only the events of graduation night. She knew how much he wanted to continue the Calhoun legacy in town, knew how much he'd hated playing football. He traced his fingertips over her hip and felt her shiver against him. Her fingertips drew shapes over his chest.

"I should drive you home."

"I know," she said, but didn't make a move to separate her body from his.

"What are you thinking about?"

She was quiet for a long moment. Her breathing grew deeper, and her hand stilled against his chest. James thought she might have drifted off to sleep. He closed his eyes. There was plenty of time to drive to the orchard. According to the book Mara gave him, as well as Gladys's insistence, the little boy would sleep through the night. The clock on his bedside table said they had at least a couple of more hours, and he intended to spend every moment of them with Mara in his arms.

"I was thinking that I wish I hadn't waited two years to come back home," she said.

James's eyes snapped open, and he twisted her hair around his hand, holding her in place. Beyond that he didn't dare move, wondering if he'd heard correctly. Moments passed. Then she sighed, and her body relaxed against his. She made the soft sound that he remembered, the one that signaled she had fallen asleep.

"I wish I'd followed you to wherever it was you went," he said to the dark room. Then he closed his eyes and slept.

SUNLIGHT TRICKLED THROUGH the open window, teasing James's eyes open. He glanced at the clock. Just after six. He should wake Mara. He flipped over on the bed, but she wasn't there. He sat up, looked around. No sign of the red bikini, no sign of her.

He got out of bed, pulled his still damp shorts from the night before over his hips and wiped a hand over his eyes.

Gone. Again.

Damn it, why did he keep making the same mistakes with her?

He checked the bathroom, but it was empty. Padded downstairs, but there was no sign of her in the living room or the kitchen. There was, however, fresh coffee in the pot on the counter. He poured a mug and stepped onto the deck.

Mara stood at the water's edge, the tank and capris from the day before covering her body. Relief washed over him. Not gone in the night, then. Not gone at all. Just not in his bed.

He could live with that.

Slipping his feet in the flip-flops he'd left in the grass the night before, James started across the yard.

"Good morning," he said when he reached her side.

"Hi." She sipped from her own mug of coffee, watching the gray sky as it shifted to pink in the distance.

"Want me to drive you home?"

She nodded, and the fact that she wasn't talking made him cold despite the warm morning.

They were outside the city limits, his Jeep eating up the miles between Slippery Rock and Tyler Orchard too fast for his liking. He glanced at her, but couldn't read her expression. He thought he caught a bit of regret in her eyes, but her feet tapped along to the happy song on the radio.

He slowed as he neared the driveway to

the orchard. Mara put her hand on his and said, "Stop."

James pulled the Jeep to the side of the drive and waited.

"I'm not sorry about last night."

"Neither am I." He was only sorry he hadn't made a move sooner, because if he had just a few weeks to convince her to stay, he would need every second of every day to do it.

"I'm not sorry about any of it," she said. "Not the weekends we stole, not that we kept it only between us. Not any of it."

He wasn't sure where she was going with this, but he thought he wasn't going to like the ending.

"I am sorry about one thing. I'm sorry I walked out in Nashville, and I'm sorry that it took me so long to tell you about Zeke."

"That's two things."

She shook her head. "They're linked. One doesn't happen without the other. It just doesn't." James's heart beat a little faster with that admission. Because if the two events were linked, it meant if she'd stayed in Nashville, she'd have stayed permanently. He could work with that knowledge.

"You can't keep apologizing for that."

"And you haven't really gotten stupid-mad about it yet."

"I may not have made accusations." He shrugged. "Besides, what's the point in getting stupid-mad?"

She shot him a confused look, that line forming between her eyebrows again. "The point is yelling, getting all those feelings out so they can be examined and dealt with."

"I can examine and deal with those emotions without the yelling or the accusing or the fighting." He'd never seen much point in either yelling or fighting. Making a case, being calm in the delivery—those were the things that got him what he wanted. What he wanted now was Mara, and he didn't need to yell or fight to get her. He only needed to convince her that she wanted to be with him. Based on last night, he was more than halfway there.

"You're a better person than me, then."

"And that is a very good thing," he said, teasing her. She smiled at that. "And we can't keep going over the same details or we'll never move forward. You walked out in Nashville. I got over it. You didn't tell me about Zeke until now." That was still sticky. He'd missed more than a year of his son's life, and that hurt. "You did what you thought you had to do. I can deal with that."

She was quiet for a long moment. Then she

opened her door. "Okay. I'll walk the rest of the way, in case they're all still sleeping."

"I think they know we spent the night together."

"Yeah." She shrugged and got out of the vehicle. "Do you still want some company at darts tonight?"

"Definitely."

"Then I'll see you in a few hours."

She closed the door and started to walk up the drive. She turned at the little path that led around the house toward the plum orchard and the backyard. When the two of them and Collin were kids, how many times did they sneak into the kitchen to steal cookies using that path?

He watched her until she was gone, then reversed out of the drive and turned onto the highway.

Halfway there, he told himself. *Just keep making your case.*

MARA GATHERED HER hair in her hands and secured it to the top of her head with a red elastic. She sat in the security office of Mallard's, making a few more adjustments to the new program she'd been writing for the place. Because the store was so small, the program was coming together more quickly than she'd imagined.

She checked the wall clock. Just after three. She'd already put in the order for the new surveillance cameras for both the interior and exterior of the store. Once the cameras arrived, she would oversee the installation. The new locks had already been installed. Everything was on track, and there wasn't much more to do today. If she left now, she could spend an hour or so with Zeke before meeting James and the others at the Slope.

It would be their first public outing, and the thought made the butterflies in her stomach swarm to life. Dinner at his house didn't count because the only people who had been around were their friends and her relatives. And his parents, but Jonathan hadn't given her too many dirty looks. By the time the group sat down to eat, the older man had been playing with his grandson as if they'd never been apart. Jonathan's seeming approval meant a lot, but it didn't mean the rest of the town would fall in line.

Despite James's statements the night before, he needed the town's approval to become sheriff. If being with her meant he wouldn't get that approval, she would have to leave, no matter how strongly her heart protested. She couldn't be the reason someone else became sheriff; the job meant too much to James. It was part of his identity.

Eventually, no matter what he said now, her costing him the sheriff position would turn him against her.

Mara shut down her computer and put her laptop in her bag. Downstairs, she saw CarlaAnn at the register, chewing gum. She was on her cell phone, and the usual teenage bagger was nowhere to be seen.

"And that is when I knew it was that Tyler girl," she was saying. She paused, listening to whoever was on the other end of the line. "Well, I can't help that that isn't what you heard. That's the way it happened, Viola," she said.

Mara waited at the door, unashamed to be eavesdropping on CarlaAnn's half of the conversation.

"You know precisely why she hasn't been arrested or charged with anything. The Calhouns are covering for her. Again."

That did it. Sheriff Calhoun hadn't covered for Mara even once. He had questioned her, but had never been able to prove anything because she and the guys had been smart enough to cover their tracks. Mara folded her arms across her chest, and her gaze fell on the new electronic security pad she had installed at the employee's entrance.

She shouldn't do it. It was childish. She was an adult.

"And you know that little bastard of hers is going to wind up just the same as she—"

Mara whirled around. She would listen to the gossip about her; after all, most of it was true. But for CarlaAnn to bring Zeke into it… That was hitting below the belt.

She booted her computer back up, opened the security protocol for the employee door and began tapping keys on the computer.

It only took a couple of minutes to make the changes, and CarlaAnn was still on the phone when she left the security office once more.

"Well, the same to you, then," the older woman said and stabbed her finger against the phone's screen.

Mara pasted a smile on her face. "See you tomorrow," she called out as she passed the register.

"You don't work Saturdays."

"I'm expecting one of the cameras to arrive tomorrow. No rest for the wicked," she said, with a careless shrug of her shoulder.

"Hmmpf," CarlaAnn mumbled.

Mara shook her head and continued out the

door. She wasn't going to let the CarlaAnns of Slippery Rock ruin her day. She'd had great sex last night, had a good day at work today, and now she was going home to play with her son. There was nothing to complain about with that kind of day.

Besides, CarlaAnn was going to get a little surprise in the morning, and despite the fact that she knew it was childish, the anticipation made Mara giddy.

She was home within twenty minutes, and Zeke met her at the door.

"Ma, ma, ma," he chanted, pushing his little fists against the screen. Mara picked him up.

"Hey, little man. I like these words you're learning," she said and pressed a kiss to his forehead. She set him on the floor and dropped her laptop bag onto a chair as she slipped off her shoes.

Zeke toddled off to his building blocks and began making a tower. She poked her head into the kitchen and saw Gran standing before the open refrigerator door.

"What are you doing?" she asked on a laugh.

"I was helping Amanda in the berry garden. It gave me hot flashes, and I'm using the fridge to cool down."

Mara shook her head. "You're nuts."

"I'm old. Give me a break."

"How was Zeke today?"

"Busy. We read a book and he decided to help Amanda in the berry garden—how he stayed so cool and I got so hot I have no idea. I think I'll go take a cold shower, see if that'll help me cool off."

"Do you want us to take him tonight?" It surprised her how easily the *us* slipped off her tongue. She kind of liked how it felt. Us. She and James. It was nice.

"You are not taking that sweet baby to a bar."

"They serve food, so technically it's a bar and grill."

"I wouldn't call what Merle passes off as food as actual food."

"But it is edible," Mara pointed out.

"All the same. Give me a half hour to shower and I'll be fine."

"We aren't meeting until seven, so take your time."

She rejoined Zeke in the living room and added a block to the tower. The little boy watched the tower for a long minute, then picked up another block from the floor. He considered it for a moment, then dropped it. His pudgy hand reached for a block in the center of the tower, and the whole thing tumbled down.

Mara shook her head and chuckled. "You know, when you pull the blocks from the tower, it always falls over."

Zeke didn't seem to mind. He simply picked up a couple of new blocks and began building again. Mara handed him a block. He examined it and let it drop. While he built, Mara talked.

"I'm going out with your daddy tonight. Your uncle Collin and Savannah will be there. And Savannah's brother, Levi. It's nice to be back here, to see everyone." Zeke kept building, so Mara continued talking. "It's different. Nice, but different. I didn't realize how much I'd missed Slippery Rock, and now I can't imagine not being here."

Zeke handed her a block, and Mara added it to the tower.

"It isn't as easy to build a life as it is to build a tower, but maybe it could be different here." What was even sillier was thinking about building a life here after a single night with James Calhoun, but she couldn't seem to stop herself. "You and I could figure out a babysitting or nanny situation for when I'm working, and I could take the shorter jobs instead of always volunteering for the more difficult ones. I'm almost finished writing the program for Mallard's, and it's really only a couple of weeks since I've been on the job. My bosses at Cannon will like that. Between jobs, we could live here. Would you like that?"

Zeke didn't answer. He just kept stacking the blocks. He picked up the last one, which was barely as big as his palm. He examined it, turning it over in his hand a few times. Then he reached up on tiptoe and placed it on top of the other blocks. He looked at Mara triumphantly.

She clapped her hands. "Good job, kiddo. You did it."

Zeke looked at his creation for a split second, then plucked a block from the middle of the stack, sending the whole thing toppling to the hardwood floor. He giggled, but instead of building another tower, he toddled off to grab the purple plush dinosaur.

Mara began picking up the blocks, putting them in the plastic storage bin according to size.

There was still a lot to work out with James. A lot to work out about Zeke, and a lot to work out with her job, too. With James's, as well. If she saw that her presence was having a bad influence on his future, no matter how badly she wanted to stay, she would go.

But for now, what was the harm in doing a little planning?

CHAPTER FIFTEEN

BECAUSE IT WAS Friday night, the Slope was busy, with most tables occupied, and Juanita hustling to keep the mugs of beer and wine-glasses filled. The seven of them—Levi, Collin and Savannah, Jenny and Adam, and James and Mara—shared a single booth near the back of the bar. Levi signaled Juanita for another bucket of beers when she hurried past.

James watched as Mara aimed her dart and let it fly toward the board on the wall. It hit in the lower right quadrant. Not a bad shot overall. It would be better if she were playing on his team, though.

"Nice shot!" Savannah high-fived Mara while Collin took position to make his next throw. They were playing girls versus guys, in deference to Levi, who was the lone single in their group.

"Not bad for a girl," Adam said. He sat in the wheelchair, peeling the label off the bottle of beer Jenny told him not to drink. He took a sip, and she shot a glare at him. "I could do better."

"You have to be able to stand to be able to shoot," Jenny said, arms folded over her chest. She sat across the booth from James, Savannah sat beside Jenny.

Mara looked from Adam to Jenny and back again. She handed her darts to Collin, who was up next, then slid into the booth next to James.

"How are things going?" she asked, keeping her voice light and friendly.

Adam spun the wheelchair around, working the wheels until he reached the jukebox.

"I'm sorry," Jenny said. "We shouldn't have come tonight. I just…he needed to get out of the house, and my mom was willing to watch the kids. He'll be okay. It's all going to be okay." Jenny didn't sound so sure, but James didn't know how to comfort the woman who had, until the tornado put Adam in the hospital, been one of the most positive people he'd known.

"Have you heard from Aiden?" he asked, hoping a change of subject would release a little of the tension settling around the table.

"He'll be here after Founder's Weekend. It was the earliest he could leave work." Jenny shot a glance at her husband, who was paging through the song list on the juke. "Adam told him not to come, but I insisted. We need someone who can run the shop. Owen and Nancy are doing their best, but they seem to think nothing has changed at the shop since Adam and I bought it from them a few years ago. A lot has changed." She eyed her husband who was still at the jukebox. "A lot has changed," she repeated.

"Anything we can do?" Collin asked from his position near the board.

Jenny shook her head. "None of you are trained woodworkers, and the shop didn't get hit with much damage. We'll be okay. It'll be okay," she said. Those six words seemed to be a kind of mantra for her.

Savannah and Mara both reached across the table, putting their hands on Jenny's. The woman offered a wobbly smile. "I'm just... going to see if I can get him anything," she said, rising from the booth. She said something to Adam, but he shook his head, turned the wheelchair toward the exit and left. Jenny followed.

James shook his head. Not long ago, Adam had been the only one of them in a relationship, and now his relationship looked to be on rocky ground. The one relationship that should have been on rocky ground—James and Mara's—seemed smooth. Almost steady. It was weird.

Not that he could call what was going on with Mara a relationship, exactly. Not yet. Sharing a kid and sleeping together while not talking about the long term wasn't the typical way relationships progressed. But, then, Mara was far from typical, and he didn't mind that at all.

Collin scored twenty during his round, but his score wasn't enough to push them ahead of Mara and Savannah. James didn't like to lose, not even a friendly game of darts, so he carefully took aim and let his dart fly. He hit just outside the bull's-eye. Nice.

He glanced behind him. "No high five?"

"We don't high-five the enemy," Mara said, with a grin splitting her face. James rolled his eyes and took aim while Mara turned the conversation to Levi. "You sure you want to play with one of them and not with us?"

"I have a feeling they'll come back," Levi said, muscled arms spread over the back of the booth. He'd been quiet most of the evening, and James wondered what was bugging him.

"Are you going to shoot that dart or just caress it to death?" Mara asked, taking a sip from her daiquiri.

James shrugged off the curiosity about Levi. If he wanted to talk, he would talk. Until then, it was time to play. James had another near miss with the bull's-eye. Crap. James handed the darts to Savannah, who needed all of ten points to cement their win, and slid into the booth beside Mara. His thigh brushed against hers, warm despite the cool air-conditioning in the bar, and he took her hand in his, threading their fingers together. She sipped from her glass.

"This is killing you, isn't it?" she asked.

"Losing a game of darts?" James shrugged. "It's just a game."

She pressed her shoulder against his. "Liar."

"You forget that I was the one who didn't care about football except as a way to get to college."

"Yeah, until you were on the field. Then it was game over for whoever was trying to guard you."

James looked at her for a long moment. "How did you know that?"

"You don't give me enough credit. I wasn't just plotting our assaults on the student body, you know. I was also considering what a certain student body would look like without all those football pads covering it."

"Now who's lying?"

She held her hands up. "No lying here. I had a crush on you long before our encounter in Jefferson City." Some emotion James couldn't quite name made her blue eyes darken to an almost navy color.

"God, between you two and my sister and Collin, it's a syrup fest in here tonight." Levi picked up his bottle and slid out of the booth. "I'll be at the bar until the next round starts." He stopped at the jukebox and slid a few quarters into it, then took the last stool at the bar.

Mara squeezed James's thigh. "As long as we're playing it straight this time, no holding back, I figured I should let you in on that secret."

"We're playing it straight?"

She nodded, and despite the glint in her eyes and the grin on her face, James knew it was what she wanted. Which was good, because Mara was what he wanted. There had to be a way to make this work between them, and he was going to find it.

"Definitely," she said. "No secrets. No omissions. We see where this takes us."

"As long as we're putting it all out there, I had a crush on you, too."

"I'm not an idiot," she said, rolling her

eyes. She finished her drink but didn't signal for another.

Savannah squealed, interrupting the conversation. One of her darts had landed dead center. Game over. He realized he didn't care.

Juanita arrived at the table with the new bucket of beers. "Whose tab tonight?"

"Mine," James said. He took his credit card from his wallet and handed it to her.

"I'll bring it right back," she said, disappearing into the crowd.

"How about a dance before the next round?" Savannah said. She'd locked arms with Collin, who leaned against the wall.

"I don't dance," he said, but he followed her to the small open area near the jukebox when the next song started. It was a mid-tempo Keith Urban song, but the two of them fell into a slow, swaying motion.

"Are you sure about this?" Mara asked, her voice quiet.

"No," he said.

She shot her gaze to his.

"We said honesty, right?" he said. "I'm not being honest if I say I don't wonder. I don't know where this goes, and I don't know how it works."

"It would be easier to go back to being

friends, I think." She squeezed his hand under the table, but didn't let go.

"Much, much easier."

She was quiet for a long time. James watched a few of the patrons. People he'd known all of his life. Thom, the mayor, was there. Bud had come in for a drink after shutting down his store at the marina. A few people he knew from high school were there—Mike Mallard with his wife. No one seemed to be paying any attention to the table in the corner.

"I don't want easy," James said, and was surprised to realize the words rang true. Life had been easy for him. He loved being a cop, but he'd never really considered anything else because of who his father was. He loved Slippery Rock; no matter what other places he visited, this was the place that called to him, so it was an easy thing to buy a house and settle into small-town life. He'd worked hard to get where he was, but he could still recognize how easy most of his life decisions had been. Like checking off the box in a sports trivia quiz. "I've had easy. I'm tired of easy."

"I've never had easy. Not that my life has been filled with stepmothers and stepsisters who made me clean chimneys or anything. Figuring out who I am and what I want, though, has never been simple. I should want easy," she said, and paused. "Why don't I want easy?"

James sipped his beer. "I could offer a few more meme quotes. 'Nothing worth having comes easily.'"

"'Except ice cream—ice cream is always easy'," she put in.

James grinned. "'All things are difficult before they are easy.' There are a million of them."

"Let's finish this conversation in private."

"I'M GLAD I'M here now. With you." Mara pulled his face to hers. They were at his house, on the back deck, watching the lake in the moonlight. "I know this isn't the best timing, because of the situation with Zeke, and your job, and my job." Want filled those clear blue eyes. Desire. "And I'm finished with the 'I'm sorry about Zeke and Nashville' conversations—at least for the rest of tonight. And tomorrow. You might have to remind me after that."

"What is it that you're saying?" he asked, even though he knew the answer.

"I'm saying that I don't want to leave Slippery Rock when the job with Mallard's is over. And it will probably be finished within the next week."

The blue deepened, and the darker pigment near her iris seemed to spark. The look in her eyes dragged him into the spell that was Mara.

"Thank God." He pressed a quick kiss to her mouth. "It's about damn time."

He'd already broken nearly every one of his rules about dating, and he couldn't seem to stop himself. Before Mara came back to town, he didn't date local girls. Hell, before Mara walked into his life, he'd dated very little in general. After Mara, or, more to the point, between their hookups, he hadn't dated at all. During the past two years, he'd had a handful of dates, none of which lasted more than a couple of hours. None of them included kissing for kissing's sake or the soft brush of a feminine hand against his under a booth at the Slope. More important, he hadn't wanted them to.

It was a little nerve-racking how much he wanted Mara, not just in his bed but in his life. Because things were bound to get hairy at some point, and there would be no place to hide. She'd been in his house, in his bed. His backyard. His lake. She was everywhere.

How hard would it be to let her go if she got

scared again? What happened if, unlike their friends, the regulars at the Slope—Thom Hall and CarlaAnn and their ilk—and the other people in town did make a big deal of their interim sheriff dating a woman who had been accused of all manner of misdemeanor crimes in her youth?

And what about when Zeke was into the terrible twos and it was a stretch just for him and Mara to see one another? Sooner or later, Gladys would want time off from babysitting or Amanda would do something teenagerish that would remind Mara of her past, then where would he and Mara be?

She'd only just come back into his life and he was preparing for her exit. Maybe that was smart, but he didn't want smart. Not tonight. He wanted her. Plain and simple.

He toed his sneakers off and kicked them away before stepping onto the cool grass.

"Let's take a walk," he said, and held out his hand. Mara took it and together they walked until their feet hit the sand. Mara toed off her sandals and stepped into the water with him.

"God, I want you, Mara." The words left a burn as they ripped from his throat.

The one thing he wanted—Mara's body beneath his, offering heat, comfort and maybe something else—wouldn't let him go. He glanced down, and her gaze pulled him further into her web. He didn't mind.

"I want you, too, James."

"Mara…"

"The timing is terrible, but I do. This is complicated and has the potential to get messy, and I don't like messes any more than you do." She put her hands on his face. "But I can't stop wanting you."

"I think that's a good start."

Her sweet, soft lips brushed his jaw, and James was lost for a moment. He forced his mind back to the surface.

"My parents' relationship has been messed up for as long as I can remember," she said. "There wasn't any room for us when they were together. I never figured out how to be with someone and keep my focus on my plans, on the rest of my life. When I found out I was pregnant, I realized I had to break that cycle. I didn't… I don't want to be the kind of person who neglects her child in favor of her other relationships."

"You're a good mom, Mara." He put his arms around her waist and pulled her to him.

"I'm trying. And I'm not going back on our agreement from the other night. This isn't another apology for running away in Nashville. I want you to know that I confronted those parental demons, but it still makes me nervous. Being a mom. And being with you."

James ran his hands through her hair. "Mar, you're the strongest woman I know."

"No, I'm not. I run when things get hard. I get distracted at work when I'm thinking about home, and at home when I think about work. I need clearly defined boundaries, and even then, I can mess things up."

"That's reassuring."

She smacked her hand against his biceps, but it was a playful smack. "If you're willing to pull me back from the brink of distraction, I'm willing to drag you into my distraction from time to time." She offered him a half grin. "Because I don't want to be without you. I don't want to move from unfamiliar hotel room to unfamiliar hotel room. Who eats dinner off a room service menu all the time? And who never has to make a bed or wash a towel because there is a maid who does all the hard work?" She paused. "I want more than that."

"You mean you don't want easy, either?"

She shook her head. "I've never had easy, remember? What would I do with easy?"

"So you're okay with upping the complication factor between us?"

She put her hands on his shoulders. "More

than okay. I'm adding *complicated* to my everyday vocabulary. Working on a security system? *Complicated*. Figuring out how to make a meat loaf? *Complicated*. Oh," she exclaimed, smacking his shoulder again. "Speaking of vocabulary, Zeke's added a string of 'ma, ma, ma' to the 'no, no, no' from the barbecue. The baby books were right. His vocabulary is starting to come, and it's coming fast."

James grinned at her abrupt change of subject. "I don't think we have any choice in the complicated department. Let me ask you this. Would you term what we were doing before as 'dating'?"

"Well, we did have meals together, even if we only rarely finished them at the restaurant," Mara said, pressing one index finger against the other. She counted off another point. "But, we did have sex, and often, and let's just concede that having regular sex requires some form of dating. So, yeah. I would say we were dating. Then."

"And now?"

"I would call darts nights and barbecues with our friends multiple-couple dating."

"And what about what we're doing right now?" He took her hand, bringing her to a little blanket in the yard and laid her down on the soft folds. He pushed his thigh between her legs as he captured her mouth with his. Her body was soft against him, but her mouth was ravenous.

"I would call this the lead-up to really great sex," she said, kissing his chin, "which we wouldn't be having if we weren't also on a date."

"See, already complicated."

"Well, we do have a kid, and this is only our, what, second date since we started dating again?"

He nibbled her earlobe.

"Do that again," she said.

He blew a gentle breath against her ear, and then playfully nibbled the lobe.

"I think I like complicated," she said on a sigh.

"Me, too," James replied. But he wanted more than her ear.

James slipped his tongue between her lips, tasting her. Her mouth was sweet from the daiquiri she had at the Slope. Salty from the peanuts on the table. She was everything he wanted, and not just for tonight.

Mara tightened her arms around his neck, pressing against him so that James could feel her breasts beneath the layers of fabric between them. He pushed his hands beneath her top so that he could caress her bare skin against the palms of his hands. Her muscles trembled at the touch.

James pushed both of his hands beneath her top, spanning her waist. She trembled again as one thumb played with the undersides of her breasts, beneath the silk and lace of her bra. Still, it wasn't enough contact. He reached up over her breasts, his hands flattening against her lace-covered nipples. They hardened to sharp buds as her tongue began to thrust with his.

The rough lace between them was too much. James pushed it aside and filled his hands with her full breasts, teasing and stroking. Getting to know the feel of her again. Mara pushed her hands beneath the hem of his T-shirt, playing her fingers against his ribs.

"I've missed you," he said. "I didn't know how much until I caught you stealing milk and cookies from the grocery store."

She opened her eyes, her gaze filled with laughter. "That was a security check, remember?"

"You say *security check*. Other people say—"

She cut him off, pressing her mouth to his.

She ran her index finger over his pecs, down his abs to rest just above the snap of his jeans.

"Let's go inside," she said. "We might be tempting fate in the neighbor department if we stay out here much longer."

"That's the beauty of this location. The distance between the houses."

She raked her nails over his abdomen, teasing him a little. James sucked in a breath when those small hands went lower, flirting with the button of his jeans. She didn't dip her hands under his waistband, just rubbed lightly.

"Distance or not, let's take this inside." She licked her lips. "I thought about you all the time, at all the wrong times, and in all the wrong ways. The more I tried to stop thinking about you, the more I thought about you. Naked, mostly."

"I'm good at naked."

"Yes, you are. I'm sure all the women tell you that."

James laughed. "I guess I just haven't been listening very well." He stood and held his hand out to Mara. She took it, and he put his arm around her waist as they walked inside the house.

He shut the sliding glass door behind them

and then pulled the drape closed. "Private enough for you?"

Mara nodded. She moved to his side and ran her hands over his chest. Down his abdomen. And then she went farther.

She walked her fingers down his abdomen and under the waistband of his jeans. "I like having you all to myself."

"You know what I'd like to do?"

"I have no idea." Technically that wasn't true. He could see by the wild glint in her clear, blue gaze that she wanted to make love to him. Why she wanted to come inside when there was only the slimmest of chances they would be seen or heard in the backyard? That was a question to which he wanted to find the answer.

"I want you to put on your uniform."

"Now who's getting kinky?"

"I thought we established that night in Nashville, with the tie, that I was already kinky?"

"Maybe if the tie had stayed knotted," he suggested, taking her wrists in his hands and then holding them behind her back. Mara watched him for a long moment, not saying anything. "Okay," he said. "I'll be right back."

While James went upstairs to put on his uniform, Mara took off her bra, putting it into her tote. Then, she arranged the pillows on his sofa. She didn't want to make love with him on the hard floor, and she knew if she followed him to the bedroom, she'd never see him in the uniform that had been haunting her dreams since he pulled up in the department SUV outside the grocery store.

James knocked on the wall separating the living area from the family room that was attached to his kitchen. Mara whirled around.

Even in the dim light, she could see the outline of the bulletproof vest under the tan shirt, and the leather belt with his gear creaked when he walked into the family room. He looked handsome and just a little bit dangerous, and a spark of attraction skittered along her arms.

"Hi," she said.

"You approve?" James asked, and did a little spin before her.

Mara laughed. She reached for him, and stepped up on her toes to lay her mouth against his. The fabric of his uniform shirt was slick against her hands, and the vest beneath it made his chest and shoulders seem impossibly wide.

James wrapped his arms around her, holding her body close to his, and despite the layers of clothing between them, she could still feel his heat. This was a bad idea. It was going to take forever to get all this gear off him, and she wanted to feel the stubbly hairs on his chest tickling her breasts now.

Hands shaking, Mara tried to undo the rest of the buttons, but the holes seemed too small. She gave up, grabbed hold of his shirt just above his belt and pulled hard. The shirttail came free, and that was one layer down. Ten more to go, she thought sarcastically.

James pulled her top over her head. "What happened to the bra?"

"It's in my bag." She reached for the button of her pants, released it and pushed the garment over her hips, along with the black undies. When she was standing naked before him, she held her breath for a moment.

He'd said he liked the changes to her body, but that was when they were in the dark. Lying down. Standing before him she felt somehow exposed. He must have read her expression, because James reached out and ran the backs of his fingers over her jaw.

"I meant what I said. You're the most beautiful woman I've ever known."

His words gave her confidence, and Mara advanced on him again. She'd wanted to kiss him in this uniform, this part of him that meant so much. But now she wanted him out of it.

"I'm going to kill this shirt if you make me do all the buttons," she said, "but if you deal with that, I'll take care of the rest."

James grinned, and slowly unbuttoned his shirt. As each released, a bit more of the black vest was revealed. James shrugged off the shirt, and stood before her wearing the bulletproof vest and the rest of the uniform.

"I thought you'd have a T-shirt under that or something."

"If I'd been planning to wear the vest and the uniform for more than five minutes, I would have. As it was, it seemed a little like overkill."

"Good call." She wanted him skin to skin with her, for the rest of the night, and getting him out of the rest of his clothes was going to take too long. Mara undid the untility belt at his waist, and tossed it onto a chair. With it out of the way, she undid the waistband of his uniform pants and pushed them over his hips. She grinned when her hand came in contact with skin instead of the boxer briefs he typically wore. "Boxers are also overkill?" she asked as the back of her hand skimmed his hard length.

"In this particular instance, yeah." James

kicked off the pants. "By the way, in addition to the boxers, I usually wear a cup. You know, for protection."

"I didn't realize Slippery Rock was such a dangerous place," she said and released the Velcro closures of his vest. The raspy sound made her shoulders tense.

"You have no idea. I actually get propositioned like this at least three times a week. Sometimes, the protective cup is the only thing between a particularly randy Slippery Rock resident and my virtue."

She dropped the vest to the chair with his utility belt, and then James was naked. All six glorious feet and two inches of him. "I should warn you, since you're without your protective gear," she said, putting her arms around his neck as she pressed her mouth to his chest, "that your virtue is in very definite danger tonight."

James picked her up, sliding her body along his until he held her face-to-face. "Promises, promises," he said and took her mouth with his.

An annoying buzz woke James from the best dream he'd had since Mara came home. It involved his uniform and Mara taking it off him. He slapped out at the annoying buzz, knocking the alarm clock to the floor. Six o'clock. Saturday morning. He needed to get ready for his shift.

With bleary eyes, he made his way to the shower, turned the water on cold and stepped under the chilly stream. The cold water had the desired effect, and he stepped from the shower a few minutes later feeling like a new man.

Mara stood in the bathroom, holding two cups of coffee and wearing the uniform shirt from last night. "Good morning," she said.

"I thought I dreamed that." He wrapped a towel around his waist.

She shook her head. "I called Gran a few minutes ago. Zeke is still asleep. I told her I'd bring muffins from The Good Cuppa for breakfast. You want to make a quick stop with me before your shift?"

James took one of the mugs from her and drank. "Can't. I skipped over a little paperwork yesterday, when I was helping with the removal at the day care. But I'm off at three, if you and Zeke want to do something."

She beamed at him. "We would love to, and you're in luck because our busy social calendar has opened up recently. The only people we're scheduling are you and…well, you're the only one on our schedule."

James put the coffee down and kissed her delicious mouth. "You're the only ones on my personal schedule, too."

She returned his kiss, and then said, "I'm glad about that."

His phone bleeped in the other room, and James hurried to pick it up. A text from the dispatcher in the next county alerted him to a situation at Mallard's Grocery. He pulled jeans over his hips, along with a black T-shirt, then the department polo that he usually only wore when he was at a conference. "Have to run. I'll see you this afternoon," he said and grabbed his utility belt and the bulletproof vest on his way out of the room.

It took less than five minutes to reach the grocery store, and there was only one car in the lot. A frustrated CarlaAnn stood at the employee entrance, hands on her hips, staring daggers at the door. When he pulled into the lot she crossed her arms over her chest and tapped her foot against the concrete.

"I'm locked out," she said, waving her hand toward the door.

"That seems more like a call to your boss than a call to the sheriff's department."

"Yes, well." She looked uncomfortable.

James stepped closer to the door. The new

locking mechanism had to be one of Mara's additions to the overall security. It included a digital keypad, and a readout which currently scrolled the words *It Figures*. He narrowed his eyes, remembering CarlaAnn's use of the phrase a couple of times the day Mara ran her shoplifting test.

She wouldn't have.

Would she?

"Let's clear the readout," he said, pressing the clear button. The words stopped scrolling across the readout. "What's your password for the lock?"

"Five, seven, four, four, zero, one," she said.

James input the numbers and the phrase began scrolling across the readout again. Crap. She'd done this. Something had to have happened between CarlaAnn and Mara. It was the only thing that made sense. This appeared to be a programming error. Mara was a programmer. Since her arrival back in town, CarlaAnn had been doing her damnedest to make Mara leave.

"I'm not sure what you expect me to do here," he said. He didn't know an override code, and he didn't think punching random numbers into the keypad would do any good.

"I don't want Mr. Mallard to know I messed

up the new system." CarlaAnn lowered her voice. "I was hoping you might, ah, help me get in touch with Mara? She installed the system, she should know how to get around it."

James blinked. The woman didn't suspect that Mara was behind the lock not working. "I could call her," he said. "If you're sure that's what you want."

CarlaAnn nodded and then began chewing on her thumbnail. "I need to get inside so I can get my drawer ready. The store is supposed to be open by seven. Customers will be here soon. Please?" she added, almost as an afterthought.

James shrugged, holding back a grin as the two-word phrase scrolled across the lock. He dialed Mara's number, and she picked up on the first ring.

"I'm right around the corner," she said before he could say anything, confirming his suspicions that she was behind CarlaAnn's lockout. He didn't want the clerk to have any more ammunition against Mara, though, so he explained what he needed anyway.

A few minutes later, Mara's SUV pulled into the parking lot and parked next to the sheriff's department cruiser.

"Hi, what seems to be the problem?" she

asked, and he had to admire the clueless note she put into her voice.

"CarlaAnn is locked out. She—" CarlaAnn stared hard at James, as if unwilling to admit it had been her idea to call Mara in the first place. James started over. "We thought you might be able to help."

Mara cocked her head to the side. "It isn't working? I just finished the programming yesterday. This is odd." She pushed a few random buttons on the console, but nothing happened.

"Could you hurry, please? I need to get my drawer set up before the first customers arrive," CarlaAnn requested, but her voice sounded snotty to James. As if she were somehow incapable of being nice to Mara. He shook his head.

"Let me try one more thing," Mara said, hitting a few more random number combinations on the keypad. *It Figures* kept scrolling across the readout. Mara blew out a breath, as if stymied by the lock. James had to admire that she appeared not to notice CarlaAnn's increasing impatience. "I don't get it, my override code isn't working, either."

"It figures," CarlaAnn mumbled.

Both James and Mara watched her closely for a moment, but the clerk didn't connect the words she had just said with the phrase still scrolling across the lock.

"What was your code again?"

"It doesn't work," CarlaAnn insisted.

"Let's just give it a try."

CarlaAnn rolled her eyes and sighed, but she repeated her code to Mara. However, Mara didn't punch in the five, seven, four, four, zero, one code. Instead, she punched in six, four, eight, nine, four, eight, not even attempting to hide the fact that she had changed the code. A tinny *ta-da* sound emanated from the lock as it clicked over.

CarlaAnn blinked. "It worked."

"Glitches," Mara said with a shrug.

CarlaAnn disappeared inside without even offering a thank-you over her shoulder.

James turned to Mara, who shrugged again. "Are you mad?" she asked.

"Why'd you do it?"

Mara frowned and considered her words for a moment. "She keeps gossiping about the security check, which is fine," she said, rushing the words before James could interrupt. "I can deal with her kind of people, but…" Mara watched him for a moment. "Yesterday afternoon, she brought Zeke into it. She was mean and whoever she was talking to was obviously not interested, and that seemed to make her even more mean."

"And you decided to get even."

"It was just a little prank."

"I'm not mad. Anyone who brings a kid into gossip deserves a little comeuppance."

"Unfortunately, she doesn't seem to get that the prank is on her," Mara said, and there was a note of annoyance in her voice.

James took her hand, leading her away from the Mallard's employee entrance. "Ah, but you do get it. Every time she annoys you, you'll know that she isn't worth your time."

"I like the way you look at things," she said, leaning her shoulder against his for a moment. "By the way, the code I used to unlock the system?"

"Yeah?"

"The keypad is like a telephone, each number is attached to a letter."

"And?"

"Put all the numbers together and it spells out 'nitwit.'"

James barked out a laugh. "You are a crazy woman, Mara Tyler. Devious and clever all at once."

"Just don't get on my bad side," she said.

James put her in the car and watched until the SUV disappeared out of sight. He got into the department SUV and turned it toward the station house. Devious and clever. How had he ever convinced himself that he didn't love Mara Tyler?

CHAPTER SIXTEEN

"AND SO I'D like to be the officer who takes the Slippery Rock Sheriff's Department into next year, and the next decade," James said, standing at the podium on the newly built grandstand. It was Founder's Weekend; the following week, the calendar would switch over to August. The special election for sheriff would happen on the first Tuesday in November. Mara had been in town for five weeks now, and her job at Mallard's was completed. They'd slipped into a comfortable routine over the past few weeks.

While they both worked, Gladys watched Zeke. The three of them went on picnics or swimming at the lake regularly. Mara and Zeke hadn't moved into his house, but they spent more time there than at the orchard.

It had been a few weeks since he and Mara had stopped hiding their relationship from Slippery Rock, and while only their families and closest friends knew about Zeke being

James's son, other people probably suspected. So far, no one had asked.

He spotted her in the crowd, carrying Zeke on her shoulders as she walked toward the grandstand. The little guy held the purple dinosaur. They really needed to give that thing a name, he thought, as he went on with his speech.

"What about cyber crime?" someone in the crowd yelled out.

James looked for the speaker. It was a tall man with closely cropped hair. He wore a state patrol officer's uniform, and James thought he looked vaguely familiar. Probably someone with whom he attended a law enforcement convention.

"We are committed to fighting cyber as well as physical-world criminals," James said.

"But you have no experience," the man said, before James could continue with his speech. Everyone in the crowd focused on the new speaker.

"We haven't been touched by cyber crime in Slippery Rock, but that doesn't mean we aren't experienced in how to deal with it."

"If the town hasn't had problems, how did you gain your experience? As a hacker, maybe?"

"In training sessions, the same as you."

Mara stopped making her way through the crowd and focused her attention on James and the newcomer.

"But your girlfriend *is* a hacker?" The crowd parted for the man, who made his way quickly to the podium.

"No, she isn't. She's a computer programmer and security analyst."

The uniformed trooper held his hands out at his sides as if he didn't understand James. "You say *programmer.* I say *hacker.*"

Mara started toward the podium, but James shook his head, stalling her.

"What's your point?"

"My point is that the people of Slippery Rock and Wall County deserve actual protection from their law enforcement staff. Since the county absorbed the town police, residents have only one place to go if there is a problem. I believe there have been problems."

"Not of the hacking variety," James said drily. He shook his head, realizing with certainty where the conversation was going. Whoever this trooper was, he wanted the sheriff's job, and he was using James's announcement speech to get the attention of Slippery Rock. Smart move.

He wanted to kick the man's ass, but it wasn't a smart move.

"You have been called to the local grocery on an attempted theft call. No arrest was made—"

"Because there was no theft. Mar, ah, the person in question was actually a security consultant who was running a sweep."

"The elusive hacker girlfriend, right?" The trooper had a mean grin on his face that James would have liked to slap off.

"She isn't elusive, and she isn't a hacker. She's right there. With our son," James said, pointing at Mara and Zeke in the crowd. Every head turned to look at Mara. She froze for a moment, then turned on her heel and walked quickly away. James wanted off this podium. He hadn't meant to tell the town about Zeke this way. Hell, he hadn't intended to tell the town the truth about his biological connection to Zeke at all. It wasn't their business. It was his.

"So you're explanation is that your—" the man made bunny signs with his fingers "—securities expert girlfriend was not, in fact, stealing a quart of milk and a package of cookies. It was all just a big misunderstanding."

"That's exactly what I'm saying."

"And was her vandalism of the water tower a misunderstanding?"

"That was ten years ago."

"And when she hacked the school district computers so that the motherboards were connected to the wrong monitors?"

"It was three cables that were switched, not a hack. And again, it was ten years ago. None of that has any bearing on my run for the office of sheriff." James turned to the people in the crowd, most of whom were now looking at him with curious expressions on their faces. "The polls open in a little over two months, and I'll be around at several town functions to answer questions between now and then. Thank you."

"And so will I. Be at those functions," the trooper said as he stepped up to the podium. "I'm Missouri State Trooper Brian Whitaker, and if you're ready to have someone outside the crooked Calhoun family running your town, I would appreciate your vote on Election Day."

Trooper Whitaker waved to the crowd, then hopped off the stage.

The crowd began to disperse, folding Whitaker into their ranks until James couldn't see him. The crowd buzzed with questions and comments and probably a lot of speculation, but there was nothing James could do about that. These people knew him, they knew his father, and some had known his grandfather.

He would make a good sheriff, and Mara's past—hell, his past—had nothing to do with how well he could run the sheriff's department.

"Well, that was interesting," Levi said, making his way through the crowd to where James stood near the grandstand.

"*Annoying* and *insulting* were the words I would choose," James said. They began to walk. A few people slapped James encouragingly on the shoulder. At least, he thought the slaps were encouraging.

"I was surprised you brought Zeke into it, though."

"It wasn't intentional. She was there and he was there and it just…came out." James looked around, but he couldn't see her. He twisted his mouth to the side. That was odd. "I wonder where she went." Probably making sure Gladys was settled with the other ladies at the bridge tournament in the basement of the Methodist church, or checking on Amanda, who was staffing the orchard's booth at the farmers' market. This was the first day the market had been opened since the tornado.

Nearly all of the renovation and rebuilding projects were completed; only a few interior walls and painting projects at the various businesses harmed by the twister remained.

"Last I saw, she was headed toward the market." The two of them started down Water Street in that direction. "So this thing is serious between the two of you?"

James nodded. Serious enough that he'd taken the ring he had with him in Nashville out of the drawer of his great-grandfather's oak credenza. They hadn't made any long-term plans, and he didn't want to rush her, but she'd told her bosses yesterday that she wanted to take a sabbatical. Mara choosing to stay in Slippery Rock indefinitely was a big step forward.

"It's the most serious I've ever been. About anything."

They reached the farmers' market, and Levi clapped his big hand on James's shoulder. "Good luck," he said, and continued on toward the Walters Ranch stand on the other side of the building.

At the orchard booth, Amanda said she hadn't seen Mara since earlier that morning. James continued looking around, but she was nowhere. Not with the church ladies playing bridge, not wandering around the marina, one of Zeke's favorite places. She wasn't at the Slope or around the grandstand.

A cold feeling swept into James's chest. Just like in Nashville, she was gone.

He unlocked his smartphone, hitting the button to call. Her phone went straight to voice mail. He tried texting, but after thirty seconds of watching his screen with no response, he decided she was definitely not talking to him.

What the hell?

A few people called out to him. He waved a hand in their direction but continued toward his Jeep as fast as he could walk. She was not going to run, not this time. This time he was going to find her, and he was going to make her talk.

No more running.

Mara rocked Zeke in their room at the orchard. He'd been fussy most of the day, and after James's stunt at Founder's Weekend, the little boy had gotten significantly more fussy. When James pointed them out, several crowd members reached for him, touching Zeke's leg or his arm. A few got into his face or hers, offering congratulations.

She wasn't angry at the congratulations. She was annoyed that James made the two of them a sideshow. She hadn't asked to be part of his campaign; it was better if she wasn't associated with it at all. While most of the town seemed okay with the two of them seeing one another, there was a very vocal minority who continued to bring up her past.

It was only a matter of time before someone brought up the bus tires and graduation night. She couldn't lie about the incident. She'd worked too hard to become a respected security expert to lie about a vandalism charge. When townspeople brought up the vandalism, his whole career could go up in flames, because no one would care that both James and Mara had repaid the school anonymously for the damage done. They would care only that James's part in the prank had caused significant monetary damage to the school.

Zeke's body was limp in her arms; he'd finally fallen asleep. She put him gently into the crib Collin had brought down from the attic. She had had to refinish it, but the heirloom crib was now one of her favorite things. She was going to miss the crib. Would miss this room with its soft lavender color and fuzzy rug.

She would miss Slippery Rock in general, and her family in particular.

She would miss James most of all.

Staying was out of the question, and she knew it was cowardly, but she had to get out, and she had to do it quickly. She couldn't be the reason James lost his chance at the sheriff's position. Mara took her suitcase from beneath the bed and began to pack shirts and shorts into it.

Once the suitcase was packed, she started on Zeke's things. Most of them fit into a small duffel. She went downstairs to pick up his stuffed animals. Mara sat heavily on the couch, running her hands over the soft fur of the lemur that Zeke liked to throw around. The Pack 'n Play was filled with Zeke's books and a few smaller toys.

He wouldn't have a room like this when they found their next hotel. She would need to look into nanny services. Contact a lawyer to set up custody and visitation schedules. It was going to be so hard to drop Zeke off with James for a weekend or a week or… God, for a holiday. And she knew once they started talking about visitation, James would also want to talk about financial support. Mara sighed.

This wasn't supposed to be easy, but did it have to be so complicated?

A car came into the yard—she didn't have to look to know it was James. The familiar rumble of his Jeep was clear through the closed windows. The rest of her family was still at the market or enjoying the afternoon Founder's Weekend events. There were a cake-baking competition and carnival games. This evening, the current high school football team would play against the Sailor Five—well, three since Aiden still wasn't in town and Adam was medically ineligible to play.

She met James on the porch, putting her index finger to her lips. "I just got Zeke to sleep."

"You took off without telling me," James said, sitting beside her on the porch swing.

Mara pushed her foot against the floorboard of the porch, setting the swing in motion. "I didn't want him to be in the middle of whatever was going on with that uniformed guy."

"He's running for sheriff. Against me."

"I figured."

"His entire platform seems to be based on your rebel reputation and my apparent inability to do anything other than what you tell me to do."

Mara nodded. That was exactly what she had been afraid of all this time—her past haunting his present. It wasn't fair. To him.

"It doesn't matter," he said, but there was a hint of anger in his voice.

"Of course it matters. This town would rather dwell on the past than deal with the present. Or the future." She shook her head. "I'm sorry. I didn't want this to happen."

"Me, either. Now that it has, we'll deal with it."

"No, we won't. I'm leaving. You can't win with me here, and you deserve to win." She couldn't keep the note of wistfulness out of her voice, and she hoped James didn't notice it. For the first time in her life, Mara didn't want to leave Slippery Rock.

The sabbatical she'd asked for from her bosses had been her first step in staying. She'd intended to use the time to set up a home office and come up with a plan to convince them to let her write security programs from here. Someone else could learn to install the systems. There would still be a few times she would have to travel, but for the most part, she thought she could make telecommuting work.

Not at James's expense, though. His dream was to be sheriff. His destiny.

"If I can't win because I'm seeing you, because we're a family, then I'll deal with that—"

"We aren't a family. We're friends who had an affair and a kid."

"We're more than that, and you know it."

"This was never going to work. I travel for a living. You run a small-town sheriff's department. You can't come with me on jobs, and I can't do the work from here," she said, putting as much sincerity into the lie as she could. Because if he knew how badly she wanted to stay, how badly she wanted to be a family with James and Zeke, she would never get him off her grandmother's porch.

She would have everything she wanted.

He would give up the only thing he'd ever wanted.

"People make long distance work all the time, Mar. People live in California but work in New York or Paris. We'll figure out how to do it."

"And, what, you'll give up your dream of being sheriff? Sooner or later, you would hate me for costing you that position. I don't want you to hate me, so I'm leaving. We'll negotiate visitation agreements and the rest of it. I'm not going to keep you away from Zeke. He loves you."

Mara loved him. She wanted to press her fist against her chest to loosen the knot growing there, but she couldn't. James couldn't know how hard this was for her.

"I love you, Mara. The job is important, but

it isn't as important as you are. You and Zeke, you're the world for me, and I'm not going to let you walk out of it. Not again."

She took his hand and squeezed it. "I'm not walking out, just walking away. I…" Mara had to move. Sitting here with James was torture. She couldn't say what she had to say while parts of her body touched his.

"It isn't fair to you," she said.

"It isn't fair to you," he said, following her to the porch rail. "You made mistakes when you were a kid. Who didn't? No permanent damage was done, not by you, anyway," he said, smirking a little. "You can't keep using your past to hide from what you want."

"I'm not using the past. That—that trooper is using my past. CarlaAnn is using my past. Your father has been very nice to Zeke and me, but even he, I'm sure, has used my past to convince you to…to…"

"To not love you? News flash, Mar. I love who I love. No one orders me around on that front."

"You know what I mean."

"What do you want?"

Mara shook her head. What did she want? It didn't matter what she wanted. It mattered what James wanted, what he deserved.

"I want Zeke to have a good relationship with you, and with my family."

James waited a moment, but Mara kept her lips pressed together. "What do you want?" he asked again.

"I want to keep writing security programs. I want to see Paris and Moscow and the Australian Outback."

"And?"

Mara sighed. He was going to keep asking her until he got the answer he wanted, so why not give it to him now and get it over with? She would still leave.

"I love you," she said, sighing. "I love you and I want to stay here with my family. With you. As corny as it is, I want Zeke to grow up here. To be bored here. To raise hell here, just like the six of us did when we were kids." She put her hands on the porch railing. "I love this place. I never thought I would, but I do. Every gossipy, boring inch of it."

"Then stay."

"James." She shook her head.

James put his index finger beneath her chin and pushed up until their gazes met. "Stay. We'll figure it all out. I can be a deputy. I can get a different job altogether. I can be sheriff. None of it matters, not without you. So stay and we'll figure it out together."

She wanted to. God, did she want to. James pressed his mouth to hers.

"Stay," he said against her lips.

Mara knew it was a mistake. He couldn't really love her, not enough to give up what he'd wanted forever. But maybe, just for a little while longer, it would be nice to live in the fantasy. She was a strong woman. She'd walked away from him before and survived. If worse came to worst, she could walk away again and be okay.

CHAPTER SEVENTEEN

MARA MADE HER way to the middle of the big conference room in the city hall building. It had been just over a week since James had outed himself as her baby daddy, and there had been no major explosions. No snarky write-ups in the local paper, no comments from CarlaAnn when Mara went into Mallard's to pick up the groceries for Gran and no more talk about her past from Trooper Whitaker.

Of course, Whitaker hadn't withdrawn from the race, either, and had called tonight's debate between him and James. The man made her nervous.

Almost as nervous as James did; she'd told him she loved him. He'd told her he loved her. They were more or less living together at this point, although many of her things were still at the orchard. She and Zeke had been spending most of their nights at James's little house by the beach.

His leather furniture was now accessorized

with Zeke's plush animals. James's back deck was littered with building blocks. He'd added a deck box a couple of days ago that held a toddler life jacket and sand toys. He'd made room in his life for them.

It was all going so well, and she didn't want to jinx it with bad thoughts, but something had to give.

Bud sat beside her. "Good to see you here tonight. Wasn't sure you'd come."

"Why wouldn't I?"

Bud pointed toward Whitaker. "He doesn't seem to like you."

"If his whole campaign rests on his irrational dislike of me," she said, echoing what James kept telling her, "it's a weak campaign. We've never even spoken to one another."

"I'm just saying," Bud said, shrugging.

Yeah, so was she. No one was listening, though, especially not James. Well, he might have convinced himself that her past didn't matter, but there were other people who didn't agree, and their ringleader was CarlaAnn.

The grocery store checker sat in the front row. She wore a pair of dark-wash jeans, fancy cowboy boots and a flowing tunic that skimmed her slim hips. She'd left her hair down. CarlaAnn turned to look at Mara, a smug expression on her face.

The woman really needed to get a grip on reality. Sure, locking CarlaAnn out of the grocery store once the new system had been installed and running was petty, but CarlaAnn had been so ridiculously petty while Mara was designing and testing the system that the action had seemed justified at the time.

"Can I ask you something, Bud?"

"Shoot, kiddo." The older man folded his arms across his chest and crossed his sneakered feet at the ankles. He wore old basketball shorts and a baseball jersey. The combination should have looked silly, but it fit Bud.

"Does it bother you that I was a little bit of a…" Mara searched for the right word. *Troublemaker* seemed wrong. She'd never been after trouble. *Criminal* was wrong—no charges had ever been filed. *Reckless* fit what other people thought, but Mara had planned all their pranks very carefully.

"Rebel?"

She nodded. "Thanks. Does it bother you that I was a bit of a rebel when I was a kid?"

"What kid doesn't have a little rebel in them? You never meant any harm, and really, none of those pranks did any significant damage."

"There was the bus incident."

Bud raised an eyebrow. "Two buses out of a

fleet of twelve were damaged, there was a full insurance payout, and…" He paused. "It's my understanding that some anonymous donor has made several endowments to the transportation department over the last few years."

"Still, the damage was…significant." And not just to the buses. That had been the first time Mara had run away from a problem. She'd done it to save James, but still. Maybe if she hadn't run then, she wouldn't have run in Nashville.

Maybe she wouldn't still be contemplating running now.

"It was a long time ago. I'm sure the statute of limitations has run out on that one."

"But if it hadn't?" she pressed the issue.

Bud shrugged. "Between the insurance money and the anonymous donors, what harm was done that hasn't already been undone? I'd say the debt has been paid."

Amanda slid into the seat beside Mara. Gran had stayed at the orchard to watch Zeke. "Did I miss anything?"

"Are you even registered to vote?"

"I registered to vote the first day I was eligible this spring, thank you very much," Amanda said, straightening her shoulders and crinkling her brow. "And since I'll turn eighteen the day before the election, I fully intend to exercise my civic duty. I am a responsible citizen."

"Who paints on sidewalks and yarn-bombs unsuspecting residents," Mara whispered. She and Amanda still had a ways to go in their relationship, but things were better between the two of them.

Amanda elbowed Mara. "They're getting ready."

Thom Hall made his way to the podium at the front of the conference room. He introduced both James and Whitaker, running through their education and experience before introducing Jonathan Calhoun.

James's father limped to the podium. "I want to thank everyone for coming out tonight, and I want to say what a pleasure it has been to serve you for the past twenty years as your sheriff. As most of you know, my son, James, has been a deputy with Wall County for several years. Trooper Whitaker has been a member of the state patrol for as many years. Both are qualified, and I am confident either one will serve this office well. Let's hear from the candidates."

The audience members clapped, and Trooper Whitaker stepped to the microphone. He talked about his years with the state patrol and his responsibilities. Mara tuned him out, focusing instead on James. He hadn't worn his department uniform, but Whitaker had.

He should have worn the uniform.

James sat calmly to the side, feet flat on the floor, hands clasped loosely in his lap as he listened to Whitaker talk about drug task forces and investigations and working with the lawmakers in Jefferson City.

"Blah, blah, blah," Amanda said.

Mara elbowed her. "Be respectful."

Amanda pretended her hand was a mouth, making a face as she pressed her fingertips to her thumb. Mara bit back a grin.

Finally he finished his speech, and James stepped up to the podium. He didn't immediately go into the speech he'd used on Founder's Weekend.

"It has been my pleasure to serve you all for the past eight years. I was a part-time campus security officer through college and after I received my degree and completed my police academy training, I began working full time at the Wall County Sheriff's Office." He pointed in his father's direction. "I've learned from the best, and I hope you'll allow me to keep working within the department that has been like a second family to me for years."

CarlaAnn glanced over her shoulder again, her gaze clashing with Mara's. Mara shook her head, and when James finished speaking, she joined with the rest of the audience to applaud for both candidates. Thom returned to the microphone.

"We'll open the floor to questions at this time," he said.

There were questions about parking on Water Street, and one resident brought up Wilson DeVries's yard, which had still not been cleared of downed trees.

"His yard could really use another yarn bomb," Amanda whispered.

"Bite your tongue, kid. You're practically related to the next sheriff, you know."

"Yeah, whatever."

CarlaAnn raised her hand and waited for Thom's assistant to reach her with the microphone. "Hello, I'm CarlaAnn Grainger. Most of you know me from Mallard's, where I've worked for the past twenty-five years."

"Is she throwing her hat in the ring, too?" Amanda asked. Mara shushed her.

"I'd like to know, from each of you, how you would deal with the problem of this town's rebellious teenagers. They've been running wild for more than ten years, and each year they get worse. What can you do to return our streets to the people?"

Mara closed her eyes and shook her head.

Leave it to CarlaAnn to make childhood pranks a criminal endeavor.

"I'm in favor of harsher laws, especially for our youths," Whitaker spoke, his voice full of authority. "Children need boundaries, and they will respond if we give them those boundaries."

James looked at the man for a long moment. "This spring all of the seniors drove tractors to school on April Fool's Day. You'd jail them?"

"Perhaps not jail. But it's my understanding that there was not adequate parking for the tractors, and that the vehicles caused serious traffic flow issues throughout the day. One of them even became stuck in the drive-through window at the Dairy Barn. I would ticket those drivers."

"I disagree. While traffic was slowed on the day in question, it was not impeded. I was on duty most of that day," James countered. "The students allowed people in faster moving cars and trucks to go around them, and in some cases waited through the light signals to allow more traffic to move around them. That kind of behavior doesn't deserve ticketing."

"There have been more serious crimes, Deputy Calhoun, don't you agree?" Whitaker asked.

"Such as?"

"Vandalism to the water tower."

"A coat of paint reversed the effects of that incident." James tapped his fingertips against the podium and looked pointedly at the crowd as if daring one of them to ask about the other pranks the six of them had pulled. This was so not okay. They were using her to get to him, just as she had predicted.

"What about the mental anguish of the child who was targeted?" Whitaker persisted in his questioning, clearly trying to undermine James.

"I'm not sure that child experienced mental anguish."

"Because one of your friends instigated the attack?"

"It wasn't an attack. It was a prank. Ill-thought out and retaliatory, but still only a prank."

"And what about vandalizing all the school buses on graduation night? Was that also only *ill-thought out*?" CarlaAnn asked, still holding the microphone.

James blinked. Mara fisted her hands in her lap. "I would label that prank a mistake. The school district has been reimbursed for any costs related to that incident. At least, that is my understanding."

"How would you know about reimbursement? Are you on the school board?"

"Ah, no," James said. He paused. "I heard about—"

"I told him that I repaid the district," Mara said. She stood, straightened her shoulders. She couldn't let him do this. Yes, James had let the air out of the tires, but he was in the bus yard that night only because of her.

CarlaAnn's head swiveled so she could see Mara, that smug smile still in place. She crossed her arms over her chest and nodded twice before taking her seat once more.

"Hello," Mara said as the crowd all turned to look at her. Amanda, still sitting in her chair, stared at Mara with her mouth wide open. "I'm Mara Tyler. Most of you know me. You don't, Trooper Whitaker, but you've obviously heard a lot about me."

"Actually, I—"

Mara didn't let him finish. "I did a lot of things when I was a teenager that I now regret, and most of them I've never apologized for. Principal Monroe, if you're in here, I'm sorry that I switched your computer cables with Miss Apple's. I was just learning about programming and networking, and it seemed like a funny thing to do. CarlaAnn, I did paint your daughter's phone number on the water tower, and I did it because I was mad at her. I never apologized to her." That was as close to an apology as CarlaAnn would get, Mara decided. Her daughter had been hateful as a teen, and now Mara knew why. It was because of her mother. "And to the town as a whole, I am very sorry about what happened to those buses on graduation night. For the past few years, I've been sending anonymous donations to the school transportation fund to pay for the damages."

She swallowed. "But James Calhoun should not be penalized for my mistakes. That would be unfair and unjust, especially to a man who has always been fair and just to the people of this town. Trooper Whitaker, you may be a great law enforcement officer, but you don't have the connection to Slippery Rock that Deputy Calhoun has." She looked around at the people in the room, most of whom she had known all of her life. "Connections are important here. The only connection I had for a long time was my grandparents, and then a sweet boy with shaggy brown hair befriended me on the playground, and as we grew up, we continued to be friends. We each had our first rides in a patrol car together—the night his father found us with paint-covered hands near the water tower."

Mara took a deep breath. "I came here this summer hoping to help my family rebuild their orchard, and instead, my family and James helped me rebuild my life. I can't now let that life harm other people." She stepped over Amanda's legs into the open aisle leading to the door. "When you cast your vote, cast it for the person you think will do the best job in the present, not in the past. A smart man likes to talk to me in internet memes, and I finally have one for him—don't judge anyone by the past, because no one really lives there anymore."

She walked as quickly as she could out of the conference room.

It was time to go, before she hurt the people she loved any more than she already had.

JAMES WATCHED MARA walk out of the conference room, stunned. She never looked back. Didn't hesitate.

She was gone.

Everyone started talking at once, but two people didn't say anything. Amanda, who was sitting in her chair with a shocked expression on her face, and CarlaAnn, who had taken her seat and was smiling broadly. Damn, but that woman was a witch.

James tapped his finger against the microphone, trying to focus attention back on the debate. "Excuse me," he said loudly when the tapping didn't work.

"Hey," Bud yelled, standing up a couple of seats away from Amanda. "Shut up so James can talk," he said, and the buzzing conversations stopped.

All the attention focused on James, and he ran his finger around the collar of his polo shirt.

"You asked if the bus prank was ill-thought out," he said, focused on CarlaAnn. "Yes, it was. But it wasn't Mara Tyler's thought. It was mine. Mara was turning on the cabin lights to run down the batteries. She thought it was unfair that seniors were allowed to skip the last week of school while the underclassmen had to take finals. Sure, that extra week's vacation was a perk for the senior class, but Mara had been determined that, after our graduation, the entire high school would get that extra week of summer break. That doesn't excuse what she was doing. What *I* was doing. Because while Mara was turning on the lights, I was letting the air out of the tires." The crowd gasped. James put his hands on either side of the podium and gripped the wood tightly. "I don't have a good explanation for that. I was young and stupid, and I never thought that letting the air out of the tires would warp the rims. And, for the record, Mara isn't the only person who repaid the school. I began making anonymous donations the year I started working for the sheriff's department. I know that doesn't change what I did, but I have made restitution. I would like to say that we all do stupid things when we're kids. I can't take back what I did on graduation night, but I can tell you that if given the opportunity to serve you as sheriff, I will continue to make up for that night."

James looked around. Trooper Whitaker looked stunned. CarlaAnn looked annoyed. His father looked shocked.

"If you'll all excuse me, though, I have something more important than this debate to deal with right now." Before he could second-guess himself, James stepped off the platform and followed Mara's route out of the conference room.

He saw her rounding the corner of city hall and took off at a run. She whirled when she heard his footsteps approaching.

"Don't. Don't tell me again that people

won't care about the things I did." She held up her hands. "The CarlaAnns of Slippery Rock are never going to let it go, and I can't let my actions do harm to you."

"The CarlaAnns of this world are sad, pathetic human beings."

"James." Mara sighed. "Please. I don't want to hurt you."

"Then stay. Because the only way you can hurt me is if you walk out again."

"You know this can't work—"

"I know we can work through this, together."

Mara sidestepped him and started walking. James stepped around her, cutting off her route.

"Your job—"

"—is as a deputy, and if I'm elected sheriff, great. If not, I can still be a deputy."

"Do you really think Whitaker is going to keep a former teenage vandal on his staff? CarlaAnn just outed the water tower thing—"

"And I outed the bus thing," he said. James took her arm. "I don't want to be sheriff only because you lied to protect me. I should never have let you take the blame in the first place. I should have owned up to what I did."

"I didn't mind people thinking I did it, because it made it easier to leave. And I needed to go. I needed to see what was out in the world, and I needed to understand who I was without Gran and Granddad, Collin and Amanda." Mara shook her head. She pulled her arm free. "I had already come up with a million reasons not to go, though. I was afraid to leave and afraid not to, and when you let the air out of the tires, I knew what would happen. I saw it as my chance. If I left, the town would blame me."

"So you sacrificed your reputation to save mine."

"Mine was already mostly broken." Mara pushed away from him. "I have to go. If I don't go now… I have to go."

He couldn't keep running around her like a crazy person. James grabbed Mara's arm with one hand and opened the back door of one of the department SUVs with the other, pushing Mara inside. He slid onto the seat beside her and shut the door.

"I'm not letting you go. I did that once already. It didn't work out so well."

"We can decide on visitation for Zeke later—"

"It isn't about Zeke. It's about me. I love you, Mara. I want to be with you more than I want to be without you. I want to live in that house by the lake and watch Zeke grow. I want to play chase in the orchard. If I'm not elected sheriff of Wall County, so be it. I'll work as a deputy or maybe go to the highway patrol."

"But it's your dream."

"Being sheriff is only one dream. Family is another. Kids. Growing old with the woman I love. Shooting darts with the guys until we're all eighty. We can have more than one dream, Mar, and the most important dream to me is you. Zeke. Collin and Gladys and Amanda and my parents are all in there, too, but you're at the front of the line. At the top of the list."

"James, I love you, but—"

"You're worth more than a career," he said, putting his finger under her chin so she had to look at him. "You're worth more than the pettiness of a woman like CarlaAnn. You're worth more than the parents who neglected you for years. They didn't break you. You're strong and smart and sexy. You're a great mom." He pressed his mouth to hers. "Let yourself have the things you want."

Her hands were trembling when she put them against his cheeks. "I want you," she said, kissing him back. "I want all the things you said, but I'm afraid."

"News flash, Mar. We're all afraid, but you can't let fear steal your happiness. You have to reach out and grab it. Hold on to it, work for it and never let it go."

She rested her forehead against his. "I do love you."

"And I love you. The rest is going to fall into place."

"Promise?"

He buried his hands in her hair, and pressed another kiss to her mouth. "Swear."

Mara put her arms around his neck and sank into the kiss. "James?" she said.

"Yeah?"

Mara tested the handle of the SUV. The door didn't budge. "Do you think you can figure us out of the back seat of this police SUV? It's a little hot in here." She waved her hand in front of her face.

For the first time, James realized what he had done. He'd locked them in the back seat of a police car. He shook his head.

"We're going to have to wait to be rescued. It could be a while. The shift change doesn't take place for—" he checked his watch "—another couple of hours. At least the windows are cracked, right?"

Mara chuckled. "We're going to make the newspaper this time, aren't we?"

James shrugged. "Probably." He rested his forehead against hers. "You know what's really serendipitous about this?"

She looked at him with a strange expression on her face. "Serendipitous?"

"Accidental?"

"I know what the word means. It just seems a little...odd to be using that word when we're locked in the back seat of a cop car."

James wrapped his arms around her, pulling her to his side. "No. It makes perfect, random sense."

"Why?"

"I fell in love with you the first time in the back of my dad's patrol car. It's kind of fitting that I get you to agree to marry me in the back of another patrol car."

"You didn't ask me to marry you."

He kissed her again, nibbled her full lower lip. "Will you marry me, Mara Tyler?"

"Yes," she said, her hands tickling the back of his neck. Mara swung her legs over his in the back seat.

James twisted a lock of her hair around his finger. He'd had the ring in his pocket since Founder's Weekend, looking for the perfect moment to give it to her. In a moment, he decided. For now, it was enough that he had Mara exactly where he wanted her. She wasn't going anywhere, and neither was he.

* * * * *

Get 2 Free Books,
Plus 2 Free Gifts—
just for trying the Reader Service!

Get 2 Free Books,
Plus 2 Free Gifts—
just for trying the Reader Service!

HARLEQUIN *Presents*

Get 2 Free Books,
Plus 2 Free Gifts—
just for trying the Reader Service!

Get 2 Free Books,
Plus 2 Free Gifts—

just for trying the Reader Service!